SUCCUBUS SOCCER MOM
A Reverse Harem Tale

by

Jacquelyn Faye

SUCCUBUS SOCCER MOM
A Reverse Harem Tale

ISBN: 978-1-945893-12-4

Published by Untold Press LLC
114 NE Estia Lane
Port St Lucie, FL 34983

www.untoldpress.com

PRODUCED IN THE UNITED STATES OF AMERICA

10 9 8 7 6 5 4 3 2 1

Dedication

For Namihei Odaira

Founder of Hitachi

You know what you did

You glorious bastard

Prologue

"Fucking snail trails. Seriously?" My lip curled as I sneered in disgust at the brass pole rising up from the stage and disappearing into the blackness of the industrial ceiling above. 'Sinamon' forgot to wipe down the pole after her last dance, and the bitch got *seriously* turned on dancing in front of large crowds. Friday nights at Full Exposure drew in vast amounts of horn-dogs, pervs, jocks, businessmen, bi-curious housewives, and hardcore lesbians. Some of them were manlier than the guys in suits that came and dropped portions of their kids' college tuition just to see a girl spread eagled in a G-string.

Well, one thing was for damn certain, I wasn't going to be pressing my hoo-ha against the slimy brass without disinfectant. Reaching up, I upended my bottle of 151 rum against it, let it dribble down, pulled my lighter out of the pocket I'd had specially sewn into the center of my studded red leather bra, and lit that bitch up.

Alcohol burns off quickly, but the blue flames were kind of pretty, and I watched for a second before leaping on and spinning amid the flames. The audience gave a collective gasp, and Ginger, the owner of our fine establishment, slammed her drink down against the bar. She had warned me about showing off, and while demons couldn't contract sexually transmitted diseases…the thought of slipping off the pole mid-dance because of some over juiced skank hag didn't seem all that appealing either. It's not like I set the stage on fire.

I held on with my legs and dropped backward, back slamming against the pole, my face a foot off the black painted plywood beneath me. I must have used too much

7

rum. The stage was, in fact, on fire. Not enough for the wood to catch, but enough to be a safety concern. For the humans in the bar, not the pole dancing demon smiling as the flames licked her face like a sensuous lover.

The DJ let half the song play while I danced in the flames, slowly lowering the volume. I ended the song with a flip off the pole, and my feet landed just as the flames dwindled down and the music stopped, my heels thudding loudly.

"Are you ready to see this flaming beauty get naked, boys and girls?"

I leaned back against the pole as the DJ's words settled over the crowd, and their thunderous response made my ears ring. Chuckling, I popped the clasp on the front of my bra and leaned forward, letting it fall off my shoulders and onto the floor behind me. Kicking it back to the DJ, I slipped my fingers in the waist of my matching panties as the heavy bass of Dragula started pounding from the stage speakers.

The guys sitting in the booths surrounding the stage surged forward, clamoring over each other to offer me their little green bills and lustful gazes. Ignoring them, I closed my eyes and shifted my panties, one side off my hip, before pulling them up tightly against me as the opening riff of the song exploded.

The rest of my dance became a blur as I got what I *really* came for. Their lust. As they showered me in bills, I fed off them like a Golden Corral buffet. The suits, the nerds, the geeks, the pervs... They all had different flavors, and with that much lust in the air, I didn't need to touch them to feed. They were launching it at me like dollar bills.

My climax started to build, and I had to concentrate to keep it at bay. Some of them might not have survived the experience, and the song was ending soon. I bent over in front of the pole and let my leather covered crotch slide down the pole to edge myself, but when I looked up, my eyes met his.

The rest of the bar faded away as he became my sole focus for the moment. Sure, there had been guys that caught my eye in the past, but not like that. Not like him. He was close to six feet, not overly muscled, not a jock. He wasn't dressed in a suit, either. His build was medium, giving him a look like he wasn't a stranger to hard work, but that he wasn't into body building. In a word, perfect. But my gaze wasn't fastened to his body, but locked onto his *eyes*. He was as human as they came, but his eyes were magic. At least in appearance. Pools of blue floating in the smoky shadows of a strip club in Orlando.

Not breaking eye contact, he moved a little closer to the stage, offering me a dollar embarrassedly, like his friends had put him up to it. His stubbled face hadn't seen a razor in days, and the image of his cheeks sliding against my thighs made me smile as I strutted toward him.

He was mesmerized as I sat down in front of him, spreading my legs with hands on my knees. "Is that for me?" I looked at the bill in his fingers and then at his crotch, which I swear swelled as he took in every inch of my body.

"Do you want it?" He didn't sound too sure.

"Yes. Please," I cooed the last word.

A bead of sweat dripped down the side of his face, sliding over his perfect skin, and getting lost in the beard he was trying to grow. "Where?"

How I heard him over the music was no mystery. I could hear mice fucking in the walls over the music. The fact he could hear me at all *was*. "Well, I don't have any pockets. You can stick it in my panties if you want."

His cheeks flushed, and he nodded, looking down at the red leathered gates to glory. With a trembling hand, he reached for the strap on the side, just above my hip, until I opened my legs and nudged his hand away with my knee.

"Not there." I reached down. When guys tried to hand me money, I usually ignored them. A few of the tastier ones that I had an interest in feeding on later, I let slide fives and tens into my waist. I'd never offered the front of them to anyone…ever. There was just something about the guy in front of me that told me I could trust him. "Here," I whispered, peeling the front of my panties away from my flesh.

He couldn't see anything, it wasn't legal for us to expose our lower extremities where alcohol was served, but the guys to his left might have gotten a peek.

The bill quivered as he stuck the corner in, brushing over my pubic hair and sending goosebumps over my legs. I cooed softly and grabbed his wrist. "It will fall out if you don't put it in all the way." I let my fingers trail down over his hand and grabbed the base of his fingers, sliding them into my panties. His knuckles grazed my lips and my lust flared at his touch.

"Would you like a dance after my set?"

He just nodded.

"I'll come find you…"

I pulled his hand free and rolled backward in a reverse somersault, landing on my feet and flinging my hair back as I stood. It was only then did I realize the song was over.

So that's how he heard me.

"Everybody, give it up for Kara!"

I bowed as the applause exploded through the room.

Scooping up most of the bills left on the stage for me, I headed for the stairs, stopping by the DJ booth and swiping my bra from the floor.

Sage was coming up at the same time, and I hugged my back to the wall to let her pass. "Holy fuck, Kara. That was *hot.* And I ain't talkin' bout the fire!"

"Shit. I forgot about that. Ginger's gonna kill me."

"Her star performer? I don't think so!" She flicked my nipple as she passed, laughing as she stepped on the stage.

"Bitch!" I couldn't help but chuckle. As far as humans went, Sage was one of my favorites.

Slipping back into my bra, I stepped out from the stage entrance and made my rounds, collecting tips from the guys too lazy to walk up to the stage. That was my excuse for traversing the whole bar in search of blue eyes.

I found him at the bar, leaning back against it on his stool, surrounded by guys nearly twice his age. His eyes were like beacons in the fog, and I stopped collecting tips when I found him.

"Hi," he said shyly as I walked up.

"Hey, yourself. Did you enjoy the show?"

The guys around him made appreciative noises, but I ignored them, focusing on him. He silenced them with a glare and then smiled up at me. "This is my first time at a club like this."

"Disappointed or surprised?"

"The former before I saw you dance, the latter after…" He blushed and rubbed the backs of his fingers absentmindedly over his lips. The same fingers that had just caressed my pussy on stage.

His eyes glazed a little when he caught my scent on his knuckles. A side effect of succubus pheromones, but there was still clarity there, too. The lights were on, he was home, but it was like he was watching a movie. Probably about a stripper.

"Buy me a drink?"

"I'd love to," he answered, and one of his friends got up and moved over to the other side of the group, letting me have his stool without me having to glare at him. A gentleman.

I sat down and turned away from the bar, facing the stage like my new friend was. I was watching Sage, he was watching me. I could feel his eyes on me like glue.

"What you want to drink, Kara?" The bartender asked in her gruff voice.

"Why do you even ask, Clove?"

A bottle of rum slammed down on the thickly lacquered bar top. I reached over my shoulder and grabbed it, twisting the top and clinking it against the neck of the beer bottle my new friend was holding.

"Cheers," he said with a small chuckle.

"Nostrovia!"

"Are you Russian?"

"Nope. Not that I know of. Orphan, so my lineage has always been questionable." I winked at him, earning myself another sexy little chuckle. He really was too damn cute for his own good. If he wasn't careful, I was going to eat him up. "What's your name?"

"Ryan."

"Huh. That's a cute name."

"And you're Kara."

I nodded, taking another swig of rum.

"So… How much is that bottle gonna cost me?" He didn't seem to care, just struggling to converse with a stripper.

"Tell you what, you buy a lap dance, and I'll buy my own drink." Truth be told, I didn't need the money and when he'd asked to buy me a drink, I'd just ordered without thinking. The bar would have charged him a hundred bucks for a whole bottle of shit rum. I could afford it. He looked like he worked at Home Depot.

"That sounds like quite a bargain." He grinned and took another sip of beer. "Tell you what, make it two lap dances. I didn't see anybody else in here I'd rather break my strip bar cherry with."

I froze mid sip. "This is seriously the first time you've ever been in a titty bar?"

"Yep."

"Virgin," I whispered, practically salivating. It was time to have some fun.

"Well, to titty bars, yes." He even fucking blushed.

I turned around and set my bottle behind the bar. "Be back in a bit, Clove."

"Okay." Clove used to be one of the top dancers, until she took a nasty spill off the pole. She started bartending while the leg healed. That was three years ago. Personally, I think she was glad to be out of the game, and her gruff nature made her the perfect bartender.

I grabbed Ryan's hand and hauled him to his feet. "C'mon. Let's go get you all turned on and stuff."

"Going to take more than a couple of lap dances…"

I took that as a personal challenge. A devious smile plastered itself to my lips on the way to the private dance area.

"So, can't help but notice all the girls use spices as their stage names. Is Kara a spice I don't know about?"

"Hey, Rocco," I greeted the bouncer outside the booths. "We'll be a bit."

"Keep it clean, Kara."

"You know me."

"That's what I'm afraid of." He chuckled and opened the velvet rope, letting us in.

I turned and looked at Ryan as I led him to my usual booth in the corner. "No. The place is owned by Ginger," I finally answered. "When the girls chose their stage names, they went with other spices. It kind of became a tradition."

"You chose Kara?"

I stopped in front of the booth and pressed myself against him, leaning up to his ear and giving the lobe a tiny lick. "I'm not some bitch who's afraid of what she does. Therefore, I don't use a stage name. Kara Day." I held out my hand.

"You really just told me your actual name? What if I was a stalker or something?"

I grinned at him and gave him an evil look. "Then, I'd have to eat you."

He gulped. "I'm not, though."

"Didn't think so. I can smell a creep from fifty yards away."

"I'm a teacher."

"Teacher?"

"High school. English."

"No shit."

He nodded.

I backed him up against the booth, pushed him gently onto it, and straddled his thighs. "You know how these dances work?"

"No?"

"It's simple. I take my top off and rub all over you with my body. Where and how long is up to me. See that camera over my shoulder?"

He glanced up at the ceiling and nodded.

"There's guys watching everything in here, so you're not allowed to touch me. I'm sorry. Good rule of thumb is to keep your hands on your seat unless I pick them up. Okay?"

Again, he nodded.

"The next song is about to begin. That's when the fun starts," I said, and unhooked my bra, tossing it on top of the booth behind him.

I probably could have sat like that for the duration of the two songs and he would have been happy. As soon as the ladies were free of their red leather confinement, he was hooked.

"You like them?"

"Very much." He nodded and didn't take his eyes off them, except to look up and flash me a smile.

"Men and titties."

"Yeah." He blushed as he finally met my eyes for a moment.

The song faded, and the next started. It was Nickelback, the group everybody loved to hate but sang along and knew every word by heart. I really dug them. Especially "Something in Your Mouth." That song was made for lap dancing.

I stood and turned around, laying my back against him and spreading my legs over his, letting my hands roam my body as I ground my ass against his lap.

"Fuck, you smell good."

"I get that a lot." I grinned at him and turned my face to rub my cheek against his, the smell of arousal wafting from his skin. My leather underpants were about to become very slippery. I gave a throaty laugh and arched my back, pressing my ass against his rapidly hardening cock. "So much for not getting turned on by a little old dance."

"It's not the dance, it's the dancer."

That earned him a treat. I rolled over, my stomach pressing against his as the hardness in his jeans pressed against my clit. I spread my legs over his and bucked my hips, giving him a little friction as I grazed his lips with my teeth.

"You're so hard."

He nodded, blushed, and looked away.

"No. Don't be embarrassed. That's the ultimate compliment."

"You must get a lot of compliments."

His wit surprised me. There was much more to Mr. Ryan than shy good looks and amazing eyes. "None that have been as sweet as yours."

"We're still talking about compliments, right?"

Blocking the camera with my body, I ran my hand over his cock. "Yes. Ultimate ones."

"I'm sure you get this a lot, but I just have to tell you. You are so goddamn beautiful. I don't know if I'm going to last two songs…"

"If you can't, don't worry about it. You wouldn't be the first guy to walk out of here with a wet spot."

"Spot? I'm thinking more like a splatch."

"Wanna know a little secret?" I lifted myself off him and let my breasts lightly slide over his face.

"What?"

"I'm so wet right now I could probably put out a small housefire."

He chuckled. "That's pretty wet."

"You don't sound like you believe me, Ryan…"

"If an exotic dancer got wet from every lap dance she gave, we would be up to our ankles in…" He trailed off, too embarrassed to say it.

"Pussy juice?"

"Yeah." He blushed.

"Put your hands on your knees," I whispered as I rubbed against him."

"You said–"

"And now I'm saying different." I bit my lip shyly.

His hands slid up from the pleather and settled on his knees. Turning toward the camera, I bent over, sliding my hands down my stomach and moving my panties to the side as I turned around. When I settled on his leg, the back of his hand was pressed against my lips. "See?"

He nodded, mesmerized as I slid back and forth across his hand.

"Do you like that?"

"I'm going to come."

"Can't have that now, can we? Not yet." I slid down his leg and dropped to my knees. Turning back to face him, I spread his legs and pressed my chest against him. Deftly, I ran my hands up his chest and back down before sliding over his legs. My hand unzipped his zipper before moving on. On the upstroke, I fished him out of his pants. He was staring at me incredulously. "See? Quick and easy."

"How much practice have you had?"

"That's not a question you ask a lady."

His face fell. "You are absolutely right, I apologize."

"No need. You didn't hurt my feelings," I answered, letting my tits dangle over his hardness. His silky hardness sent a shiver of pleasure straight from my nipples to my clit. "How close are you?"

"Very. I'm sorry."

"Don't be. I wanted you to be." I got up off the ground and straddled him, trapping his cock between us and blocking the view from the camera. I arched my back, pressing my nipple against his lips as I looked up and winked at whoever was watching the monitor. With my left hand, I slid my hand down my stomach, gripped his cock and lifted my hips. With one swift movement, he was inside me and I was leaning over him, fucking him in the booth.

"Holy fuck."

"You gonna come?"

"Yes. Quick, pull it out!"

"It's okay. It would be a cold day in hell before I got pregnant." *With a human. Without a bit of magic.*

He started breathing heavy, and his face contorted with every movement of my hips. Within moments, his seed was splashing inside me as I milked him dry. Not just his cock, his energy, too. I sucked it in and came on top of him, pressing my face against his neck.

"Are you sure we're safe?"

I could see the worry in his eyes. Not of just getting me pregnant and showing up with a court order for child support. No, there was something deeper. I chuckled when I realized he was worried about catching something from sticking his dick in a stripper.

"Don't worry. I'm on birth control, not that I ever need it. This is farther than I've ever gone…with a customer." I let my lips graze his.

"Don't suppose you'd want to have dinner sometime," he managed to stammer.

"Ryan… Are you asking a stripper out on a date?"

"Do strippers date?"

"We do."

"Then, yes. Kara Day, would you have dinner with me on Sunday?"

"We just happen to be closed on Sundays. So, yeah."

His grin was interrupted by his very wet cock slipping out of me.

"Mmm." I reached between us, getting my fingers *very* wet and slipping them between my lips. "You want a taste?"

Chapter 1

The sound of the alarm going off made me groan, sit up, and start crying. Without looking, I reached over and slapped it off and flopped over face first on the bed, trying to dry my eyes on the pillow. *His* pillow. He'd been gone for over a year, and I was still having the same dreams every night.

Succubus dreams weren't like mortal ones. We remembered every sensation, sound, scent, and scene as we relieved the moment. It was a survival mechanism for us when we had droughts between feedings. We could actually get a little juice from the dreams themselves, and it had been over a year since I'd fed.

To say I felt like shit was the understatement of all time. I did have a stash of power, tucked into my own little corner of Hell, but I'd been skimming from the top of it for the past year. I'd promised myself not to touch it again. I'd have to live off the dreams or go out and face the world.

"Come on, Mom. Get out of bed. We're going to be late."

Without looking, I flipped my boy child off. He cackled as he closed my bedroom door and went to fix himself some sugar puffs or whatever the fuck kids ate for breakfast.

Ryan's picture frowned at me from his nightstand. Not really, but it wasn't hard to picture him being disappointed in me from the human afterlife.

"Don't judge me," I told him, and reached over, running my finger down his cheek. "How the hell do you expect me to survive with two kids without you? Bet you didn't think of that before you went and got killed."

A year. That's how long it had been since I'd had a conversation with my Ryan. My perfect, loving, tender, annoyingly sweet hubster. After I'd met him in the strip club, we'd had our date. And hundreds more. Eventually, he moved into my house, and we got married. *That*, in and of itself, was almost unheard of for succubae. We weren't the marrying kind. And to have a child with a mortal was an almost unforgivable sin. Hybrid offspring were... unusually unusual. Half-demon, half-human hybrids. Cambion.

Luckily, Ryn and Karl, my fifteen-year-old offspring, hadn't really manifested any demonic abnormalities as of yet. I wasn't looking forward to that day, let me tell you. They thought their mama was just as human as their recently deceased father. They were in for quite a shock. The birds and the bees were going to have to be replaced with the horns and the tails. If it were set in stone exactly what the traits of cambions were, it would have been a lot easier if I had a timeline. Either way, we needed to have a chat soon.

I still couldn't believe I let Ryan talk me into having them. I'd planned on only giving him one, but of course, I'd been blessed–and by blessed, I mean cursed–with twins. They were funny, smart, gorgeous, and had a *wicked* sense of humor. Karl was a miniature Ryan with longer hair. It kept hanging in his face, but was almost long enough to ponytail. I couldn't wait for him to ditch the manbun. Ryn was my mini-me. A little thicker, but not chubby. More muscular. But seeing her face and hair was almost like looking in a mirror. Except for their eyes. They both had Ryan's eyes.

Luckily, they were low maintenance, or I'd have hitched a ride straight back to Hell after Ryan was killed in a motorcycle accident.

Succubae sucked at parenting. We usually paid people to raise our offspring, but Ryan had made me swear upon all that was unholy that I would never do that to our kids if anything ever happened to him. Who knew that day would actually come? What could I say? I was a sucker for him.

My heart heaved. It usually did when I was having melancholic mornings after having particularly vivid dreams. The other day, I'd dreamed of our wedding. Stripper bridesmaids had caused quite the uproar with Ryan's family. He thought the whole damn thing was funny as hell.

He hadn't even tried to get me to quit stripping. I needed it to feed. In fact, he hadn't even *suggested* that I stop. When he found out what I really was, he wasn't surprised. "You had to be. No woman can exude that much raw sexual energy and be human," he'd simply said when I finally broke down and told him. I'd made myself tell him *everything* before we got married.

From that day on, he was the only man for me. Human or other. I hadn't wanted anybody else. Feeding from their lust as I danced at Full Exposure, I went home to my sweet, sweet Ryan and sated myself on his cock.

And then he was gone. Taken by a drunk driver who thought those medians on the highway were just a suggestion. He'd hit Ryan head on and killed them both. He was lucky. If he'd survived, and I'd gotten my hands on him... They never would have found his body. Hell, he might even still be alive, just fervently wishing he wasn't. He took my love from me, that deserved five lifetimes of torture.

My bedroom brightened as my eyes flared in anger.

With a groan, I got up out of bed, heading for the kitchen. That's where humans insisted on keeping the coffee maker. On the nightstand seemed like a more logical place to me, but what the Hell did I know? I was just a demon. Humaning was hard. They had so many rules and inhibitions, it drove me insane.

Ryn handed me a mug as soon as I exited the bedroom. I blinked in surprise. "Morning, Brat."

"Morning, oh giver of life."

I chuckled and followed her back into the kitchen. She scooped some eggs onto a plate with toast. "Is that for me?" I was joking. The kids knew I never ate breakfast.

"Make your own." She stuck her tongue out at me. "Wait. Isn't it *your* job to make *me* breakfast?"

"Dream on." I reached over and snagged a piece of her toast as she walked by and set her plate down in her usual spot at the nook table.

She frowned and held her fork up in a threatening manner. "I will shank you."

"Try it, pipsqueak, and you'll be eating your eggs out of the side of your head."

"Most parents don't threaten their children and steal their food," Karl said as he sat down with his bowl of cereal. Ryn loved eggs. Karl, not so much. He was like me when it came down to eating breakfast.

Ryn stared at her plate, suddenly quiet.

"You okay, kid?"

"Yeah. Just had another I miss Dad moment."

Nodding in understanding, I took a swig of my coffee and stared out the window. All of us had gone quiet, each remembering Ryan. "So…excited about your first day of school?"

They both shook their heads. Not that I could blame them. They had suffered last year, the school they attended was a non-religious prep academy. The same one their father had taught at. Since the day they started kindergarten, they got up with him, went to school with him, and came home with him. With him gone, they were lost. That part about me being a shitty parent became quite evident. Their attendance last year hadn't been the most stellar. I tried to distract them by taking them places—the mall, the beach, anywhere but there. It reminded us way too much of him.

I'd been tossing around an idea in my head. Maybe it was time to get the kids thoughts on it. "So. I was thinking…"

"Didn't we tell you not to do things you weren't used to?" Karl grinned at me and shoveled a heaping spoonful of Sugar Puffs into his mouth.

I dipped the tip of my finger into his soggy cereal and flicked it at him.

"Ewww. Now, I'm gonna smell like milk all day!"

"Don't pick on your mother. She was thinking about you."

Karl looked at Ryn. "Oh, boy."

"What?"

"Usually, when 'rents say they've been thinking about you," Karl said with little enthusiasm, "it means that they're about to drop a bomb on you in your best interests. Unfortunately, what said units think is best for you is usually something that is going to suck monkey balls."

I nodded. That was a fair assessment. Karl never ceased to amaze me. "Well, you're wrong in this case. I was thinking not only about you, but of you, too. Why I wanted your input to see if it was even feasible."

"What?" Ryn scooped the last of her eggs into her mouth. "Wait. Let me guess. You want to go to the mall today and want us to go with you, skip school."

"Well, shit. That idea is *way* better than the one I came up with. Let's just do that instead." I winked to let her know I was kidding.

"Just tell us, Mom."

"You guys want to move?"

They both stared open mouthed for a moment. Then they looked at each other.

"Where?" Karl finally asked.

I shrugged. "Don't know. Anywhere but here. Too many memories in this house, and I just can't seem to get away from them."

Karl reached over and put his hand on my arm, nodding in understanding. "Can we move someplace that has seasons? I've always wanted to see snow."

"It's snowed in Orlando before."

"Flurries don't count," Ryn chimed in.

"Do you want to build a snowman?" I sang the question and earned two sets of eyerolls. My mission for the day, accomplished.

"Actually, we kind of do. Dad used to talk about moving all the time."

"He did?" That little tidbit was news to me. Demons liked warmer weather. The thought of snow actually kind of freaked me out a little. The thought of freezing my nipples off scared me a lot. Ryan knew that, and that was probably the reason he never asked, or brought it up to me. "Where?"

"Everywhere. The thought of moving to a little town with actual seasons was one of his favorite story topics."

"So, you guys seem a little excited. You're okay with this?"

"Wish you hadn't waited until the day school started to bring it up, but yeah." Ryn pushed her plate away. "Did Dad have any family anywhere?"

Ryan's parents had died when he was in college. He had distant cousins and an aunt and uncle. I'd met them at the wedding, but he never really talked about his family much. I never brought it up, because I was a friggin' demon. I'd originally told him I was an orphan, and being a succubus, that was pretty close to the truth. I had a sire and a dam, both of noble demon lineage. But as soon as I was brought into being, they handed me off to a wet nurse. They'd done their responsibility and procreated. The rest was up to me. If they saw me sitting around lamenting the demise of my late human husband and conversing with my half-human offspring, they probably would have been mortified. "Yeah, but I don't know where. Or even how to get in touch with them. They weren't exactly close."

"So, anywhere we want?"

I nodded. "You guys pick, and I'll start looking for a house. As long as it's not in a different country. That would open a whole can of worms."

24

"That's fine! We find your terms acceptable." Ryn grinned. I had a feeling she already had a place in mind. "When?"

"As soon as possible. No sense starting the school year if we're moving."

"I've seen you go to some great lengths to avoid taking us to school, but this one tops it all." Karl started laughing.

"What? If I didn't wanna take you to school, I'd still be in bed."

"Uh huh."

"I'm a great mother who takes pride in the education and wellbeing of her children!"

They both started laughing.

"I'm being serious here! Just you watch. When we get to the new house, I'll get you all enrolled, and might even volunteer at the school. Not like I have a job anyway."

Karl turned to his sister. "Oh my God, Ryn. Could you imagine her with all the other moms?"

"Remember when she had to take you to your soccer game because Dad had parent teacher conferences?"

"And ended up missing them trying to persuade the cop to not arrest Mom?" They were both having trouble speaking around their laughter.

"You two are hilarious." I picked up my mug and went to make a refill.

I had just hit brew when the twins chimed in together, the freaky way twins often did, "We want to move to Boston."

"Huh?" I turned slowly to see if someone had replaced my kids with insane replacements. "Why you wanna pick like as far away as possible to move? And how did you decide so quickly?"

"We've actually thought about it before. It's because of Dad."

"Because he went to college there?"

They nodded.

"The whole point of moving was to get away from all these painful memories, and you want to move to where he went to college?"

"We won't actually be in college for four years..." Ryn took a sip of her orange juice. "Plus, we have no memories of Dad *in* college, just wondering what he was like when he was there. That's a lot different and makes me kind of happy."

"Us," Karl added.

I stared at them for a good long moment, until the Keurig sputtered the last of my coffee into my mug. Turning, I gave them my answer. "Fine. That kind of makes me happy, too. *But* we're not living *in* the city. We'll find a suburb. Nice house with a picket fence and no nosy neighbors."

"Can we get a dog?"

"No."

Chapter 2

With a nervous laugh, I turned the key in the brass deadbolt on the outside of the worn, but presentable, door. "This is it. You little shits nervous?"

"Why would we be? It's a house, not school."

"Yeah, well, you're starting tomorrow," I retorted, and pushed the door open. "Go pick your rooms, the movers weren't that far behind us when they stopped for gas."

It had taken us two days just to drive from Orlando to Bickering. The kids had groaned when I showed them on a map how far it was from Boston, but I refused to move any closer than that. Human cities, really large ones, enticed way too many supernatural creatures to call it home. Yes, we lived in Orlando, but only two percent of that is downtown. The rest is hundreds of little suburbs spread out around it, and the only thing downtown was businesses, bars, and restaurants.

"We could have at least moved to Salem," Karl reiterated for the thirteen-thousandth time since we'd headed north. "At least that place has some history. Bickering is a hipster mecca."

"Which is what we are," I said, and took my first step into our new home.

Ryn whistled in appreciation. Our house in Orlando was gorgeous, but modern. The houses in Bickering were older, but a different kind of beauty. Grandiose, with wood floors and crown molding. Studies with wood walls. I'd fallen in love with it on the realtor's website. It had put a huge gaping hole in my funds, but at least we had a nice house. I took consolation that once the house in Orlando sold, some, if not most, of that money would funnel its way back into my bank account. If not, I could always start stripping again. I did kind of miss it. And the endless stream of sustenance.

"Okay, maybe Bickering isn't so bad," Karl said as he looked up at the landing above, the polished oak banister, and the vaulted ceiling with ornate lighting illuminating the entrance with a warm glow.

"Glad you finally see it my way. Go look at the kitchen."

"Why bother? Not like we use it."

I winced at the little jab. Mother of the Year, I was not. A fact that they never let me forget. Not out of spite, I think they appreciated my hands-off approach, but sometimes I think they got a little jealous of their friends who still had both parents and ate dinner at a table, talking about their day. Or staring at their cellphones like most families.

"I'll burn you something for dinner."

"I'm good. Chinese is fine." He grinned and headed toward the stairs. "Gonna go pick my room."

"Not the big one with the bathroom, that bitch is mine," I called up after him.

Ryn, in an uncharacteristically tender moment, hugged me before taking off after her brother. I didn't even get a chance to awkwardly pat her on the head. My usual response when they displayed affection.

I was lucky they didn't hate me, but then again, I wasn't around much when they were younger. They spent the day with Ryan at school, and then when they came home, we ate dinner before I went to work. They were basically his kids. I was just the egg donor and incubator.

"Damnit, Ryan," I whispered, and started up the stairs. Until the knock on the front door and the chime of the doorbell stopped me. Sighing, I walked back to the heavy wood door and flung it open.

"That didn't take you long–" I stopped and blinked. I'd been expecting the movers, not a middle-aged couple standing there bearing a cake…

"I know! We'd heard the place had sold and that you'd be moving in tonight or tomorrow, so I had a cake all prepared! Welcome to the neighborhood, neighbor!" Her shrill voice didn't match her looks. She had the typical suburban chicken-butt haircut, dirty blonde, but her ends were frosted platinum. She might have been athletic in her youth, but looked like she enjoyed eating. Not fat, nor chubby. Frumpy. Her face was positively beautiful, almost cherubic.

"Uhhh…."

"Oh, silly me! I'm Karen, and this is my husband, Rick!" Rick, on the other hand, had the typical dad bod. I found myself smiling at his warm brown eyes, stubble, and khaki pants. I was guessing he was in the insurance business. Maybe an optometrist. His brown curly hair was cut close, and he was *tall*. Almost six-and-a-half feet.

"Kara." They stared at me for a moment, until I realized they were waiting for an invitation inside. "You want to come in?" I pulled the door open and stepped back.

"Oh! We'd love to!" Cake-laden Karen stepped inside and whistled. "Oh my God. I am sooo jelly of your floors! Ours are tile. Marble. Venetian. Easier to keep clean, and they don't scratch, but they cost a fortune!"

"I can only imagine."

Rick shot me an apologetic look for his overexuberant wife. "So, what brings you to Bickering?"

"My kids picked it out on a map."

They both started laughing. "You have kids?"

I got that reaction a lot. I was sixty human years old, but most people mistook me for a college student. Even my kids were wondering why I wasn't getting older. I was hoping their powers would manifest before I had to sit down with them and have the talk. The one where I told them about what their mother was, not the one about dicks and hoo-has. I gave that one to them already. They were

29

both eleven, and curious, when I'd sat them down. "Yeah, two."

"Wait, you're serious?"

"Of course. Can I take that from you?" I motioned at the cake in her hands.

"They must be babies..." She handed it to me, and I led them toward the kitchen.

"Fifteen."

"*You* must have been a baby! Wait... They're both fifteen? Twins?"

"Yep." I paused a moment at the bottom of the stairs. "Kids! Come meet the neighbors!" Whether they came down or not, I didn't really care. I was just being polite and didn't give a crap if Karen believed me or not. "I wasn't a baby, though. Got pregnant when I was twenty-five."

I heard Karen skid to a stop behind me. "You're *fourty*?"

No, sixty. "Yep." I turned and gave her a smile over my shoulder. At least *that* I could prove. My driver's license had my fake age on it.

"Wow. You keep in great shape..."

"I had to. Used to be an exotic dancer."

You could have cut the silence in the hallway with a chainsaw. I flicked on the kitchen light and set the cake down on the granite countertop. Whoever had owned the house before I bought it had completely redone the kitchen. At least I wouldn't have to worry about the stove blowing up in case I needed to reheat a pizza or something.

"Exotic dancer?"

"Yeah. Stripper." I grinned at her, waiting for the explosion. It usually happened when I told people what I used to do for a living. I wasn't shy, and I wouldn't lie. People just sucked.

"Oh my God!"

Here it comes... Meltdown in 3...2...1...

"My girlfriends and I have been trying to take a pole dancing class for-ev-er. Do you think you can teach us?"

Huh? Wait... "What?"

"Yeah! There's a ton of studios with classes in Boston, and there was *one* in town, but they closed a year ago. We've been trying to get one of the larger ones in Boston to open a studio here, but so far, we haven't had any luck! Do you think you could teach us?"

"Uh...sure." *What the fuck?*

She fucking squealed and grabbed my hands, jumping up and down. "You *have* to come over for dinner tomorrow! I'll introduce you to the girls!"

"Okay."

"Bring your kids! We'll introduce them to ours, even if mine are a little younger. We have a boy who is thirteen and our daughter is fourteen!"

"Can't wait." I managed a weak smile and to keep the Taco Bell we'd had for lunch down. We'd lived in our old house for thirteen years. I'd waved at our neighbor twice. Never did learn her name.

The kids skidded to a stop in the kitchen, their socks sliding over the hardwood. "What was that noise? Oh. Hi," Karl said, and smiled at the neighbors.

"Kids, this is Karen and Rick from next door. Say hi."

Ever polite, a trait that they picked up from Ryan, not me, Karl shook both their hands and introduced himself. Ryn did the same, but a little less exuberantly.

"We'll introduce you guys to Billy and Madison tomorrow!"

My kids stopped in their tracks and turned to stare at me. I shrugged. "They were nice enough to invite us over for dinner. And give us cake. Want a piece?"

"I'd love one, but we should probably wait for the plates and silverware to show up, Mom."

"Oh. Right. Good call."

The doorbell went off, and I fervently hoped it *was* the movers and not more neighbors. "So, what school are you going to go to? Have you enrolled yet?"

Karen wasted no time grilling the kids for info as I walked over to the door and opened it. "Howdy, neighbor."

The guy standing alone in my doorway was six feet of sexy. No dad bod, dark brown hair with eyes to match, stubbled beard. He was dressed in khaki pants, too, but he wore them a hundred times better than Rick. I nearly drooled. It wasn't that I was interested, but... Never hurt to start hunting my next meal. If I didn't feast soon, I was going to start having problems controlling my powers. Demon bodies had ways of ensuring our survival. It wasn't always pretty or survivable to everyone around us. Better to get over the funk I'd been in. Ryan would have wanted it that way. "Hi."

"Did I see Karen and Rick come in?"

"Yeah. They're in the kitchen."

"I'm sorry," he whispered, and gave me a little smile. "I'm Daniel, your other neighbor." He reached out his hand, and I took it in mine, letting his energy wash over me as I took a little sip. It wasn't enough to feed me, but it might keep the dreams at bay for a day or two.

"Would you like to come in?" *Me,* I finished the sentence in my head. I gave a little gasp at the thought. Maybe I was losing my mind. Or maybe I was just hungrier than I thought. Either way, it was the first sexual thought I'd had about another person besides Ryan in a *very* long time. Maybe it was time. He wasn't coming back.

The familiar pain gripped my heart, and I let it. It would always be there, that I knew. But how I let it affect me, that was something I *could* control.

"Maybe some other time. When you have furniture." He chuckled.

I looked over my shoulder and then back at Daniel. "Good point."

"I'm just teasing. I'll let you guys get settled in. I'm assuming that was your younger brother and sister with you?"

"You spying on your neighbors, Daniel?"

"Just the extraordinarily cute ones." He leaned against the door frame. "I'm kidding. I was watering the flowers when you pulled in."

"Most people pee inside."

"I was using a hose…"

"I'm impressed." I laughed a little. At his expense, I admit, but it had been so long since I'd had a meaningful, flirty conversation.

"Oh, I have a feeling the neighborhood is about to get a *lot* more fun… Glad to have you."

"You haven't. Yet…" I tucked my bottom lip under my teeth and turned away. "When we get settled in. I'll have you over for…dinner."

"I'd like that."

"You say that now. You haven't had my cooking." I panicked a little inside. *Maybe I should have Ryn cook. She can make eggs. Roasted meat and vegetables shouldn't be much harder.*

"I'd like that. I'll bring dessert."

"No need. I'm sure we can find you something sweet to munch on."

He blushed and blew out a puff of air as he tried to wrap his mind around my innuendo. "And will your uh…husband be joining us?"

And then he had to go and ruin the moment. "No." I shook my head.

"Sorry. Divorced?"

"No. He was in an accident. A year ago."

He frowned. "I'm sorry."

I held up my hand. Not really wanting to hear it. I'd been having such a good time. "Getting past it. Part of the move."

"Gotcha. Took me a while just to get over my divorce. And I hated her. Sleeping alone…sucks."

I nodded. "That it does. Goodnight, Daniel." I smiled and slowly shut the door, giving him ample opportunity to move out of the way.

"Goodnight, Kara."

"Was that Daniel?" Karen chirped behind me.

Plastering a smile on my face, I turned to her. "Yes. He stopped by to introduce himself."

33

She leaned a little closer. "That boy is primo. All the divorcées are after him and his landscaping tools, if you know what I mean!" She giggled conspiratorially.

"His cock?"

She sputtered and blushed beet red.

"What?"

"Nothing! Yes. That's what I meant," she answered defeatedly.

"He was attractive." I took one more glance at the door, vaguely wishing he had stayed.

"Oooh. Somebody has a crush!"

"Crush? No. I just found him attractive and wouldn't mind fucking him."

When I turned back to Karen, she was as white as a ghost and her mouth was hanging open.

"Are you okay?"

"You sure do know how to speak your mind…"

"Saves time." I tilted my head, hearing the sound of airbrakes outside the house. "Finally. The movers are here. Would you like me to see if I can find the coffee maker?"

"No! We'll let you get to work. Are your kids going to school tomorrow?"

"Yes. I have a meeting with the administrators tomorrow about their enrollment. And I have to pay their tuition." After researching the school system…a private academy sounded like the much better option.

"It's expensive, I know. But totally worth it!"

"Your children attend Brentworth?"

"Yes! Most of the neighborhood kids do."

"Isn't that convenient…"

"It is! Especially since it's so close. I'm president of the PTA!"

"Of course, you are."

She nodded. "Tell you what, I'll meet you outside in the morning. I take the kids to school. You guys can hitch a ride with us, and I'll introduce you to Mr. Marshall. The principal."

"That would be great," I said with about as much enthusiasm as I could possibly fake.

"We'll see you then! Rick! We're leaving."

"Yes, dear. Night, kids."

"Night, Mr. James."

"Your husband's name is Rick James?"

"Yes?"

"That's super freaky." I giggled at my own joke. If I had a thousand hands, I still couldn't count the number of times I'd danced to that song on my fingers.

"What is?" Karen seemed genuinely confused.

Sighing and counting to ten severed heads, I found my smile. "It's a song. By Rick James. Never mind." I was saved by the sound of the doorbell. For the third time. In one night. Maybe it wasn't too late to move back to Florida.

Chapter 3

"You're uh...wearing that. To meet the principal?"

I looked down at the silk shorts and matching top I had slept in. "Yes? Why?"

"You might want to put something else on. Longer," Ryn said with a giggle.

"Why?"

"Because. That's um...very clingy."

"Too sexy?"

"Mom! You can see your..."

"Hoo-ha?"

"Uh huh."

"Fine." I trudged upstairs and found a pair of jean shorts in the same box I'd pulled out my sleepwear. It was going to take us a month to unpack everything, and I was already exhausted. The juice I'd managed to drain from Daniel was long gone. We were up until one in the morning just getting everything in the house.

I took the stairs down two at a time. Rick and Karen were probably out front already, and I had a feeling if we were late, that would be tantamount to murder.

"Better?"

Ryn closed her eyes and lifted her eyebrows, shaking her head. "A little."

"What's wrong with these?"

"Those aren't shorts, it's a belt with leg holes. Never mind. Come on." She turned and walked out the front door.

"Where's your brother?"

"Out here already."

I slipped on my flipflops and walked outside. And froze my fucking nipples off. When you spend sixty years living near the equator, mornings in the north can be a little different. Even if it was August. The door slammed shut behind me, and it would have taken me ten minutes to dig out a jacket anyway. I crossed my arms over my chest and walked down the driveway.

Karen and her two kids were parked in the street at the end of the drive, waiting impatiently.

"Sorry," I heard Karl mumble to Karen as he climbed in the back of her maroon minivan.

"Shit. I forgot my coffee."

"There's coffee at the school! Come on, lazy bones. The kids are going to be late!"

She was so fucking chipper, I wanted to rip the mailbox out of the ground and stab her in the face with the pointy end.

"My goodness! Don't you have a jacket?"

"Still packed," I grumbled, and walked around the van, getting in the front seat next to her.

"Oh, sweetie. You're gonna freeze!"

"Tell me about it," I managed to stutter through chattering teeth.

She reached over and punched a few buttons on the dash, and I was rewarded with a stream of warm air blowing on my face. "Better?"

"M-m-m-much."

She giggled and put the van into gear, gunning it and speeding toward the front gate. I nearly ripped the 'oh shit' bar off in a fit of panic as she rounded the corner. Luckily, the school was only a few blocks away, and Karen skidded the yuppy-wagon into a spot right in the front of the school. "Just in time!"

"You can say that again. I was just about to pee."

"You should have gone before you left the house!"

Ignoring the crackhead behind the wheel, I opened the door and spilled out of the Toyota Sarcophagus, grateful for the chill of the ground against my hands to calm my nerves. I rose from the ground just as Karl got out of the van and gave me a sympathetic grin. "That was fun."

"I'm having you tested for drugs, boy child."

"High on life, Mother." He chuckled and slung his bag over his shoulder, heading for the front door.

"You two, get to class. I'm going to show Kara and the kids to the front office."

"Yes, Mother." The slightly younger children waved goodbye to us and headed inside. Karl opened the door for them and waited for us. It looked warm, if vaguely smelly, inside. I wrinkled my nose as I started walking toward the yellow glow of the halls of Brentworth Academy.

"I know," I heard Ryn whisper to Karen.

"Know what?" I asked over my shoulder.

"Your shorts…" Karen sounded almost apologetic.

"What's wrong with my shorts?" I looked behind me at my butt.

"Kara… I can see your buttocks."

Ryn started snickering.

"So?"

"You're meeting the principal of your children's school. You should have dressed up."

"You should have seen what she *was* wearing." My daughter was such a helpful little imp.

I shrugged and headed for the door. Ryn mentioned something about a bra, but I wasn't really paying attention. I wanted nothing more than this morning to be over with, so I could go back to bed and dream. I'd woken up shaking, and not in a good way. I was at my limit, and the stress of the move didn't help in the least.

The receptionist behind the glass window gave me one look from what she could see *above* the counter to the top of my head and frowned. "Can I help you?"

"Yes. Enrolling my offspring."

"Offspring?"

"Yes. It means children."

"Are you sure you have the right school?" She sneered until she saw Karen walk in behind me and stand next to me.

"Good morning, Margaret. She's here to see Mr. Marshall."

"You know this woman?"

"Know her? She's my neighbor. We're practically *sisters*."

I practically vomited in my mouth.

"Name?" She grabbed the handset from the black phone on her desk.

"Yours? I believe it's Margaret."

"Your name. What is *your* name?"

"Kara Dell. Mr. Marshall should be expecting me." He better damn well be for the amount of money I was about to hand him. I had the folded-up check in my shirt pocket. Looking down to make sure, I laughed. The check was covering one extraordinarily hard nipple. The other one was tenting the silk shirt I was wearing. I looked like a fucking unicorn. At least I figured out why my child and neighbor were discussing bras as we walked in.

"Mr. Marshall, I have a Kara Dell here to see you." There was a pause as she listened to whatever he had to say. "Mrs. Stanton and Mr. Blake. Got it. I'll send her in." She hung up the phone and wrote something down on two scraps of papers, handing one to each of the offspring. "These are your homerooms. I'll have the runner show you where they are." She stood up from her desk and looked at somebody inside the office. "Mr. Hansen, show the new students to their classes and then get to yours."

"Yes, Miss Steinger." The door to the office opened, and a boy, probably the same age as mine, motioned with his head for the kids to follow him.

"Bye, Mom," they said, and gave me a small smile before following the skinny kid.

"Remember having to walk them to their classes on the first day? I miss them being that little."

"No."

"You didn't?"

"My husband was a teacher at the children's school. He took them to and from. Raised them, too. He wanted kids so bad."

"You divorced now? I'm surprised he didn't fight for partial custody."

"He's dead."

"Oh my God, Kara! I'm sorry."

I held up my hand, not wanting any sympathy from anyone. "It's okay. I don't like to talk about it. Car accident."

"I understand," she said quietly, and didn't say another word. We stood there awkwardly until the sound of a door inside the office broke the silence. A moment later, a balding head poked out.

"Mrs. Dell?"

"Morning," I grumbled.

He gave me a once over, and I swear his eyebrows twitched. "Please come in," he said, and held the door open. His face fell when he saw Karen. "Morning, Karen. What can I do for you?"

"I'm here with Kara." She pointed at me.

"You two know each other?" He was asking me, not her.

"Neighbors," I explained, and rolled my eyes.

He *hmphed* and nodded, leading us into the sanctum of the inner office. I spun and caught Margaret checking out my ass. I blew her a kiss before following Karen into the principal's office.

"Well, let me start by saying how very glad I am that you have chosen to enroll your children in Brentworth Academy's long heritage of education–" He stopped talking when I held up my hand.

"I did my research and everything I read pointed me to your door. Sort of crunched for time, we just got to the house last night, and I have a billion things to do. I trust you to take care of my offspring." Reaching into my pocket, I pulled out the check and set it on his desk. "Is there anything you need from me?"

His eyes roamed my chest, and he finally caught my eyes. "No. Not unless you would like a tour of the school?"

"I'm hardly dressed for that. I was lucky to find this outfit in one of the boxes," I lied smoothly. There had to be a Starbucks around. Maybe I could entice Karen into stopping on the way home.

"Very well, then. Should you have any questions, feel free to contact the school."

"Oh, Margaret and I are already friends. Thank you, Mr. Marshall."

"It was a pleasure, Mrs. Dell." He stood and offered his hand. I shook it, resisting the urge to wipe it off on my shirt as I turned and walked away. The man was a creep through and through. I momentarily wondered how many MILFs he'd had under his desk to get, or keep, their kids enrolled in the snob school. Then I realized I really didn't want to be thinking about his cock in *anybody's* mouth. Shud. Der.

"Coffee? I'm buying," I asked Karen as we exited the office, making it a point to pull my shorts even higher as we walked past Margaret.

"I'd love some!"

"Starbucks?"

"Right around the corner."

"Convenient."

"We must have a toast to a new school year full of fun! You certainly know how to make an impression. I thought I knew how to be rude to that stick in the mud. You elevated it to an artform. You should have seen his face when you stopped him mid-speech."

"I found myself unable to look at his face. He wasn't looking at mine, anyway."

"Well, yes. Any guy would be staring at your chest. You should have worn a bra."

"Keeps the guys distracted."

She chuckled and keyed the locks to the van. We got in, and she drove a little slower—NASCAR instead of Formula 1. She circled around the Starbucks three times until she got a parking spot by the front doors, cutting off another minivan to get the primo spot. Amazing the lengths humans went to, to avoid walking fifty fucking feet. It was a wonder Karen didn't weigh more. Pole dancing and Zumba must have been paying off.

We walked up to the counter, and the twenty-something, curly-haired kid stared openmouthed at my chest. Finally remembering he could get fired for ogling the customers, he raised his eyes. "Um. Morning. What can I get started for you?"

"I'll have a venti coffee, black."

"Black?"

"Yes. I like my coffee like I like my men."

"Black?"

"Hard to swallow."

He blushed a furious crimson color and started frantically punching buttons on the register. I caught a slight charge from him imagining me deepthroating, and I relished in the taste. He'd been around the magic beans for too long, they were starting to flavor him, as well.

"Are you together?" He looked to Karen.

I answered him. "Like as in a couple? I tried one night when she was drunk. Made it to second base, but then she remembered she likes guys. So, not for lack of effort on my part. But I'm paying for her coffee."

His slight arousal swelled, as I imagined other parts of him did as well. I would have bet twenty bucks he was going to head straight to the bathroom after we got our coffee and rub one out. Maybe, if we sat close enough to the bathroom, I could collect some of that purged lust.

If I followed him into the bathroom, I could drink straight from the source…

Bad, Kara. Don't need a reputation as the barista blowing bitch on your first day. I need to slow down. Good things cum to those who wait.

"You okay? You want to get something to eat? You look a little hungry…"

"You have no idea, Karen. I feel like I haven't eaten in a year…"

43

She blinked at me rapidly, leaning closer. "Huh."

"What?"

"Must have been the sunlight coming in or something, but it looked like your eyes were glowing red for a second."

Shit. Fuck. I was hungrier than I thought.

"Mornin', ladies."

Karen turned. "Daniel! We were just having coffee. Won't you join us?"

"Don't mind if I do. Have a meeting at ten, so I can slack off for a bit. You don't mind, do you, Kara?"

"Not in the slightest." *Fuck yes! Breakfast.*

He ordered, and we grabbed a booth by the window while he waited for his coffee. "Girl, if you don't carpe his diem, you're gonna be sorry. He's single, but I don't see him staying that way for long. Every bitch in heat in our neighborhood has tried to bag that boy with everything from casseroles to brownies."

"They used food?"

"How else are you supposed to entice a man? Think they want to eat take out for the rest of their lives?"

"Give them something sweeter to eat."

"Cupcakes?"

"Cuntcakes…" I was treated to a mid-morning caffeine shower courtesy of Karen's shocked sensibilities.

"Did you say…"

I nodded. "The way to a man's heart isn't through his stomach, Karen. It's through his dick."

"That might be the way to his bed, sweetie, but not his heart. Why buy the cow when the milk is free?"

"Why buy the whole pig, just for a little sausage?"

"Pardon?"

"Karen. I was married. It was the happiest I've ever been in my life. I'm never going to recreate what I lost, so why even try? I came here to move on, not move in." I looked at Daniel, who gave me a smile while he waited. "He has definite recurring snack qualities, but it's time to broaden my taste buds again."

44

"I hate you right now."

"Because you think I'm a slut."

"Hell no. I'm jealous." She blushed and sipped her coffee.

"Of what?" Daniel asked as he slid into the booth next to me.

"How gorgeous Kara is. Can you believe she's forty? I'd swear she wasn't old enough to drink."

He gave me a little surprised look. "Really?"

I nodded and took a long swig of my coffee.

"Holy hell. How do you stand to chug it when it's that hot?"

I blinked at Karen. It had been a while since I'd had coffee with complete strangers. Ryan knew I could chug boiling water without so much as getting a blister. In fact, I preferred my coffee scalding to hot, it had way more flavor. "Hot things never really bothered me."

"Me, neither," Daniel said and grinned.

I chuckled softly and leaned a little closer. He smelled absolutely divine, and he wasn't even aroused yet. Yet.

"Aren't you cold?"

"Fricking freezing. I have a jacket, in a box, in the house somewhere."

"I have a sweatshirt in the Jeep, if you want to borrow it."

"It's okay. It's warm in here, and I'm heading home after this."

"Unpacking?"

Zoning out for a moment, I was almost overcome by the miasma of lust coming not from Daniel, but from the bathrooms. The barista I'd teased had succumbed to my torture, and was in the bathroom furiously pounding his meat. If I closed my eyes, I could not only see him, but the little fantasy he had going on in his little head. Karen and I were on our knees, kissing each other around the shaft of his cock. My lady parts practically spasmed under the table.

"Yes," I managed to answer Daniel a little breathlessly. Grinning, I took another sip of my coffee.

"You okay, Kara? Your face is a little flushed. I hope you're not getting sick."

I was watching the show in my head and not really listening to Karen. The kid was edging himself, taking his fifteen-minute break a little early. He wanted to make it last...

Absentmindedly, I set my hand down beside me, I'd been closer to Daniel than I realized, and it ended up on his thigh. "Just a little dizzy. Long night," I managed to stammer.

"I bet. I'm free after my meeting if you need help moving furniture or anything."

Score. "I'd love to. The movers put everything where we wanted, but it's where we *thought* we wanted it. It was late, and I couldn't ask them to stay and shuffle it around."

"I'd be glad to help."

"What time?"

"Should be free around lunch time."

"I'll order delivery. Least I can do is feed you."

"Don't forget, you owe me dessert." I didn't miss his subtle reminder and flashed him a little smile.

"I would never forget to feed you dessert."

"Awww. I have a Zumba class at noon, or I'd help, too."

I turned from Daniel and raised my eyebrows at Karen. Her face flushed when she realized what I had planned.

"Well, next time," she said, and sipped her coffee nervously, just as the kid in the bathroom got a little too close to the edge.

I could feel his cum seeping from the tip of his cock onto his hand as he used it for lube, making long slow strokes up and down his length. My nostrils flared as I caught the earthy scent all the way at our booth. My lips parted, and my tongue slid over my lips.

I'd forgotten my hand on Daniel's thigh until his arousal hit my senses. I groaned as I sat back in the booth, sliding forward just a bit until my jean shorts dug into just the right places. A tiny quake shivered through me. A fact that didn't go unnoticed by Daniel. He leaned over and whispered in my ear. "Did you just come?"

"A little," I grinned at him.

He chuckled and kissed the lobe of my ear. "How?"

I turned my face to his and whispered in his ear. "I've been on edge all morning. My shorts are rubbing my clit."

He nodded in understanding. "Want me to call off my meeting?" He said it loud enough for Karen to hear.

Glancing over at her, I almost laughed. She was staring at us over her cup of coffee, watching in rapt fascination. "No. That's okay. It will give me some time to unpack and find the necessities."

"Longer shorts?" Karen asked bemusedly.

"Sheets," I replied honestly. I didn't mind sleeping on the bare mattress last night, but there was no way I was fucking on it.

"Oh. Wow." She shuddered like she was living vicariously through me.

Daniel chuckled. "Well, I should get this meeting over with so I can help you move that furniture."

"Come on over whenever you get back. I'll be around."

"See you then." He gave me a sly smile, got up, and headed for the door.

The kid in the bathroom blew his load at the same moment, and I threw my head back and came with him, taking all his pent-up lust and energy back into me with one long, quiet shudder. I bit my lip as I sat up and saw Karen was wearing the same expression I was.

"I think I just had an orgasm," she said quietly, glancing around nervously. She had obviously been caught up in my backlash.

"Why?" I asked innocently.

"Why? The two of you! That was the hottest thing I've ever seen! No games, no doubts. You two knew what you wanted and made it quite clear. You just met him last night! How is that even possible?"

"Easy. He's divorced, I'm a widow. We're using each other."

She blinked in surprise. "And you're okay with that?"

"Why wouldn't I be? I have needs, too."

"Looks like your needs are about to get filled..."

I chuckled. "Hopefully, he'll fill more than my needs... I'll let you know."

"You fucking better." It was the first time I'd heard Karen swear. She sounded almost like an addict.

Chapter 4

Ding dong.

If my doorbell was going to be going off that much, I needed to find something a little less annoying sounding. I set my coffee down on the counter next to the Keurig I had gleefully found while rummaging through boxes, and headed to the door before they pressed the button again.

"Sorry, meeting ran a little longer than I expected," Daniel said as soon as the door opened, giving me an apologetic look.

"No worries. Come on in. Coffee?"

"Please." He looked around the entrance and living room. The furniture was about the only neatly placed items in the house. Boxes were strewn everywhere, labeled by room. "Love what you've done with the place," he said with a chuckle.

"Yes. I was going for disaster chic with a little bit of apocalyptic Feng Shui. Think I nailed it."

"I'd say you nailed it. With every missile strike."

"Oh, come on. It's not *that* bad."

"I'm teasing," he said, and held up his hands defensively as we walked into the kitchen. "Nice furniture. I mean that."

"Thanks. The hubster decorated our last house. I have all the fashion sense of a stripper."

"I didn't see any poles."

"It's coming next week. Putting it up in the bedroom, though. Figured the HOA would complain about putting it in the front window."

"Yeah, the Donaldsons might bitch. Especially after Mr. Donaldson has a heart attack when he walks Mr. Whiskerbiscuit."

"They seriously named their dog that?"

"Whiskerbiscuit the Third. Mrs. Donaldson believes in a strict pet diet of half the food off her plate. She takes the dogs for brisk morning drags, since their little feet have trouble reaching the ground."

"That's horrible!" I couldn't help but laugh as I put the pod in the machine and hit brew. "Cream and sugar?" I started to panic, not knowing where they were or in which box. I had the powdered creamer, but had yet to make a trip to the store. It hadn't been a priority since I drank mine black.

"Black is fine," he said letting me off the hook. I knew he was, because he'd ordered it with both at the coffee shop. Daniel was sweeter than he looked. Not that he looked bitter, but he was a cross between bad boy and businessman. I wondered what he did for a living, and finally, my curiosity got the better of me.

"How'd your meeting go?"

He frowned. "Not as well as I'd hoped."

"That sucks. What do you do for a living?"

"Software developer. I was meeting with a potential investor. They're willing, but for a larger cut than I was willing to give." He saw the lost look on my face. "Blah, blah, blah. Boring stuff."

I was, in fact, sorry I'd asked. My eyes must have glazed over.

"So. What about you? What's does Kara do for money?"

I tilted my head in confusion. "Stripper. I wasn't kidding when I said that was my fashion sense."

"Holy shit. Really?" He didn't seem turned off, merely curious.

I was grateful it had come up before we went any further. People tended to react badly if they found out you were a stripper *after* you started dating. Or fucking. If they found out before, they were either good with it, turned on by it, or ended it before it started. Ryan was a rare find. He wasn't just good with it, he got turned on by me dancing for other people, as long as it didn't get out of hand. At the end of the day, I was his and his only, and I was good with that.

Now... I was a succubus. Falling head over heels with a human was a once in a lifetime event. I'd never tie myself down like that again. And no more offspring. Ever. That fucking hurt.

"Yes. Does that bother you?"

He sat down on the barstool in front of the kitchen counter and thought about it for a moment before answering. "Nope."

I pulled the mug out of the machine and set it in front of him. "You sure? Not that I'm employed right now, and probably won't be seeking employment, but it's who I am. I take my clothes off and dance for people for money. No jealousy flare ups when you think about it?"

"Kara?"

"Yes?"

"I like you. I like you a lot, and I have from the moment I saw you last night. I'd love to date you. My social life since the divorce has been...almost nonexistent. I work crazy hours and hardly ever see my kids. It's one of the main reasons my wife left me for her personal trainer. I'll probably never have the desire to get married again. Are you okay with that?"

"Yes?" I didn't understand the question.

"Well, I'm fine if you want to take your clothes off and dance for other guys." He grinned at me and then narrowed his eyes a little, not angrily. "In fact," he looked down at his lap, "I seem to like that idea very much..."

I walked around the corner of the counter and looked. He wasn't rock hard, but I could definitely see the outline of his cock through his trousers. I lifted my eyebrows in appreciation. Definitely not a little sausage. I laughed and leaned against the counter beside him. "What about seeing other people?"

"An open relationship?"

I nodded. We'd literally just met, and to be discussing relationships rules and boundaries before we started dating was kind of gross. I just really didn't want any misconceptions before we did. He was my neighbor. Did I love him? No. Was I attracted to him? Yes. Did I want to sit on his cock and suck every ounce of lust from him? *Fuck yes.* Did I want him getting all possessive and jealous? Fuck no. Best to nip it in the bud.

"If you want to date other guys, I'm fine with that. Hell, I knew my wife was fucking her trainer for three years before she left me."

Ding. Ding. Ding. We have a winner.

"What about you? You ever cheat on your wife?"

"No. I barely had time for her."

"So, if I date other guys, you're not going to date other women?"

He laughed. "Why would I? Not going to find anybody else as hot or intriguing as you."

I set my coffee down on the counter next to his and leaned over, locking my lips to his. When his tongue slipped in my mouth, I sucked it like I wanted to suck his cock.

"Fuck, you're hot," he managed to stammer.

"Abnormally high body temperature. It's why I freeze my fucking nipples off when it's cold outside."

He chuckled. "I meant sexy. And beautiful. But yes, your lips are warm."

I leaned in closer and whispered in his ear. "You should feel my pussy."

The semi-visible cock covered by his tan trousers throbbed against the fabric. He liked that idea. A lot. "Let's get your furniture moved first."

"I lied. The furniture is fine where is."

"You lied? Why?"

"Because I wanted you."

"I'm good with that." He grinned.

I knelt on the ground and turned him to me, reaching out and unzipping his pants. "So, you won't mind if I do this?"

"No. I'm pretty sure I'll like it."

He was hard enough to make it difficult to fish him out through the opening in his pants. And long enough it made it even more difficult, but I loved a fucking challenge. It was the first cock I'd seen in the flesh, so to speak, in a very long time. I stroked its velvety hardness and practically drooled at the lust pouring from him. Without batting an eye, I enveloped the tip with my lips and hummed in happiness. He swelled even harder, the taste of precum dancing on my tongue.

"Kara…"

"Mmmhmmm?"

"It's been a while. I'm just warning you."

I sucked him all the way in, letting the velvety smoothness of his tip guide him into my throat. When my nose was nestled against his pants, I slowly pulled him back out and began pumping him with my fist. He shuddered as his cock drooled. He wasn't the only one, either. The romper I'd put on right before he got there was positively soaked between my legs. My pussy wanted him almost as much as I did.

"Kara…" He groaned my name more than spoke it, and I felt him throbbing against my tongue. I pulled all but the tip of him out of my mouth and stroked him one handed, suckling on his head like a candy.

The first spurt hit me in the back of my throat as his lust burst into me harder than his cum. I reached down with the hand I'd been steadying myself against his leg with and slipped it up under the loose part of my romper and slid a finger inside me, burying it deep and hitting the spot. I shuddered as he climaxed and moaned against his cock.

The second surge poured out of him like liquid fire, salty and sweet, coating my tongue. The third and fourth were quick spurts that I swallowed with the rest of them. Then he began to shudder as I tried to suck more out of him. He screamed my name and came one more time, thick and heavy. I pulled him from my mouth and stood, showing him the treat he'd given me before swallowing it down.

"Holy fuck. Holy fuck."

I had fed so well. Rubbing my hands over my breasts and belly, I let the warm fuzzy feelings wash over me.

"Mmm. Did you like that?" I straddled his legs and kissed him. He didn't shy away from his taste in my mouth, our tongues dancing against each other, slippery and hot. I reached down and grabbed him, not as hard as he was, but still firm, and rubbed him against my soft cotton covered mound.

"That was incredible," he answered lazily.

"Want to have your dessert before lunch?" I wiggled my eyebrows at him.

He stood, easily lifting me with his arms and setting me down on the counter. The mugs slid as he pushed my ass back and tugged at the front of my jumper. "You should have worn something with a little easier access," he chided, and sat back down on the stool, scooting closer.

Luckily, the outfit was loose enough for him to grab the crotch and move it to the side of my swollen lips.

"So, fucking wet," he said, mesmerized as he stared. He leaned forward and scooped his tongue into my hole, ladling my wetness into his mouth and groaning at the taste. "So fucking sweet," he added, and dove in for another taste.

I leaned back on the island, propping myself up on my elbows to watch him as he ate me. One hand held my romper out of the way, the other he used to part my lips with two fingers and pull back the hood with a third. He kissed my opening, letting his tongue dip inside me again before travelling up the valley between my lips and lightly flicking my clit. Then his lips found it and gently sucked it between them, sliding his tongue from side to side over the very end of it inside his mouth.

"Daniel, don't stop," I gasped out, grinding myself against his face. "You're going to make me come."

"That's the plan," he whispered against my flesh, blowing air across my nub as he saw me shudder against his breath. Then he circled it with his tongue and opened his mouth, completely covering it, and using long swipes of his tongue to drive me insane. Shifting my weight to one of my arms, I reached down and grabbed a fistful of hair, pulling him against me harder as he assaulted my flesh with his mouth and tongue.

I started panting and bucking in time with the swipes of his tongue. Then he slid lower and shoved his tongue inside me. "Daniel!" My thighs closed around him as I fucking came. He didn't let it end, either. While he fucked me with his magnificent tongue, he slid his finger over my clit and gently swished it from side to side as I gave up trying to hold myself up and dropped back as my legs spread, and I came again.

"Did you like *that*?"

I held up a finger, begging him to wait for my answer as the stars began to fade from my vision. He stood up and slid me off the counter to his lap, straddling him on the barstool as his lips found mine. While he kissed me, he reached behind me and lifted my ass, fingers sliding under my romper. When he lowered me, his cock nudged my entrance.

"Kara..." He seemed to freeze.

"Worried about getting me pregnant?"

He nodded shyly. "And other things."

Laughing, I whispered into his ear, "I can't get pregnant, and it's been over a year since I've been with anybody. Every last test I've ever had came back negative. I think you're safe."

He blushed, hating to have to ask.

"What about you?"

"You're my first since the divorce, and ditto on the other stuff."

I pulled myself onto him, driving his cock inside me.

We stayed in that position for a few minutes, enjoying the kissing until I started to roll my hips. I was amazed he didn't slip right out of me. I was that wet and burning with the need for his seed. I wanted him to fill me. "Come in me," I whispered against his lips.

"You want me to fill you?"

"Yes."

His head lowered, breaking the kiss as he pressed his forehead against mine. The hand under my jumper began pulling me against him harder and then slid down, his fingers grazing the point of our junction, collecting my wetness. Then they moved to my ass, fingers gliding over the rippled entrance. I was starting to pant when he pushed the tip of one in.

"Unnnngh," I groaned against him. "Yes."

"You like your ass played with?"

I nodded, not trusting my voice.

"Have you ever had a cock in there?"

Again, I nodded, but whined the word, "Yes!"

"Do you like it?"

Again, just a nod.

I felt his cock tighten inside me. We were both getting close again. "Can I fuck you in the ass sometime?"

I pulled back and saw the want and need in his eyes. It made me smile as I sucked up some more of his lust. "Only if you promise to come in me when you do. Then I want you to fuck me some more, your slippery cock sliding in and out of my ass. Would you do that for me?"

"Kara. There isn't much I *wouldn't* do for you."

My lips found his, and I sucked his tongue into my mouth as another orgasm started, triggered by our fantasizing. I hoped he was up for the challenge. I wanted him to fill all of my holes.

"Fuck," I moaned as I pulled away from the kiss. "Fuck, fuck, fuck. Fuck me. Harder. Come inside me, Daniel."

"I am," he groaned as he started breathing heavy, his hips thrusting him against me as I rode him over the edge.

He let out a groan of ecstasy as he erupted inside me. I put my legs around him and pulled myself forward, driving his cock even farther in as I came, too. When he finished emptying himself, I lay back against the counter, his cock still buried in me. I wasn't sure what was better, the fucking or my belly full of lust. That round had gone a long way in filling the tanks, but I was nowhere near full power. It was like eating a full course meal after starving for weeks.

"That was fucking amazing. I swear you were milking me."

I squeezed his cock with the muscles I'd spent years working out. I was waiting for the day when they introduced Kegels as an Olympic sport. His eyes widened in surprise. On the outside, succubae were completely human in appearance. On the inside…we were built a little differently, evolved for pleasure and feeding from lust. Human males never assumed we weren't human, just gifted. Unless our skin color changed, our wings and horns sprouted, and we were taking their life with the last of their energy and lust. We could literally fuck a human to death, much like a vampire could take a humans last remaining drops of blood.

Personally, I didn't like shifting, and I'd never killed. But some succubae made it part of their regular feeding. That was a stupid way to get busted, and they didn't give the humans enough credit for their intelligence. It might appear that the human had a heart attack. But if enough of them had heart attacks with a woman matching the same description every time… They were bound to get caught.

The sound of the front door opening and shutting got us up pretty quick. I slid off Daniel's cock, and he stood up, getting his cock back in his pants just as the kids walked into the kitchen. I slid my jumper over myself and prayed I wouldn't leak. To be safe, I turned on the sink and splashed a bit of water on myself. Multiple wet spots would be much better than one.

"Hey, Mom." Karl stopped and looked at Daniel. "Hi?"

"Hey, sport. I'm Daniel, your new neighbor."

"Oh, hi!" He nodded and slung his backpack off and onto the floor.

"Greetings, boy child. How was school? Where is your sister?"

"Talking to some of her friends outside. Is there anything to eat?" He opened the fridge and frowned at the void. "I thought you were going to the store?"

"I was unpacking and socializing."

He sighed. "At least you found the coffee maker." Karl nodded at the only item that had actually made it out of a box. That, and the bedsheets that didn't get used.

"You drink coffee?" Daniel asked, a little surprised.

"No. But you try to be around my mother before she's had caffeine. She's a demon."

I almost choked on my surprise until I figured out Karl was being figurative instead of literal.

"How was school?"

"Sucked. But Rynnie and I joined the soccer teams. That sounded kind of fun, since we didn't play last year. It was either that or lacrosse."

"Did you walk home? I would have picked you up."

"We were going to, but Karen picked us up, since she had to get Billy and Madison."

"Those are her offspring?" She had mentioned them, but I wasn't really paying attention.

"Yes, Mom. Those are her offspring."

"That was nice of her. Do you want me to pick you up tomorrow?"

"We get done with soccer practice at five."

"Okay. Remind me in the morning."

"I'll text you at 4:45, since you'll probably forget in between."

"I would never..."

"How many times, Mom?"

I sighed, not wanting to continue an argument I was about to lose with my fifteen-year-old child. Succubae knew how to pick their battles. "A couple."

"Seventeen. Last year."

Daniel chuckled, and I shot him a warning glare. "You may not have noticed, but I'm a horrible mother."

Karl shook his head, walked up to me and hugged me. "No, you're not. You're just kinda forgetful. A lot. Sometimes."

"Thank you, offspring." I patted his head.

The front door opened again and Ryn's voice echoed shrilly through the house. "Mom, there's some old guy out here that says the grass is three-eighths of an inch too long."

"I am not old!"

"And that would be Mr. Donaldson. Want to borrow my mower?" Daniel chuckled.

"I'll hire a service tomorrow."

"Don't. Wait until the spring. The weather's cooling down, so should the grass. I can take care of it until it snows."

That came as something of a little shock. I wasn't expecting him to offer. It was kind of sweet. "You don't mind?"

"Not at all. I was going to mow mine this weekend. I'll let Mr. Donaldson know on my way out."

I walked over to him and gave him a small hug, nothing overtly sexual. I wasn't sure how the kids would respond to me dating. It seemed like a good idea to get their take on it before announcing it to them. "Thanks, Daniel."

"My pleasure, Kara. Walk me out?"

Nodding, I followed behind him, patting Ryn on the head as we walked by, and pulling the door shut behind me. "Dinner tomorrow?"

"Wouldn't miss it. Pick you guys up at six?"

"Guys?"

"Aren't the kids coming with us?"

"I was going to leave them at home and have them order pizza."

"Oh. Okay. Then yes, I'll pick you up at six." He turned and faced me, looking at the window beside the door. "Okay to kiss you, or you want to talk to the kids first?"

Sighing, I nodded. "Kids first. They're watching through the window, aren't they?" I could feel them behind me.

"Yep."

"Yes, I should probably tell them about you before we kiss in front of them. Or have dinner with them."

"Then consider this a verbal kiss of my affection. Have fun at Karen and Rick's." He chuckled and walked down the driveway to talk to the neighbor about the grass.

"See you later, Daniel."

He waved over his shoulder, and I found myself smiling at him, even though he couldn't see me. The door opened, and Ryn poked her head out.

"New boyfriend?"

"Huh?"

"That guy. He's your boyfriend, isn't he?"

I turned back and smiled again at Daniel, who was pointing at his yard to Mr. Donaldson. "You okay with that?"

"Hell yeah. It's about time. I was gonna upload your pic to Tinder in another week."

"What's a Tinder?" I turned around and motioned her back into the house.

Chapter 5

I hung up the phone with Ginger, and a smile plastered itself on my face.

"That sounded serious." Daniel cocked an eyebrow at me.

"It was," I answered and took a small bite of food. I was nearing my limit. Unlike vampires, Succubae could eat food, and we did draw a little nutrition from it, but we couldn't survive on it, even if we had to.

"Gonna tell me about it?" Daniel teased.

"After dinner," I said with a grin and motioned to his plate.

Instead of reaching for his fork, he reached into his pocket and pulled out a small velvet covered box, setting it on the steakhouse table in front of me. "Happy Dinnerversary."

"What? That's not even a thing."

"It is now. Our fifth dinner out together. Figured that deserved something special."

"Daniel!" I picked up the box and opened it, gasping. Ruby earrings glinted under the lights over our table. "They're beautiful."

"You're kind of hard to shop for. I couldn't see you wearing diamonds, but for some reason the rubies seem to fit."

"You shouldn't have!" I meant it. Human males tended to gift extraordinary things to succubae, and while I should have been expecting it, I felt guilty. A man looking for investors did *not* need to be buying ruby earrings.

"Kara, the past two weeks have been incredible. I've had the time of my life, and I just wanted to say thank you."

I sniffed and wiped my eyes. Yes, demons could get a little mushy. We weren't evil...most of the time. We just loved what we loved.

I plucked out the hoops I had in my first holes and replaced them with his gift. "How do they look?"

"Beautiful, just like the woman wearing them."

Blushing, I got up, walked around the table, and kissed him. If he could be sweet, so could I. I sat back down and saw the time on my phone. "Shit. We need to hurry."

He chuckled. "Don't let Karen scare you. Open house at the school isn't that big of a deal. You don't have to be there when it starts."

"I know. She just really wanted me to be there when it did. Hard to say no to her."

"She can be a little pushy."

"To say the least. But she means well. Unlike the other women in the neighborhood." I frowned. In the two weeks we'd lived there, the vast majority of them gave me dirty looks, outright sneers, and one finger.

"It's not you, it's me."

"Isn't that supposed to be my line?"

"It better never be," he said with a chuckle. "No, when Samantha moved out with the kids, they were circling me like vultures. I may have let it out that you and I were dating to get them off my back... I'm sorry."

I held up my hand. "No. I'm glad you did. Now I won't have to hide their bodies."

"Awww. You do like me," he answered.

"A little. Yeah." I smiled.

"Can I get anything else for you?" The waiter kept looking down at my lap, trying to get a glimpse of the panties I wasn't wearing under my very short skirt. Unable to help myself, I spread my legs a little.

"No, just the check please."

There was an awkward moment of silence as the waiter ogled my not so private parts, mouth agape. I drank in some of his lust and topped off the meal. Daniel was trying hard to cover up his grin.

"Right away, sir," the waiter finally said, shaking his head and wandering away.

"You flashed him, didn't you?"

"Would it bother you if I said yes?"

"Not at all. That's kind of fucking hot." He chuckled. "Black panties?"

"What panties?"

He groaned and adjusted himself, giving him room to grow. I wiggled my eyebrows at him and took a sip of my wine. "You get another boyfriend yet?"

I shook my head. "Nope. Haven't really been looking. Someone's been keeping me very sated lately."

"It's a tough job..." He took another sip of wine and then got a serious expression on his face. "Kara?"

"Yeah?"

"Would you do me a favor?"

"Don't get another boyfriend?" I had a feeling, even with his speech in my kitchen, that the topic might come up again, that he might change his mind. I struggled to hide the sudden disappointment I felt.

"No," he said softly. "Honestly, the thought of you being with other guys...kind of excites me. Am I sick?"

Relieved, I let out a little bark of laughter. "No. Not at all. You'd be surprised how many men do."

"Really?"

"Yep. Almost every one of the strippers where I used to work were married. Their husbands would come and watch their wives dance. Then they'd bring guys back to their house. Sometimes, marriages don't work out without a little help."

"Is that how you made yours work? You speak of him almost reverently, when you do."

"Ryan was almost perfect. I miss him every day. I never thought I would see myself settle down, let alone have children. I would have given him the stars in the sky if he'd asked. But no. I would dance and the thought of me showing myself off, exposing myself, excited him. But that's as far as it went."

Daniel nodded. "I'm sorry for your loss."

"So, what was it you wanted me to do for you?"

"If you do find yourself interested in another guy and decide to start dating… Please, tell me? Don't keep it from me. I'd rather hear it from you than find out. Does that make sense?"

It did. Perfectly. "If your ex had told you she wanted to date her personal trainer, you would have encouraged her. Instead, she went behind your back, and it bothered you."

"Ate me up inside. And you're a hundred-percent correct. I would have. Instead, she thought she was being sneaky, but it was so easy to tell. She thought I was a fool. Maybe she was right. I should have confronted her the first time I found out."

Nodding, I gave him a sad smile. I wasn't the most sympathetic person in the world, I was a fucking demon. But I still felt bad for Daniel. He deserved way better than that.

"Tell you what. Since we're in a relationship, I'll let you meet them first and see what you think about them before I even think about dating them. We'll kind of do it together. That sound good?"

He blinked at me and tucked his lower lip under his teeth, finally wiping a tear from the corner of his eye. "Did I mention how glad I am I met you?"

"Once or twice."

"Thanks, Kara." He let out a sigh that didn't sound like relief.

"What?"

"I hate going to these things."

"Oh. I didn't know. I wouldn't have dragged you along."

"Don't be silly. I have to go anyway."

Something wasn't clicking. "Your kids?"

"Yeah. They go to Brentworth. You can meet them this weekend if you want. I'll have them until Sunday. Much to their disappointment, I'm sure."

"So, what was the sigh for?"

"Seeing the ex."

"She's gonna be there?"

He nodded.

"Oh, this gonna be *fun.*"

"Your check, sir."

∞ ∞ ∞

We were even later because we had to park three school districts away from the front fucking doors. Five minutes late equated into twenty with the fifteen of walking. I shot Daniel a dirty look. He kept laughing. "Think of it this way. We're fashionably late."

"My feet hurt," I lied. I could have walked the entire distance barefoot over metal Legos and not batted an eyelash, I just wanted the promise of a foot rub later. And leg rub. And various points in between.

"I'll massage them for you when we get back."

Score. I smiled as my ploy worked to perfection. "I'm holding you to that."

"Deal," he replied, and ran his fingers down my back. It had warmed up a little, not quite warm, but I wasn't shivering and turning blue, either. The blouse I wore was completely backless, and his fingers sent a shiver up my spine. "You look amazing."

I smiled at him over my shoulder and pulled my skirt down for the tenth time as we walked under the ancient oak trees. Their leaves were just starting to change colors, and they reflected the light from the streetlamps beautifully. The smell of fall was lightly perfuming the night. It was officially my favorite time of year.

It was eerily quiet, too. Too quiet, in fact. The only sound was our footsteps as they clicked against the concrete of the sidewalk splitting the perfectly manicured grass marking the academy grounds. Instinctively, I went into defensive mode. We were being hunted.

"What's wrong?" Daniel stopped and looked around, sensing my unease.

"Nothing," I lied. "Let's keep going." I grabbed his hand and started taking longer strides toward the front gate.

"Now you're freaking me out. Especially with the attacks."

I stopped walking. "Attacks? In this neighborhood?"

He nodded. "There was even one in our subdivision a week ago. It's been all over the news."

"I don't watch television." I didn't. Tried a few times and got so bored, I fell asleep. Movies were a different story. I liked movies.

"How do you get your news?"

I blushed in embarrassment. Keeping up with current events wasn't a big priority when you would never grow old and die. "I don't."

He blinked in surprise. "Well, I'll let you know of any potential dangers in the area in the future."

I nodded, and the hair on the back of my neck stood on end. Subtle currents in the air warned me a fraction of a moment before the attack came. I spun Daniel and covered his back with my own body, spreading myself as much as I could. Claws raked my back, and I hissed in pain, pushing my human toward the door and turning to face the attacker, but meeting only empty air.

"What the fuck happened? You're bleeding!" He rushed over, and I turned away, trying to keep him from seeing the wound that was probably already healing.

I held up my hand for silence and *listened.* Whatever had hit us moved inhumanly fast. Vampiric speed. I should have taken the attack head on to get a look at what we were dealing with. From the speed of the attack, I had to guess vampire or elf. Vampires were territorial and might be trying to drive me out of town. Elves just didn't take kindly to anything demonic and would often attack on sight, unless some sort of agreement could be bartered or bought.

Demons left each other alone, unless it was a challenge for power.

"You missed. You might as well come out, and we can discuss this or end it."

A shadowy figure stepped from out of the shadows of an oak some distance away. I took one step toward it, and it vanished, not into thin air, but in a burst of speed. It had to have been a vampire.

With its departure, it took the vague feeling of danger with it, and I relaxed, taking a deep breath and judging Daniel's reaction. He had seen the vampire vanish, too.

"What the fuck was that?"

"Nothing good, but it's gone now. Let's get inside." I fervently hoped that would be the end of it and Daniel's questions. I hadn't even remotely planned on telling him what I was. I should have had a contingency plan in place in case something like that happened. But I didn't. I'd grown too complacent. Other than the occasional visit from supernatural beings to Full Exposure, I'd stayed completely away from the community. The ones who visited the titty bar usually took one look at me and ran. Not to brag, but succubae weren't pussies. Most of the others gave us a wide berth. The vampire that attacked us probably didn't know what I was.

"Why do I get the feeling that you know what's going on but aren't telling me?"

"Do you trust me?"

"Of course, I do."

"Then trust me when I tell you, you don't want to know."

"Can you at least tell me why the gouge marks on your back are completely gone, along with all the blood that was pouring from your wound?" He stopped walking.

I turned to him, closing the distance between us. "I'm going to give you time."

"Time for what?"

"Time to decide if you want to know. It comes with an epic warning, too. Everything you think you know will get

67

thrown out the window, and it might even change how you feel about me. Think about that for a few days. If you still want to know, I'll tell you. Deal?"

He nodded, not quite believing me. I could see it in his eyes. "You're kidding, right?"

"No. You saw what just happened." I turned around and headed for the school. I'd meant what I said, even though I was being a little melodramatic. Deep down, on some level, humans believed in the supernatural. There was a reason books and movies about demons and vampires were so popular. Humans *wanted* them to be real. Unfortunately, they went from being afraid of them to wanting to fuck them. Worked out well for us, not so much for the humans.

"Okay. I'll think about it." He fell into step with me and took my hand.

At least he wasn't afraid of me. Yet. Only time would tell, and it wouldn't be the first time a human had found out what I really was, freaked, and ran away. Or attacked me. Or sent a priest to my house. One even tried to set me on fire. A demon. Dumbass.

In fact, Ryan had been the very first to accept me without hesitation. He'd been a *little* freaked out when he found out, but that didn't stop him from loving me. I missed my Ryan every damn day.

I looked down at Daniel's hand and smiled.

He noticed and frowned. "You were worried I was going to freak out, weren't you?"

"It wouldn't be the first time."

"If you were dangerous, I'd probably already be dead. And don't think I didn't notice you protecting me back there."

"You're really not afraid." If he was, I would have smelled it on him. There were two scents that we loved above all others. Lust and fear.

"Nope. Not of you. Whatever that thing was, yes. I couldn't even see it move. How did you know it was going to attack?"

68

"Could just feel it, don't know how to explain it."

"Spidey sense."

I laughed, having seen all the Marvel movies. "Yep."

"Cool. I'm dating a superhero."

I stopped walking and tugged his hand, halting him in his tracks, too. I shook my head. "No, Daniel. I'm no superhero. More like a villain who just doesn't care about money or power. I just want to be left alone, especially now, since I am responsible for the welfare of my offspring. If you stand out too much, you draw attention. Too much attention, and you get killed. And everybody around you. Low profile is my motto. I just want to be happy."

"Funny. You just sounded like a superhero."

I growled in frustration. "Daniel, I'm a bad guy!"

He pulled me closer and kissed my forehead. "No, you're not. You might not think you're a hero, but you're my hero. Shall we go inside?"

"I don't know if there will be room in the school for all those people and your over-inflated opinion of me." I let a little smile curve the corner of my mouth. "Come on. Let's go."

"Vampire?"

"What?"

"Are you a vampire?"

"No. Now quit guessing. I'll tell you in three days if you still want to know."

"Deal."

Chapter 6

"Kara!" Karen shouted my name from across the school gymnasium and clicked her heels across the polished wood until she was standing in front of Daniel and me. "Did you run into traffic? I didn't think you were coming!"

"We got held up at dinner and then had a bit of a walk to get here. We were only five minutes late, and it turned into thirty."

"Uh huh. You two were making out in the parking lot!"

I could have kicked myself for not thinking of that excuse. "Thanks for bringing the kids."

"Oh, no problem! I put them to work helping set up. Punch is over by the stage!"

"Hey, Mom." Ryn slithered up behind me and hugged me from behind.

"Greetings, girl child."

"Did you have fun on your date?" She gave me an impish look.

"I did."

"So did I. Hi, Ryn."

"Hello, Mr. Lewis."

"Oh, just call me Daniel."

She blushed and nodded.

I think my girl child has a crush on my boyfriend. I grinned in pride. "Where is your brother?"

"Talking to the cheerleaders." She rolled her eyes.

Again, I was filled with an overwhelming sense of pride.

"Well, have fun. If Mrs. Stanton bitches about me, she's lying, and I didn't do it."

"All right. Stay out of trouble, youngling." I patted her on the head.

Ryn took off, and Daniel chuckled at my awkwardness. "Why are you so rigid around your kids? They're not going to bite."

"On the contrary. They are half me and may very well bite one day. I suggest you use caution and keep your hands and feet away from their mouths at all times."

After the incident outside the school, he didn't know if I was joking or not, until I chuckled evilly. The relief was real.

"Ryan raised them. They were with him morning to bedtime. I worked nights and hardly ever saw them. Then when he died, I didn't know what to do. I didn't know how to be a mom. I still don't."

"Well, a good place to start would be calling them by their names instead of girl child or offspring." He chuckled softly.

"When I look at them, I am so proud and in awe by who they have become, I can't seem to get the words out."

He leaned over and kissed me on the cheek. "And that makes you a *great* mom."

My cheeks were ablaze.

"They really are good kids, Kara. So stinking smart. Like scary smart. And they're more like mini adults than kids," Karen whispered, almost in awe.

"Thank you. Wish I could take credit."

"Hello, Daniel." The voice behind us wasn't snide, but it was close. Disdainful might have been a more apt description.

He tensed beside me, and I wrapped my arms around his and turned us to face his ex. It had to be her. No other woman on the planet could have caused him to react that way. I hoped. "Oh, you must be Samantha. I've heard so much about you." I threw in an amused chuckle. It was worth it to see her face when she saw me clinging to Daniel's arm.

"Uh… Who are you?"

72

"Samantha, this is Kara."

She blinked at me repeatedly in shock. "You had a long-lost daughter?"

"Ha. No. I'm his girlfriend."

"You brought your teenage girlfriend to your children's school? Have you lost your ever-loving mind, Daniel?"

"Oh, boy. I'll be over there." Karen pointed at the punch and took off like she saw a display of Girl Scout Cookies.

I wasn't a tall woman, demon, whatever. Five-and-a-half feet to be exact. When she had the ball sack to berate Daniel in the middle of the school in the middle of the open house, I figuratively swelled to twice my height. She stepped back as she felt the anger flow from me. If she was lucky, I wouldn't release my lust and have her banging the corner of the punch table until she got arrested. So many of my powers had started flooding back now that I had the lust to spare, and I would gladly use them to make her life a living hell.

"Actually, my kids go here," I said evenly.

"You. Have children? Adopted from a previous marriage?"

I was done. "Ha! You're hilarious! But with a little makeup, a good foundation, and a little less time in the tanning bed, you might not be." The truth was, Samantha was *very* pretty. Her hair was almost as dark as Daniels, sleek and pulled up in a neat ponytail. Her eyes were green, skin perfect, lips glazed and soft looking. She was flawless, for all I could see. Her outfit left a little to be desired, and for that I was grateful.

Her mouth dropped open, she shivered as my words sank in, and then her eyes widened as she started sputtering.

"Articulate, too. Come on, Daniel. Let's go get some cookies and punch."

"See you Friday, Samantha."

There was a frustrated stomp behind us as we walked away, followed by a strangled, "Gah!"

"Gonna hear about that one later," Daniel chuckled.

"Sorry." I wasn't. But he didn't need to know that.

"Don't be. Totally worth it."

The school's principal managed to intercept us on the way to the punch bowl. "Evening, Mrs. Dell. Wasn't expecting to see you here tonight."

"Hi, Mr. Marshall. Are my children adjusting to Brentworth okay?"

"Oh, yes. Just fine. Your son, Karl, is a gifted soccer player. And your daughter is the rising star of the girls' team, too. I must say, I was delightedly shocked to see two players of such magnitude from the same family."

Of questionable lineage, I finished for him. In my head. "Thank you!" *Go fuck a goat, you piece of shit.* "We were just about to get some punch. Won't you join us?" *Please say no.*

"Sadly, I am making my rounds. A lot of parents want to speak to me this evening."

Suck your butt, you mean. "I can imagine. Well, I won't keep you then." I stepped around him and pulled Daniel with me.

"I don't think he likes me very much."

"He doesn't like anybody very much."

"He liked my check, though."

"He likes everybody's checks." Daniel laughed and grabbed the ladle out of the punch bowl and pulled two clear plastic glasses off the stack beside it. For what we paid to send our kids to the school, there should have been a punch fountain and cookie cannons. But at least they looked homemade. I snagged a chocolate chip while Daniel loaded our glasses.

"I should have brought some vodka," I muttered as he handed me mine.

"Aren't you a little old to be spiking the punch bowl?"

"Who said anything about sharing?"

He clinked his glass against mine. "Happy new school year."

"How do you like the cookies?" Karen rejoined us, leaving her little circle of friends shooting me dirty looks standing next to Daniel.

"Very yummy. Did you make them?"

"Of course! The PTA provides all the snacks and drinks for events like these."

"And by PTA, you mean you, right?"

She blushed. "Hard to find good help these days. Especially with everyone so busy with extra curriculars."

"I'm actually going to the kids' soccer games this weekend."

Karen and Daniel both stared at me.

"What?"

"Just trying to picture this," Karen said with a scared smile.

"And how it's going to end." Daniel was grinning.

"Probably with me drinking. Either of you want to go with me?"

"Can't. Taking my kids downtown," Daniel said apologetically.

"And we're planning the Fall Festival this weekend." Karen actually pouted like she wanted to go.

"No worries. I'll survive."

"It's not you we're worried about." Daniel raised his glass in a toast.

"Daddy!"

Daniel's surge of joy was palpable, even before the smile appeared on his lips as he turned. A little brunette in a blue dress was streaking across the gym floor and practically leapt into his arms. "Hey, Munchkin." He hugged her tight.

"What are we doing this weekend?"

"Going downtown, like I promised."

"Haymarket?"

"You betcha."

"Yay!"

He set her down, still holding her hand. "Abby, this is my friend, Kara. Kara, this is Abby."

I bent over and offered her my hand, but she kind of slid behind her father. I would have taken offense, if she hadn't given me a shy smile. "Hi."

"Aren't you adorable."

"You're pretty."

Heat flared from my face. I wasn't used to being embarrassed, but the youngling managed to do it with two words. It was one of the reasons I wasn't that fond of children. "Thank you."

"Where's Vincent?"

"Talking to some girls."

I laughed.

Unfortunately, it drew the attention of Abby's mother. She finally noticed her daughter talking to us, said something to the people she was with, and made a beeline straight for us. "Abby, I told you not to wander off."

"I saw Daddy."

"Yes, well you get to spend all weekend with him."

"Go ahead, Munchkin. I'll see you Friday night."

He pulled her hand, leading to her mother, but Abby refused to let him go. Definitely Daddy's girl. It would be interesting to see how his son reacted to him. "I was bored. Can't I stay with Daddy while you talk to your friends?"

There was so much her mother *wanted* to say. I could feel it oozing off her like the cheap ass perfume she was wearing. Most of it probably had to do with me, judging from the nervous glances she kept giving me. Instead of giving her a threatening stare, I feigned disinterest. It worked like a charm.

"Fine, but we are leaving in twenty minutes." She turned back around, re-engrossing herself in the conversation with her friends. Friends who were staring at me with borderline hostility. I sneered and turned around, heading back toward the punchbowl. That's where all the cool kids hung out, anyway.

I heard some mumbling, and then Daniel softly called my name. "I'll be right back. The munchkin needs to use the bathroom. Be okay by yourself for a minute?"

"I wish. Karen will probably want a status update." I hooked my thumb over my shoulder and gave him exasperated sigh.

He grinned and led Abby toward the double wooden doors off to the left. I dumped a little more punch in my cup and leaned against the wall behind the table.

"Mrs. Dell?"

I turned my head. A man wearing the classic blue polyester coaching shorts with a white polo shirt was giving me an inquisitive look. It was the first time I'd ever seen someone look impressive wearing coach shorts. He filled them out nicely, just like his shirt. It practically stretched over his pectoral muscles, but didn't give him the impression of being a meat head. He was fit, toned, but not overly bulging. With the shaggy head of blond hair, and soft brown eyes, he was gorgeous. "Yes?"

"Oh good!" He visibly relaxed and reached out his hand. I took it, returning his meaty shake. "I'm Coach Drake."

"The soccer coach?"

He chuckled, nodding. "Boys soccer. The girls have a different coach."

"How did you know who I was?"

"Your son gave me your description. Just wanted to introduce myself."

"What did he say about me?" I narrowed my eyes suspiciously.

"Blonde woman who looks ridiculously young and stands out in a crowd, no matter where she goes." He coughed. "A very apt description for a fifteen-year-old boy."

"I don't stand out..." I was almost defensive.

"Trust me. You do. Especially in this school, and believe me, that is a compliment."

I liked Coach Drake, already. Not for the compliment, but for his down to earth attitude and realization that mother hens sipping punch and gossiping really did kind of suck. "Oh. I believe you," I said with a throaty chuckle. "Punch?"

He shook his head. "I've been here for almost ten years. If I never have another sip of punch again, I'll die a happy man."

"You've set the bar kind of low."

"I've become jaded in my old age."

"Old? You don't look a day over thirty."

"Ouch. I'm only twenty-two. See what working here does to a man?"

I was staring at him blankly and narrowed my eyes when he started chuckling.

"Kidding! I'm thirty-five."

"You had me. I was about to run and jump off the nearest cliff." I wet my lips with another sip of punch.

"Please don't do that." He said it very seriously.

"It's okay. I can fly." I wasn't lying, but he didn't need to know that.

"I bet you can."

He smelled like aftershave, up until that moment. Then I caught a whiff of attraction, peppered with a hint of lust. Coach was attracted to me, but wasn't being a creep about it. I had yet to catch him looking at me anywhere but into my eyes.

I gave him a grin, just as Daniel returned with Abby. "Welcome back," I said to him.

"Good to be back." He nodded at Coach Drake. "Hey, Brady."

Apparently, they were on a first name basis. "What's going on, Daniel."

"You two know each other?"

"Since..." Drake paused to look at Daniel. "Seventh grade?"

"Sixth, I think."

"Holy crap. You guys went to school here?"

"Not at this school. But yes, in the area. Salem."

"Salem High!" Drake made a weird mascot noise. I tried not to shudder. Luckily, he was cute. Damn cute.

"What did we say about doing that in public?" Daniel tried to sound stern but failed miserably. His laughter gave it away.

"Meh. This isn't public. This is suburbia."

A smaller hand grabbed onto mine. I blinked down in confusion at Abby who was smiling up at me. The shy little girl who wouldn't even say hi to me had gotten awfully comfortable, really fast. I gave her a small, awkward smile back and squeezed her hand gently, careful not to fracture her small bones. Drake noticed.

He looked from me to Daniel. "Are you two…?"

"Yes," I answered. Honestly.

"That's awesome!" He seemed to be genuinely happy.

"She is," Daniel agreed, giving me a wink.

Blushing, I looked over my shoulder. Samantha turned and looked at me at the exact same moment. Then she saw Abby holding my hand, frowned, and started stomping in our direction.

"Abby, let's go." She stopped halfway and started motioning at her daughter to walk toward her.

"Go ahead, Abby," I said softly. "I might see you this weekend."

"Okay." She smiled at me one last time, hugged her dad, and took off toward the bitch in spandex. Samantha was going for the sporty look, but only managed to show off the fact that she was wearing granny panties under her leggings.

"Thank you," Daniel whispered with a smile. "I should go say goodbye to Vincent. I'll be right back." He leaned in and gave me a kiss on my cheek. "If you're wondering about Brady, it's a yes from me." He wiggled his eyebrows as he pulled back and headed toward the bitch stomping toward the exit.

"I told him not to marry her." Brady watched them go.

"The heart gets what the heart wants."

He nodded before he turned back to me, and his face darkened. "Don't hurt my friend. Please. I don't think he can handle another divorce." He looked over at me out of the corner of his eye.

"Not that kind of relationship."

"You're not..."

"Fucking? Yes. Dating? Yes. Looking to get married, no. We've both been there and done that."

Brady just nodded. "No offense, but good. His life is too hectic for marriage."

"I know. He told me what she did." I nodded in the direction they had gone.

"He and I got married the same year and divorced the same year." He sighed, sadly.

"Your wife run off with her personal trainer?"

"No. She got addicted to meth. Kicked her out when she got arrested for the second time."

"Humans can be weak when it comes to drugs. I've seen it firsthand."

"Hospital? You have that nurse vibe."

"No. Strip club where I worked."

"As a..."

"Stripper."

"Woah. No wonder you don't fit into this crowd." He chuckled heartily before pausing. "Karl told me what happened to his dad. I'm sorry."

"Thanks." I let it go at that. "Offspring?"

"I'm more of a Rancid kind of guy, but I'll listen to them."

Luckily, I understood his band reference and gave him a small smile. "Do you have any?"

"Kids?"

I nodded.

"No." He didn't elaborate, and I let it go. "Well, it was a pleasure meeting you. I'll see you this weekend? Karl said you're coming to his game."

"Wouldn't miss it for the world." Only because I promised the kids. There was one thing I would never break. My oath.

Chapter 7

My sunglasses were so dark, even I was having trouble seeing through them. But they were a necessary evil. I didn't do well in sunlight. Sure, I didn't burst into flames, and walking from the car to wherever I was going wasn't a problem, but sitting out under the bright morning sunlight for three hours, watching kids play soccer, I would have been lucky not to end up blind. Carefully, I opened my lawn chair and plopped my ass down, gleefully taking a sip of my tumbler of vodka and orange juice. Mimosas were for pussies.

The girls' game was up first, and I clapped and cheered with the rest of the parents when they took the field. Might as well try to fit in. A little.

"Hey, Mom. The guys and I are going to the park next door."

"Okay. Don't do drugs, blah blah blah. Be back for your game."

"I will. Text me if the coach needs me."

My ears, and my interest, perked up. "Oh. That's right. He's got to be here today, doesn't he?"

"Yeaaahh. Little hard to have a game without a coach."

"I'm sure you could manage, sweetie."

"Sure, Mom. I'll be back." He took off running.

"Dude, your mom is hot. And cool."

"Shut up, Timmy."

I chuckled under my breath.

"Fancy meeting you, here."

I turned my head and looked up over the rim of my sunglasses at Coach Drake. "Didn't think you'd be here this early. The boys' game doesn't start for an hour-and-a-half."

"I know. I like to watch the girls' team, too."

"Well, aren't you just chock full of school spirit?"

"Hardly. They have a shot of going to the state championships this year. And their coach is top notch."

I looked out at the field. There was an angry looking blonde woman giving last minute instructions to the somewhat nervous looking kids. "Got the hots for her?"

"Hardly. She's my older sister."

"Really?" I gave him a shocked look.

He nodded. "We both played for our schools, and both enjoy teaching."

"Huh. You gonna stand all day?" I noticed the lawn chair in his hand.

"Just waiting for an invitation. Where's Daniel?"

"Downtown with the kids."

"Ahh." He shook out the chair, opening it expertly and setting it on the grass next to mine. "Well, hopefully he won't get too jealous when he finds out I got to spend the morning with you."

"Nope. He's not the jealous type."

Brady frowned. "No. He's not, is he?"

"You care for him."

Brady nodded without looking offended. "One of the nicest people you'll ever meet. Too nice, if you ask me. He let that bitch, Samantha, walk all over his ass."

"And now you're worried I'll do the same." I wasn't guessing, I could feel the anxiety coming off of him. "That's why you came to sit next to me."

"Guilty." At least he had the decency to blush.

"Brady?"

"Yeah?"

"Never mind." I took a sip of my drink, not really wanting to divulge Daniel's secrets if he didn't want me to.

"If you're going to tell me that you are free to date other people, don't. I already know. Daniel called me last night." He chuckled.

"Then what are you worried about?"

"Honestly?"

"Of course."

He cleared his throat, clearly uncomfortable talking to someone he just met about that delicate of a topic. "That you will."

"Date other people?"

"Kind of."

"I'm confused."

"Kara, do you know what a cuckold is?"

I grinned. "Brady, when it comes to sex and relationships, you could consider me an expert."

He nodded. "Daniel is…"

"Daniel likes the idea of me dating other men. It stimulates him."

"Obviously."

"Then what's the problem?"

"Most wives in that situation tend to take it to the…extreme."

"Gangbangs while the hubster holds the camera?"

Brady's eyes widened, and he started sputtering. Clearly, I had taken the wrong avenue. "No! I mean, maybe. Not the point I was trying to make, though."

"What?"

"They like to berate their husbands. Tell them how useless they are, and how they can't satisfy their needs. Shit like that."

"Oh, Daniel has no worries in that department." I chuckled happily.

"So, you are satisfied?"

"Yes. When I'm with him, completely."

"Then why date anybody else? If you don't mind me asking?"

"Because I don't want to be tied down to one man. It's not in my…nature. I made concessions for my husband. I stripped. I got horny. I came home to him and him alone. Those days died when he did."

"And how do your children feel about you dating other people?"

"That is not up to them. Whatever I do, I do discretely. They don't even know I was a stripper."

"You're a very interesting person, Kara…"

I shrugged, taking another drink. "Boring is boring. The world would be a better place if people would just ditch some of their inhibitions."

He chuckled. "Some people need them."

"What about you?"

He thought about it for a moment before shrugging. "I try not to let them rule me."

"Good." I almost jumped. As soon as I said the word, the moms on our side of the field jumped up and started screaming excitedly.

"Your daughter just scored a goal."

"Really? Good for her."

"Uh…aren't you going to cheer for her?"

"Should I?"

"She might like it…"

I looked at the field. My daughter was surrounded by her new friends and grinning at me. "How?"

"Yell her name and clap. Tell her good job."

"Yay, Ryn! Good job!" I clapped, and the smile on her face doubled in size. My heart twitched, and I wasn't sure why.

"See? Not so hard, now was it?"

"It wasn't. But I don't feel so good."

"What's the matter?"

"My heart feels funny."

"That's called pride. Don't worry. You'll get used to it."

Wasn't sure if I wanted to. The feeling was…quite disturbing. I took another drink to wash it away.

He glanced over my shoulder, and a shadow crossed his face. I couldn't tell if he was worried or angry, and I didn't ask. When he looked back at me, he lifted an eyebrow. "You're awfully thirsty."

"No. Just like vodka."

"You…have…vodka in there?"

"Yes! Who the fuck drinks straight orange juice? That shit tastes like battery acid."

"Well, you're not supposed to have alcoholic beverages at the school sporting events, but since ninety-eight percent of the whack jobs behind us are probably sipping chardonnay out of their Powerade bottles…I'll let it slide."

"Want a sip?"

"Please."

I handed him the white plastic bottle with BITCH FROM HELL printed on the side, and he took a swallow, choked, and handed it back.

"You sure you put OJ in there?"

"Splash for flavor."

"As I said, you're interesting."

"Thanks." I grinned at him.

Brady looked over my shoulder, frowned, and turned his attention back to the game. "Almost the end of the first period."

"Who's winning?"

He glanced over at the scoreboard. "They are. Your daughter's goal was the only one so far. They have three."

I glanced at the opposition. Their girls seemed taller, burlier, and older. "Those girls look like they are in college."

"No, but their team is all seniors. Inner city school with a lot more students. Varsity and junior varsity, so the younger kids sit out the games unless they're *really* talented."

"That hardly seems fair."

"Don't worry. They're only winning by two. Second period is where the game really happens."

I just nodded.

The whistle blew, and the kids headed for their seating. Brady's sister didn't seem too happy, but looked like she was trying to inspire the kids, rather than scream at them. It wasn't their fault the opposing team was comprised of middle-aged kids. "When should I let Karl know to get his ass back here?"

"Tell him thirty minutes. As long as they're here before the game starts. They at the park?"

I nodded and relayed his message, tucking my phone in the tiny purse I carried when absolutely necessary. "Could you watch my stuff? I need to run to the ladies' room."

"My pleasure."

I got out of the lawn chair, noticing Brady's eyes were fastened to my ass. "Everything okay back there?"

He looked up at me, busted. "Yeah. Your skirt is rather..."

"Short?"

"Yeah."

"If I didn't want to show off, I would have worn jeans."

"I'm sure that would still be an impressive sight."

"Mr. Drake. Are you flirting with me?"

He blushed and started sputtering. "I'm sorry. That was rather inappropriate."

"Inappropriate is my middle name." I laughed and headed to the bathroom, smiling to myself. He and Daniel were close friends. That opened up a whole world of possibilities. Especially since Daniel had already waved the green flag in his direction.

Opening the bathroom door, I almost collided with the blonde woman walking out.

"Excuse me," she sneered, and exited around me, not even giving me the opportunity to move out of the way. Not that I would have. I made myself an immovable object, and her shoulder collided with mine. Getting a little satisfaction of the *oof* noise she made, I walked in and let the door shut behind me.

Few things in this universe stank quite as much as public restrooms. Didn't matter if they were used by men or women, or both. They all reeked. Public restrooms at sporting event fields were abysmally worse. Drawing a breath through my mouth, I held it until I was done, and my hands were washed.

Technically, I could hold my breath indefinitely. One of the perks of being a supernatural entity. It became uncomfortable after a few minutes, and I didn't like to do it. When I hit the door and it wouldn't open, I didn't panic, but there was no way in hell I was breathing in the stench. I pushed on the door, and the groan of metal became much more important than worrying about odors. I managed to peer out of the centimeter-wide gap I'd made and saw the hasp they used to lock the doors at night. Pressing my face against the door, my worst fears were true. Somebody, probably the bitch who tried to shoulder block me, had locked the padlock that had been hanging on the open hasp.

Laughter, muted by the door and distance, set my blood on fire. Drawing back my arm, I open-palmed the door right at the level of the latch. My hand struck, dented the metal door and pulled a good chunk of the wall off with it. Concrete and metal went flying. Calmly, and coolly, I walked out of the bathroom pretending nothing was amiss. I refused to even look at her. A mortal screaming in fear was never a good thing in a public place. I'm sure she would have seen her death in my eyes. Revenge was much better when they weren't suspecting it.

Flopping back down on my lawn chair, I reached over and grabbed my drink from Brady. I should have brought two.

"Everything okay?"

"Little trouble with one of the mothers. Problem solved."

"Is she still in one piece?" He chuckled.

"For now. Feeling cute, might rend her later, haven't decided."

"Which one was it?" He sat up and looked over his shoulder. "Let me guess. Blonde at the concession stand, glaring daggers at you?"

"Yep."

"That's Marissa Hodgins. Teaches the local cheer classes, and the mother of the previous star player on the boys' team."

"Previous?"

"Until your son joined the team."

"Oh."

"That, and she's probably not too happy seeing you sitting next to me. She probably thinks that's why your son is doing so well on the team..."

"She thinks I'm fucking you?"

He blushed but nodded.

"Want to have dinner tomorrow? I'm meeting Daniel."

He seemed a little confused. "You want to have dinner with both of us?"

"Yes."

"If you don't mind a third wheel?"

"Not at all."

If the bitch wanted to talk about me, I'd make for damn sure she wouldn't be spreading lies.

∞ ∞ ∞

Seeing your offspring hoisted up on the shoulders of his teammates was not something I ever would have expected to make me sniff and rub the corner of my eye. They had played the boys team from the same school that had trounced my daughter's team, and won in the last few seconds of the game. Karl had kicked the ball between the legs of one of the players charging him, jumped and spun as the child passed him, and landed just a few feet from the ball. He reached out with his *left* leg, giving it a sweeping kick that put it in the upper left hand of the goal, completely out of reach of the goalie.

Having the parents of the other kids patting me on the shoulder and screaming in my ear in excitement wasn't exactly normal, either. I had to consciously retract my talons before smiling at them over my shoulder.

"That was amazing!" One of the dad's seemed overly excited. Then I realized he was looking *over* my shoulder. At my tits. Taking a small sip of his lust, I smiled and headed for the gate. Karl was being deposited on his feet just on the other side.

Excitedly, Karl came running through the gate and nearly tackled me. "Did you friggin' see that?"

"I did," I answered with a small chuckle, patting him on the head. "You were great."

"Thanks!" His face got a little serious as he looked around. "Where's Rynnie?"

"She went to the park with some of her teammates."

"Good. Then she didn't see."

"See what?"

"Us winning the game. She was pretty depressed that they lost theirs."

"You're a very sweet boy, but I'm sure she would be happy for you. She played amazing as well, but their opponents were, more than likely, recruited from the jungles of the Amazon."

"Yeah." He nodded in agreement. I was glad it wasn't just me who saw the difference in the female teams.

"Should we go get some pizza?"

His grin was answer enough. "I'll go get Ryn. Meet you at the car!"

Smiling at his back as he headed for the park, I was utterly grateful for an end to the soccer induced hell I'd been subjected to.

"Need a hand?"

"Hey, Brady," I answered without turning around. "Thank you, but I can manage to carry an aluminum framed seat all by my lonesome." *Or a small bus. Definitely a hunky soccer coach. Especially if he were chained up...*

"I know you can, I was being all gentlemanly."

"Then you should have thrown me over your shoulder, slapped my ass, and taken me to the back of your van."

"Truck."

"Even better. Especially if you have an air mattress."

"Nope. Nor a topper."

"That's okay. I don't mind people watching, but I'm not getting my ass bruised."

"If I didn't think you were totally joking with me, I'd be seriously drooling over my shirt right about now." He folded his chair up and gave me a nervous chuckle.

You have no idea, mortal... "Yep. That's me. I'm such a tease," I answered drolly.

"Wait, you were serious?" His eyes bulged out of his head.

I gave him a wicked grin, shrugged, and headed for my SUV. His eyes were burning holes in the back of my skirt, I could feel the heat from his gaze. Not to mention, I could smell his lust, which the cool wind at my back was wafting toward me and hardening my nipples with its delicious aroma.

Then, I saw my vehicle sitting in the grass on four deflated tires. The lawn chair slipped from my grip as red tinged my vision.

"What's the matter?" Brady caught up to me, and even the delicious smell of his arousal didn't cool my murderous mood. "Oh. Shit." He passed me and set his chair by my bumper, walking around my car, inspecting the damage. "Well, the good news is they weren't slashed. Somebody just let the air out of them. Would you be impressed if I told you I had a compressor in the back of my truck?"

Hope fluttered through me. "Impressed? I'd blow you if you did!"

"Damnit. Makes me wish I had an air compressor in the back of my truck."

"You don't?" The hope fluttered away. I think I might have actually pouted. I'd been looking forward to blowing him.

"No. I just asked if you'd be impressed if I did." He blushed in embarrassment. His joke having taken a horribly wrong turn and smashing into oncoming traffic. "But I can run you down the street to the Home Depot and buy one."

"That would be...delightful. Let me text the kids." I whipped out my phone and let my fingers fly over the keys at inhuman speed.

"You're going to leave them here?" His voice left little doubt that would be bad parenting.

So much for the blowjob. "No! You don't mind if they ride along, do you?"

"Not at all."

Chapter 8

"So, let me get this straight...You're dating Daniel. The most eligible divorcée in Shady Oaks, if not all of Bickering, and now you're screwing around with Coach Drake? The second one on the same list? *And* you have Daniel's permission?"

"Well, not that I need his 'permission,' but I do have his blessing." I nodded at Karen and gave her an impish grin as I pulled the red plastic cart out of the corral. "He thinks it's kind of hot."

"It is. But I still hate you," she answered with a little pout, pulling a second cart out for her. The pout lasted all of three seconds, the exact time it took her to eye the discount bin in the front of Target. She squealed and made a beeline for the display of Halloween merchandise.

"Technically, we're not screwing around. Yet."

"But he gave you a ride to the hardware store, and then inflated all your tires for you?"

"Yes."

"He wants you."

"I know."

"Lucky bitch. Ooh! These are adorable!" She reached into one of the bins and pulled out three wooden carved pumpkins and unceremoniously dumped them in her cart.

"I'm going to grab a coffee. Want anything?"

"Grande caramel macchiato, extra shot, half nonfat, half soy, extra caramel."

I stared at her with half-lidded eyes, resisting the urge to slash her throat and let her life's blood drain into the black coffee I was about to purchase.

She looked up and saw the look on my face. "Coffee's fine…"

"Cream and sugar?"

"Please."

I nodded and turned around, heading for the Starbucks by the registers. Taking a sigh to calm my nerves, I got in line. Thankfully, it was only three people deep and only took a few minutes to get my order in and take my place at the serving counter.

"Two coffees for Kyra."

"Kara."

The eighteen-year-old barista blinked at me in shock. Apparently, she wasn't used to people correcting their names. Surprisingly. One would think they would actually get a round of applause with every one they got right. I made a mental note to start doing that, if it ever happened. Usually, I was Cora.

"Cream and sugar are over there." She pointed at the small countertop by the carts.

"Thanks," I paused to look at her name tag that said, 'Mary.' "Marie," I finished, and picked up the coffees, walking away before the poor girl registered what I said.

"Are you following me?"

I smiled as Brady's voice slithered over my neck like lips. Shuddering, I looked over my shoulder at him. "Since I was here first, I should be the one asking that question."

"How do you know you were here first?"

"Because if you were here when I got here, I would have known it and come found you."

He grinned and leaned against the coffee station. "Fine. I just walked through the door and saw this hot girl pouring milk in her coffee."

"Friend's coffee."

"Her friend's coffee. I couldn't resist saying hello."

"The bigger question is, what brings you to Target? I thought this store was reserved for lonely housewives."

"Alana needed some stuff, so I drove her."

"Alana?"

"My sister. Your daughter's coach." He looked around. "Where are the kids?"

"Playing with Karen's. Her husband is watching them."

He chuckled. "Rick's a nice guy. I'm assuming that coffee is Karen's?"

I nodded and snapped her lid back on, stuffing the cup into one of those cardboard thingies so she didn't scald her human skin. "Want to hang out with us?"

"No. I'll let you go. I'll see you and Daniel for dinner on Friday?"

I nodded and gave him a quick kiss on the cheek. "Thanks again for everything you did yesterday."

"My pleasure," he answered dreamily and absentmindedly trailed his fingers over his jaw where I'd kissed him.

I just chuckled. The kiss was for taking me to get a small air compressor for my car. The pleasure for actually inflating my tires and making sure I got home would come later. When he did.

Bumping his hip with mine, I headed back for the discount bins. My cart was there, but Karen was across the aisle, standing in front of a rack of sports bras and staring at me jealously.

"I swear you're a magnet. They find you no matter where you are."

"He's shopping with his sister."

Karen nodded knowingly. "Yeah. He moved in with her when he got divorced."

"She's not married?"

"No. She's a...uh. She likes women."

"They can get married, too, Karen."

"Oh! I know that, silly. I meant she's not married to anybody."

"And you were letting me know she likes women."

"Yes."

"Why?" I wasn't angry, just curious. I was a succubus. Lust was our bread and butter. It didn't matter if it was loaves or biscuits. We just loved sandwiches.

Karen shrugged, embarrassed. "I don't know. I'm so used to hanging around people who would have been shocked by the revelation. I forget stuff like that doesn't faze you at all." She took her coffee and set it in the holder in her cart, frowning slightly.

"Do you want me to pretend to be shocked?"

"No. I like this better."

Our discussion kind of felt like when Ryn had scored the goal, or Karl had won the game. Karen won a small victory, and I was almost proud. Instead of making a big deal out of it, I gave her a small smile and pretended to rifle through the sports bras beside her. Why anybody would wear one of the gods' awful things was beyond my comprehension, but then again, I didn't have large breasts or engage in sport activities. I'd stick to free fall or lingerie.

"Oh, that's adorable!"

I stopped rifling and looked at the neon pink monstrosity in my hand. "It looks exactly like every other one on this rack."

"But it has a bow printed on the front."

"You need help, Karen."

She giggled. "Come on. I want to look at shoes."

We headed toward the shoe aisle, each of us pushing our own coffee laden cart. She stopped short, and I almost slammed into the back of her, swerving my cart into the aisle at the last moment and avoiding a major wreck on the highway. "Karen!"

"What?"

"Slow down. Drive responsibly."

"These are what I was looking for, though!" She pulled a pair of white tennis shoes out of the box, from the middle of the rack, and ran her finger along the pink swoosh.

I looked down at her feet. She was wearing the exact same pair. "What's wrong with the ones you're wearing?"

"I scuffed the top in Zumba class."

I'd had enough for one day. "I'll be in electronics." I needed a new phone and to keep my sanity, anyway.

"Okey dokey."

I waved over my shoulder, gripped the cart, and pulled my coffee from the holder. I started guzzling it, hoping the caffeine would get rid of my rapidly increasing headache.

It took me a moment to find the electronics department, but thankfully, it was mostly empty. I needed a break from people. Parking my cart in front of the display of cell phones, I regretted not bringing Karl. He kept up with technology and knew the latest models of every brand, from gaming console to televisions. He would have pointed at the phone I should buy. "Maybe, I'll just wait."

Daunted, I turned my cart and looked down the main aisle of home décor. Brady wore a disinterested expression while his sister was picking out a floor lamp. Even bored, he was hot. His hair wasn't long, but it wasn't short either, pushed back and messy. I wanted to run my fingers through it.

He was wearing a white T-shirt stretched over his chest and a pair of jeans that had seen better days. They would have looked much better off of him. Leaning back against the counter, I paused to watch the show. He wasn't even aware I was drooling over him.

Until he turned his head and caught me watching the Brady Show. He blushed and waved, pointed at his sister and rolled his eyes. She was oblivious, focused solely on the selection of lamps before her.

It was time to have a little fun.

Letting my hands slide down over the front of my skirt, I let the hem slip between my fingers and gave it a little tug upward. His eyes were directly connected to it and widened as I brought it higher and higher, stopping just below the lips of my pussy and letting it go. You could see the disappointment, and relief, in his eyes. He looked around nervously and gave me a look like I was crazy.

Maybe, I should take one more look at the cell phones.

Turning, I bent over the display. He had to have been getting an eyeful, but it wasn't time to look yet. The show had just begun. I ran my finger over one of the more expensive models and bent over to see if they had any in stock in the locked case below. I had to hold myself up with my hands to make sure I could see the tiny little model numbers printed on the box. From the angle I was bent over, Brady had to have a pretty good view of my box, too.

Someone coughed behind me, and it wasn't Brady.

Looking over my shoulder, I grinned at the nerdy looking sales guy standing there, averting his eyes like a gentleman. "Can I help you find anything?"

"Just looking. Thanks."

"Well, if you need anything, I'll be right over there." He pointed at the kiosk in the middle of the department.

"Will do. Thanks."

He smiled and walked away. I looked over at Brady. He was red and practically crying with laughter. He still had a bulge in his jeans, but he was laughing.

I shrugged and lifted my skirt, giving him an unobstructed view before dropping it, and pushing my cart toward the Halloween section. I could feel his lust behind me, racing to catch up.

"I can't believe you did that." He fell into step beside me.

"Neither could the clerk."

"You're going to be in his dreams tonight."

I stopped at an endcap, pretending to peruse the pumpkin colored garland and lights. "It's not his dreams I want to be in."

"Why do you want to be in mine?"

"Well, you're playing hard to get. Might as well be in your dreams." I let go of the garland and pushed the cart around the corner, entering the main decorating aisle. Pumpkins, black glittery cats, and green faced witches assaulted my senses.

"You're dating my best friend. I'm playing not to get."

"Then what are you doing here?"

"Can't seem to stay away from you. I'd be lying if I said I wasn't attracted to you. But I won't hurt Daniel."

"And I've told you, Daniel is okay with it."

"So he says. But what if he isn't?"

"You haven't smelled his lust when he thought about it."

"Um...smelled? Ew."

"Seen. I meant to say seen." I barely managed to refrain from smacking myself in the forehead.

He nodded, unsure if I was telling the truth or not. "Well, we'll find out on Friday," he said determinedly.

"Don't you trust me?" I grinned and ran my finger over his chest.

"Would you trust you if you were me?"

"Indubitably." My finger didn't stop at the waistline of his jeans, and I felt him harden under my fingertips. "He trusts me."

"He wants you. Has nothing to do with trust."

"More with lust?"

He nodded, his breathing going a little shallow. "Either way, we're in the middle of Target."

"Afraid your sister is going to come looking for you?"

"No. She'd probably just roll her eyes, be jealous of me, and walk away. I'm more worried about security."

I unzipped his fly and let my fingers slip inside. "You mean those cute little guys in red shirts with walkie talkies? I'm not into little boys. I like men." I stood up on my tip toes and let my teeth graze his bottom lip as I fished him out the front of his jeans.

"Kara!"

"Yes, Brady?" I started some long, underhanded strokes. His cock was just as magnificent as I'd imagined. And I'd imagined it often.

"We're going to get caught."

"Hmmm. The Halloween aisle is kind of busy. Maybe we should move." I didn't let go of him, just turned and started pushing my cart to the back of the store. We rounded the corner and kept walking until we were in the inside garden department. I stopped behind one of the endcaps facing the back wall of the store and dropped to my knees before he could protest.

Drawing him toward my mouth, I looked up at him. He wasn't going to be protesting anytime soon. Maybe ever.

He whispered my name, but it wasn't to stop me, it was in pleasure as my lips slid slowly over the tip of his cock. His lust filled my nose as his hardness filled my mouth. I moaned and let my free hand slip under my skirt, diving between my swollen lips and spreading my wetness over my clit as I started sucking him.

His hips found their own rhythm as I pumped him with my fingers and suckled him with my lips. His hands slid through my hair as he held me, practically driving himself inside me. "Fuck, Kara… I'm not going to last."

I squinted up at him in pleasure, letting him know that was exactly what I wanted. His cum was only part of it, his orgasm was everything to me. I wanted it more than he did.

His hands made fists in my hair as he erupted in my mouth. Lust spread through me like heroin in my veins. My fingers danced over my clit as I brought myself off right after him. Eyes close, breathing through my nose, I drained the last of his cum from his cock and swallowed before pulling him from my mouth.

"Holy fuck, Kara."

I stood up, wiped my lips and gave him a sexy smile. "See? Not so bad, was it?"

He shuddered and fumbled with his pants as he tried to stuff himself back inside. He just chuckled, raised his eyebrows, and let out a long sigh. "That was, and I'm not going to lie, fucking amazing."

"No. That was a fucking blowjob. The amazing fucking comes later."

He shivered, his eyes fluttering as the thought danced through his blood-deprived brain. "Wow."

"Careful, Brady. Don't come again…"

He blushed in embarrassment as I laughed and wrapped my arms around him, gently nibbling on his ear.

"I really hope Daniel is going to be okay with this."

"He will be."

"I hope so. I really don't want to let you go now."

"But I'm holding you."

His arm slithered around me and pulled me harder against him. He shifted his head back until his eyes met mine. "But I'm not letting you go."

"If you want to keep me, you have to lick me."

He let go and dropped to his knees. I'd been speaking metaphorically, but he lifted the front of my skirt, his eyes drinking me in before he closed them and let his tongue slither between my lips. I mewled as his tongue flicked my clit, and he lowered my dress. Getting his feet beneath him, he stood back up and looked me in the eye. "There. I licked you. You're mine."

I leaned in and kissed him deeply, tasting myself on his tongue. "No. You licked me. Now you are mine."

"I'm good with that."

∞ ∞ ∞

Want to have dinner with me and my kids?

I blinked at Daniel's message on my phone. We'd been officially dating for two weeks. I'd met his daughter and his ex-wife. Neither instance had even phased me, even if his daughter did make me a little uncomfortable with her human cuteness. The thought of having dinner with them terrified me. A fact that didn't go unnoticed by Karen.

"You okay?" She paused emptying her cart and gave me a worried look.

"Daniel wants to have dinner."

Her eyes narrowed and she looked over my shoulder at Brady in line with his sister a few registers over. "You didn't..."

Confused, I looked behind me and saw who she was looking at. "Yes?"

"Wait... You *did*?"

I nodded, still confused. "Yeah. In the inside garden section while you were looking at shoes."

"You had sex with Coach Drake in the middle of Target?" Her voice raised in intensity and pitch the further she got into her sentence.

"No!"

"Oh, thank God."

"But I blew him. And he licked me a little."

"Kara!"

"What?"

She stared at me for a moment, shook her head, and gave up. "You're not feeling guilty?" She pointed at my phone.

"For the blowjob? No. It was quite nice, actually. He was sooo hard and smelled absolutely delicious—"

She held up her hand, not wanting the gory details. In public. "Then what are you worried about?"

"His kids."

"Brady's?"

"He doesn't have any. Daniel's."

"What about them?"

"He wants me to have dinner *with* them."

That was the point that Karen started laughing uncontrollably, drawing the attention of every person in line at every register. They all stopped to see the cackling madwoman at register five.

"Are *you* okay?" It was my turn to start worrying about her. And her sanity.

Her raucous laughter faded to chuckles and then drifted off as giggles before she wiped her eyes and caught her breath. "Yes. You're just hilarious."

"What did I say?"

"You. You blew your kid's soccer coach in the middle of the garden section, and you're worried about eating in front of Daniel's children?"

"Yes!"

"Why?" She started putting the rest of her purchases on the conveyor belt, oblivious to the cashier listening to her intently. She even focused her unbelieving gaze to me to hear my answer.

"Because kids are creepy."

"Kids are *not* creepy! You have two of them. How can you even remotely think that?"

"Because they are. My kids, too. When I'm around them, I never know what to expect, what's going through their little undeveloped minds, or how I should act around them. I would rather battle an angry horde of demons barehanded! At least I know when *they're* going to gut me."

She sighed and gave me a sympathetic look until she noticed the cashier wasn't ringing up her stuff. "Enjoying our conversation?"

The girl blinked in embarrassment and started sliding things over the scanner.

Karen *tsked* and turned back around. "Seriously, Kara. Just be yourself. I saw that little girl take to you like a duck to water. Kids can sense goodness in people."

"Or evil."

"Yes. They tend to shy away from that."

"Not always." I chuckled under my breath.

"Anyway, be yourself. You'll do fine. Just..."

"What?"

"Call them by their names, not child, or anything like that." She stuck her tongue out at me.

Sighing, I drank the last of my too cold coffee and debated getting another one while I waited. I hadn't found one thing I wanted, other than Brady's cock, in the entire store. "This is going to be awkward."

"Only if you let it."

I nodded and waited while the cashier bagged Karen's stuff and processed her payment. Karen pushed her cart toward the door without another word. As I was passing by the cashier, she tentatively stopped me by touching my arm and looking around. It was just her and me. "Did you really?"

"Blow a guy in the garden section?"

She nodded shyly.

"Yep."

Something akin to relief washed over her. "That is so awesome!" She smiled and seemed to pull back into herself.

"It really was. You should try it sometime." I gave her a wink and left her there, daydreaming.

The lust-fueled daydream was the perfect little snack...

Chapter 9

Daniel sighed as he got back into the car and pulled his door closed. He stared at his ex-wife's door for a moment and put the car into reverse before turning and looking over his shoulder as he backed us out of the driveway.

I let out the breath I'd been holding since we pulled into the parking lot of Chuck E Cheese's.

"You okay?" He chuckled as he put the car into drive and headed back toward our side of Bickering.

"I survived. Your kids are sweet."

"Even the boy?"

I nodded reluctantly. To call him standoffish would have been akin to calling Hitler determined. He hadn't even pretended to approve of his father's and my relationship. The glass of water I'd "accidentally" knocked off the table into his lap hadn't done wonders, either. "Yes! He was a darling." *Little troll.*

"You did great." He flashed me a proud grin and put his hand on my thigh.

"As I said, I survived."

"You should have brought Karl and Ryn. Vincent wouldn't have had a moment to spare for you. He would have been flustered by your daughter."

That thought made me smile. Next time, I would.

"So, how was your day?"

The moment had come. I'd been waiting all day for the time to finally rear its horny little head. I leaned over the center console and put my lips as close to Daniel's ear as I could. "Ran into Brady at Target…"

He visibly shivered in his seat. "Oh?"

"Yep."

"How'd that go?"

"Do you want me to tell you?"

He turned and nodded a little *too* eagerly.

I licked his ear and whispered, "It went fine and ended up with his cock in my mouth..."

He corrected his steering just before he clipped the garbage can at the end of the driveway we were passing. "You did?"

"Yes."

He groaned in pleasure. "Where?"

"In the store."

He did a doubletake. I reached down and ran my hand over his hardness. It surged under my touch.

"Well, I was going to ask if you were *really* okay with everything, but your actions are speaking volumes."

"Okay? That is fucking hot."

"Oh, it was. And then he licked my pussy."

"Did you come?"

"Nope. Brady was too afraid of getting caught. There's always our dinner on Friday. If you want to watch..."

"You...want to do stuff in front of me?"

His voice quivered, but I couldn't tell if it was from interest or fear. I needed to tread lightly. "Only if you want me to. Of course, you can join in. Or we can keep our dinner friendly, and you can take me home and fuck me. I'm happy with whatever you want, Daniel."

"I definitely want to see that. Would you want to have both of us at the same time? Is that something that interests you? I don't want you doing things just to please me." He was so serious, and I was trying *so* hard not to laugh.

"No! Not two dicks. I'm afraid!" I lost it.

He blushed. "Guess women have their fantasies, too. Sorry."

"Don't be. You're fucking adorable. Tell you what. You take the lead during dinner. I'll dance to whatever tune you want."

"You're pretty fucking perfect. Anybody ever tell you that?" He saw the answer across my face and gave me a little sympathetic squeeze of my thigh. "Well, he wasn't the only one," he said, and gave me a wink, eliciting a smile out of me.

"Thank you."

"Nope. Thank you."

"For what?"

"Telling me what happened."

I nodded. "No secrets. I promise."

His face darkened. "Coffee?"

"Uh oh. Sure? Why?"

"Because we need to talk, Kara."

The possibilities of the topics of discussion quickly ran through my demon brain. Only one of them could have caused his reaction, and I did a quick calculation. "Has it been three days?"

"Yep."

"Shit." A little stab of icy fear pierced my heart. "Make it a drink drink. Coffee ain't gonna cut it."

"As my lady commands." He turned on Elm St, heading for what passed for downtown in Bickering.

We rode in silence while I contemplated how much to tell him, opting to keeping my oath to keep no secrets from him and hoping he didn't react as badly as I thought he would. Humans enjoyed their mundane existence while dreaming about magic and monsters. Unfortunately, when faced with the reality of the truth, they had difficulty coming to terms with their illusion of supremacy. They also had a tendency to lash out. Often with pitchforks and swords.

He pulled into the parking lot of a yuppy bar. There were no grungy taverns in Bickering. They probably didn't even serve domestic beer within city limits. Just craft IPAs and vodka made out of grapes. I looked up at the neon sign on the side of the building. "Hop 2 It? Seriously?"

He snickered. "We can go to The Crafted Brew if you prefer?"

"Hop 2 It is just fine…"

He pulled into a spot close to the door and shut the car off, the engine *ticking* as it cooled, and we sat there for a moment. "Do you want to go in and talk over drinks, or talk here and *then* go get drinks?"

"Go inside, drinks, then talk." I needed some liquid courage.

"You're afraid?"

I nodded, unable to talk, let alone look at him. I just stared blankly at the stone wall of the craft beer hipster mecca.

The backs of his fingers gently stroked my cheek. "What are you afraid of? The truth can't be that bad."

"Daniel," I started without turning. "People think they want the truth, but when it's handed to them, they have a tendency to freak."

"I promise you, I won't."

"I promise you, you will."

"Let me just say one thing before we go have those drinks and you tell me everything. You're not human. There isn't a single, solitary doubt in my mind. Not after seeing you heal and the way you protected me. What *exactly* you are, I don't know. Nor do I care. I've already come to terms with it, and I might as well know the rest."

"Fine. Don't say I didn't warn you."

"Yep. Come on." He opened his door and got out, shutting it quietly as I sat there for a moment more, doubting what I was about to do. My contemplation gave him enough time to walk around the car, open my door, and offer me his hand. The hand I might be touching for the very last time.

Damn that vampire. If he hadn't attacked, everything would be fine...

"Come on, Kara. I'm not going to bite."

I let him pull me out of the car. He gave me a smile and led me to the tinted-glass front door with the name of the bar emblazoned on it with gold swirly letters.

"Hi! Welcome to Hop 2 It. Bar or table?" The tiny, bubbly brunette hostess tilted her head while waiting for our exuberant answer.

"Booth, please," Daniel answered.

She grabbed a couple of beer menus and separate food menus and walked us toward the back of the somewhat crowded place. "Here you go. Delaney will be here shortly to take your order. Our special tonight is pretzel nuggets with Bavarian mustard, the cream cheese and jalapeno stuffed Betterburger, and our Daily Draft is Goat's Head Eel Feel IPA."

She left us after we sat, and my head was spinning from trying to decipher the words that had flown from her mouth like some sort of archaic spell to summon a fraternity demon named Kyle. "Was that English?"

"Kind of. I'll be skipping any beer named Eel Feel, though." He raised his eyebrows and browsed the beer menu, letting out an exasperated puff of air.

Picking up the menu, I stared over the edge of it at his face. He was engrossed in the beer selection, while I felt like running away. Just as I was seriously about to bolt, Delaney blocked my escape to take our order.

"Hi! What can I get you started with to drink?"

"I'll have a Danube Salted Caramel Dragon's Blood."

"Huh?" My eyes flickered to the beer menu to see if that was really a thing, or if he was just fucking with me. He wasn't. It was right up at the top. I missed the days of lager, ale, and stouts. Instead of names, beers had morphed into potions.

"And for you?" She gazed at me expectantly.

"Vodka on the rocks, three olives, and make it dirty."

"I'm sorry, we only serve craft brews…"

"Oh, fuck no." I looked at Daniel. "Aren't there any real bars in this town?"

He covered his smile with his hand and shook his head. "Unfortunately, no."

Sighing, I handed her my menus. "Whatever's the strongest."

"You got it!"

"Give us an order of the nuggets, too. Please."

"My pleasure!" She took his menus and bobbled off, her head swaying in every direction as she walked.

"As you can see," I said to Daniel staring after our waitress. "Not everyone you meet is human. Take her for example. She's a Funko Pop."

He laughed, but then leaned forward. "You're kidding right? She's human?"

"Sadly. You must be so proud."

He visibly relaxed. "So. Spill it. What are you?"

"Still don't have a drink. And I'm not sure there's enough beer in this place to calm my nerves enough to spill my guts."

He reached across the table and took my clenched hands in his. "I'm telling you. You have nothing to worry about. I'm not going anywhere."

"That's what they all say."

"Did your husband?"

"No. But we *lived* together for a year before he figured it out."

"And did he freak when he did?"

I thought back at the moment and smiled. No, he hadn't. He patted me on the head and asked if I thought he was stupid. Then he kissed me and did other things to me that broadened the smile on my face and made me shift uncomfortably in my seat. "No. He didn't."

"Well, I won't either. As long as you're not some soul sucking demon who is going to leave me a dry, withered husk." He laughed at his own joke until he saw my face fall.

"Daniel…"

"Holy shit. On second thought, let's wait for those drinks."

Unfortunately, we didn't have to wait long, and Daniel ordered another round before she set the first glass down on the table. When she left, he started guzzling his beer. I took it as a cue to do the same, and as soon as the liquid fire hit my tongue, my eyes widened in surprise. It didn't suck. "Wow," I muttered, and stared at the half-empty glass I was holding in front of my face.

"Good?"

"That's not beer."

"Some of them are really good and have alcohol contents higher than most mixed drinks."

"Not the way I mix drinks."

He laughed. "I can imagine."

We polished our beers off without another word and the waitress brought round two and a tin bowl full of pretzel nuggets with a cup of mustard. "Ready to order, or do you need a few minutes?"

"I think we're going to stick to pretzels and beer. We ate dinner earlier."

"Sounds good! Flag me down if you need anything else." She left us staring at the buttery looking nuggets.

I reached out and gripped one between my fingers, dunked it into the sauce, and popped it into my mouth. The salt burned a little, but the taste was exquisite. What they said about demons and salt was completely true, damn television. However, it would take a lot more than the coating of a pretzel nugget to do me any harm. It was kind of like eating habanero peppers.

"Okay. Start talking, Kara."

I chewed and swallowed, washing down the nugget with the last of my beer from my first glass. Gripping the second tightly, I held it in front of me. "Where do you want me to start?"

"First thing's first. What are *you?*"

"A demon."

"Like snarly, bitey, horns, and wings?"

"I have horns, wings, and a tail, but I don't bite. Unless you ask me nicely…"

"You're a succubus!" He stared at me in shock. Almost as much as I was staring at him.

"Yes!" I almost dropped my beer as my eyes widened in shock "How did you know?"

"Kind of clicked. You're a stripper. You *really* like sex. You're beautiful, and that is almost an understatement."

I blushed at his compliment. "Thank you."

"I can't believe I didn't figure it out sooner. So, what was that thing the other night that attacked us?"

Shrugging, I took a sip of beer. "I think it was a vampire, but I can't be sure. Didn't get a close enough look at it."

"You're really not human." He seemed to be talking more to himself than me. "You really are a demon." He looked up at me, wide eyed, but I didn't smell any fear from him.

"Yep."

"You've fed from me. I've felt drained... In more ways than one," he added with a small bark of laughter.

"It's how I survive. I can eat food, but I don't really get anything from it."

"But never enough to harm me." He wasn't asking, he already knew the answer.

"I could if I wanted to. Fucking you to death is literally an option, but not one that I've ever used."

"Why?"

"Because I like you. A lot."

"Do you?"

"Of course. We wouldn't be sitting here having this conversation if I didn't." His question stung a little. More than I cared to admit.

"Good. I like you a lot, too." He softened the blow with a genuine grin. "What about other people?"

Forty-five years ago, when I had first come into my power...there had been an accident. I hadn't killed him, but it was close, and it had never set well with me. I swallowed nervously and nodded, not wanting to lie to Daniel. "Almost once. On accident. I couldn't control my abilities when they first manifested."

"You weren't always a succubus?"

"Yes. But for the first fifteen or twenty years, we're in our larval stage. Human in appearance and ability."

"Oh, God! Your kids…"

"Are half. Cambions, we call them. Some manifest powers, some don't. Either way, what they are separates them from those around them."

"That's why they seem so mature and smart."

I smiled at his compliment. "Yes."

"So, what else is real?"

"Just about everything you can imagine. They're all out there." I motioned toward the front windows. "Hiding. Some not so well. It's why the occasional story pops up in the news. They mostly live in big cities. It's why I chose Bickering instead of Boston. Close, but not close enough."

He let out a sigh and sat back in his side of the booth. I took another pretzel bite and swallow of beer, blinking in surprise at my now empty glass. I'd been so engrossed in our conversation, I didn't even remember drinking it. He motioned for the waitress and pointed at his empty glass.

"You're handling this quite well." Technically, I wasn't sure how the hell he was handling it. His face had become a mask of introspection, and I had no idea what he was thinking. He could be planning on dousing me in gasoline and shooting lit matches at me for all I knew.

"Kara, I saw it with my own eyes. The vampire, I mean. What you're telling me is nothing new. I even figured out what you were before you told me. It was all…sort of anticlimactic? I know I should be scared, and I know I should be freaking out, but I'm not. Does that make sense?"

"No," I lied. It really didn't make sense. He should have been screaming in fear and blabbering about checking himself into the loony bin. Maybe humans were watching too many supernatural movies. It was almost as if they were *waiting* for it to be real. There was only one thing I could do. I reached across the table and took his hand.

He didn't pull away. He didn't cringe. And he wasn't staring at his hand in revulsion. He had accepted what I was. He had accepted me.

Chapter 10

"Are you sure about this?" The realtor gave me an imploring look with her doe-like eyes.

Taking one last look around the studio, I nodded. After Daniel's and my discussion at the brewery the night before, I had caught sight of the dance studio across the street. The vacant, empty dance studio with stripper poles lining the front window. It was the studio that Karen had mentioned closed down due to lack of interest. In a town like Bickering, I could see it happening. But the previous studio was lacking one thing. Me. The previous owner probably had never set foot or crotch on a stripper pole in a professional manner in her life. "Yes. I'll take it."

"And I'll draw up the paperwork." She stared at the check in her hand. The check for the exact asking price. "I'll call you with a closing date."

"As soon as possible, please." The studio hadn't depleted my funds, but they were lower than they'd been in twenty-plus years. Selling the house in Orlando had just become a priority. I'd been putting it off as sort of a safety net, something to go back to in case either I or the kids found Bickering completely unbearable. Things had progressed well enough that the kids would literally have to drag me away kicking and screaming. I was happy, and I had a feeling they were, too.

"I'll shoot for Monday or Tuesday," she answered with a grin, and slipped my check inside her leather-bound notebook. "Is there anything else you wanted to look at while we're here?"

I'd seen everything, even the small studio apartment above. Unless there was a hidden cache of bondage equipment in the basement, we were done. "No. I think I'm good. Thanks, Connie." I held out my hand to the forty-something brunette real estate agent with cute lips and curvy hips.

"No. Thank you!" She motioned for the door.

Locking it up behind us, she coughed nervously as she turned around. "Are you going to uh…be offering the same kind of classes?"

"Pole dancing?"

She nodded. Almost eagerly.

It looked like I had my first customer. "Yep."

Relief washed across her face. "Oh, thank God. I had been building up my courage for months, and just as I was about to sign up…the previous owner moved to Boston and opened up shop there. That's way too far for me, and I took it as a sign that it wasn't meant to be." She blushed cutely.

"Well, there's not much in the way of renovations. I love the interior, so I won't be changing much. Just some signage, permits, and licensing. Maybe a couple coats of paint. I hope to be open within a month."

She practically bounced with joy. "I'll be sure to let my friends know!"

"Thank you. I'll see you early next week, then?"

"You betcha! Good luck with *everything*!"

I smiled as she headed for her car, got in, and pulled out into the practically deserted street. Then, I sighed at the frantically waving hand in the Dunkin' Donuts window across the street. Smiling at Karen, I crossed the street without looking.

Ignoring the squealing tires, swearing, and the look of absolute horror on Karen's face in the window, I kept walking and opened the door as I relished in the happy smell of coffee as it hit my senses.

"Jesus Christ, Kara! You almost got hit."

"Meh. I had plenty of time. He was just being overdramatic," I lied. The truth was, I had agreed to help Karen with some PTA bullshit at the school after my meeting with the realtor. I'd also forgotten about that and stepped out in front of the car, hoping it would end my suffering.

"Well, be more careful! You gave that poor man two heart attacks." She frowned and slapped my arm. I let it go and didn't gut her on the spot. "Get your coffee, we need to get going."

"I bought it."

"The studio?"

"Yep." I motioned toward the register. She grabbed her coffee and drained it, tossing it in the bin and standing beside me.

"You're going to open a pole dancing class?"

"Yep."

She squealed with excitement, earning us stares from the people trying to enjoy their coffee and donuts in peace. "Sign me up!"

"I figured." I chuckled and ordered two coffees to go.

"Wait 'til the girls hear about this!"

"Well, keep it under wraps until the deal is done."

"My lips are sealed!"

Uh huh.

We grabbed our coffee, and she drove us to the school, skidding to a stop in one of the front spots. Peeling my fingers from her dashboard, I got out of the car as quickly as I could. "How many speeding tickets have you gotten?"

"This year?"

"Never mind. So, what are we here for?"

"It's a surprise!"

Groaning, I went inside.

Karen waved at Margaret at her desk. I blew her a kiss. "Seriously, Karen. What are we doing?"

She sighed. "I sort of volunteered you."

"For what?"

"The Fall Festival. We ran out of volunteers to fill all the positions, and your name might have come up…"

"Karen?"

"Yes?"

"What did you do?"

117

She gave me a wan smile and opened a door just past the administration offices. There were long folding tables arranged in a U shape. Principal Marshall was seated at the head of the bend and every seat was filled except for the two to his right. Karen proudly walked around the table and took the one closest to him, motioning me to take the remaining one.

"Oh good. We can *finally* get started," Marshall said drolly.

"Sorry we're a tad late. Traffic was horrible," Karen lied smoothly, and smiled at the people around the table. The only other face I recognized was Brady, seated at the very end of the table to my right. He gave me a smile as I sat. "Everyone, I'd like to introduce my neighbor, Kara. She's volunteered to head up the haunted house!"

"I did?"

"You did." She nodded and smiled.

I'd take it out of her hide later. And she was babysitting my kids for the rest of eternity. All I could do was narrow my eyes at her briefly before smiling uncomfortably at the rest of the people seated around the tables. "Hi."

Brady looked like he was about to piss his pants. He had covered his mouth with his hand and flashed me a sympathetic, yet amused, look.

"Well, that should be everything. Coach Drake is, as always, in charge of contracting the carnival rides." She smiled at him and clapped. "Marissa Hodgins, ticketing." She nodded her head at the blonde seated beside Brady.

I froze, recognizing the name. The bitch who had locked me in the bathroom at the soccer field. The bitch who was after Brady. Smiling, I waved at her. She had the common decency to ignore me. *This is going to be fun.*

She rambled off the other people in the room and their respective responsibilities. I lost interest in what Karen was saying, choosing instead to sit calmly next to her and stare daggers at Marissa. It was amusing—every time she turned back, I was there, staring at her. It was childish, I know, but she locked me in a public restroom. She was lucky I didn't nail her bleached anus to a wall.

"Well, that's everyone and everything. Let me know if you need help with anything, and let's make this the *best* Fall Festival in Brentworth Academy history!"

Two people clapped. I wasn't one of them.

As soon as we were done, I walked around the table to Brady, who just happened to be engrossed in a very uncomfortable looking discussion with Marissa.

"We should grab a drink tonight, to discuss it," she finished saying as I walked up behind her.

"Unfortunately, I have plans tonight," he answered, and smiled at me over her shoulder.

"I was just coming to confirm. See you at dinner tonight?" I grinned at him happily.

"Wouldn't miss it for the world," he answered, just as Marissa turned and saw me behind her.

"You're having dinner...with Brady Drake?" It almost sounded like she couldn't believe it.

"Yep."

"Well, if you'll excuse me, I have to go vomit," she said under her breath, and ducked around me.

"Bulimia is no way to reduce the size of your ass. Try squats."

Her head snapped to the side, and she outright snarled at me. "Cunt," she whispered, and walked off.

"You are what you eat, asshole." I whispered my response, but projected enough to be sure she could hear me.

Marissa flipped me off over her shoulder and left the room. I was heartbroken.

"Be careful," Brady said almost worriedly.

"Why? She gonna lock me in a bathroom again?"

"Again? Is that what happened at McKorkle Field?" He paused to cock an eyebrow at me. "Want me to say something to her?"

119

I couldn't help myself and laughed at his chivalry. "No. Trust me. Any problems with her, I am more than capable of taking care of myself."

"Just be careful. She has a lot of friends and can make your life a living hell."

"And I can drag her into the depths of hell, have her flesh flayed from her bones, and torture her for twenty lifetimes." I chuckled to let him know I was kidding. Kind of.

"Well, are you going to introduce me?"

Behind me was Alana, Brady's sister. I'd seen her from afar, but never been introduced. Turning, I offered her my hand. "Hi. I'm Kara."

"Dell? Rynnie's mom?"

"The one and only."

"Pleased to meet you!" She pumped my hand harder than her brother had when he'd introduced himself to me.

"Oh, don't act like you didn't know, Sis. Not like I haven't told you about her a thousand times."

"I know, but this is the first time I've put a name to the face. I mean she's been so inconspicuous. Especially in Target. You know, ducking behind displays and what not."

She wasn't being bitchy, she was teasing, and confirmed it with a smile. I liked Brady's sister.

"Well, I'm sure I'll see you around." Her touch lingered as she pulled her hand from mine and left the room. In fact, Brady and I were the last ones in the conference room.

"I think my sister likes you." He rolled his eyes, unimpressed.

"If you're worried I'm going to leave you for your sister, don't."

"I'm not, but it wouldn't be the first time."

"Oh, don't get me wrong. I'd fuck her, but I wouldn't leave you to do it."

"Uh…"

"Would that bother you?"

"No. Girl on girl is hot, just don't expect me to watch." He made a gagging noise.

I laughed. Succubae *rarely* had siblings, so incest wasn't a thing we ever thought about, but I could definitely see how humans would have an aversion to it. Ryn and Karl were friends, but they rarely even hugged. I shuddered at the thought of anything ever going on between them and curled my lip in distaste. "Don't worry. I won't offer."

"Won't or wouldn't?" He tilted his head at my choice of words.

"Depends on whether you'd have a problem with it." I grinned at him wickedly.

"Not at all." He gave me a quick kiss. "Gotta get to class. See you tonight?"

"Abso-friggin-lutely." I sat back on the edge of the table and smiled at him sultrily.

"Minx." He chuckled and left, just as Karen came back into the room.

"Well, that went well…"

"Karen?"

"Yes?"

"Run."

Chapter 11

"I'll have the pound-and-a-half lobster, baked potato, and some sort of veggie, I don't care which."

The blonde waitress stared at me for a moment while she processed the information. Finally, she wrote it down and looked at Daniel.

"I'll have the steak, medium, with a potato and side salad."

"Loaded?"

"Not yet." He chuckled at his own joke.

"I meant the potato, sir." She must have been new to the service industry, awkward and unsure.

"I know. I was kidding. Yes, please."

She looked back at me, biting her lower lip and trying very hard to stare at my eyes and not on my almost exposed breasts in the purple silk camisole I wore under my jacket. Carter's was rather stuffy, and I had taken off my black jacket before we even sat down. "How did you want your potato?"

"Loaded." She nodded and wrote it down, finally looking at Brady sitting next to me.

"I'll have the Cajun pasta."

"Good choice." She nodded and wrote it down, picked up the menus, and headed toward the kitchen.

"She was a little nervous," Daniel said with a small chuckle.

"Don't pick on her. She's probably new."

He nodded at me. "Yeah. I think so, too. We eat here all the time." He paused to point between himself and Brady. "Never seen this one before."

"Nope," Brady concurred.

"So, you two dated before little old me came along?" I grinned and took a swallow of my wine.

Brady laughed, but Daniel looked embarrassed. More so than he should have. I cocked an eyebrow in intrigue, but let it go. I'd been teasing, but I would have bet money they had experimented in their youth. My pussy liked that idea. A lot.

Daniel was sitting on the other side of the table from Brady and I, having lost the hastily cast game of rock, paper, scissors they'd used to decide the seating arrangements. If the booth were a little bigger, the three of us could have sat on the same side. Instead of getting to touch both of them, I put my hand on Brady's thigh and smiled at Daniel.

"So, where are you taking me after this?"

"Dancing or a movie?"

"Hmmm. Not a huge fan of dancing, and a movie seems kind of lame for our first double date."

"What would you suggest?" Brady took a sip of his beer.

"Any titty bars around?"

He spit his beer and quickly covered the top of his glass with his free hand, saving Daniel from a beer shower.

"Titty bar?" Daniel stared at me incredulously.

"Yes. Strip club?"

"I know what a titty bar is, I was shocked you wanted to go to one."

"Why not? I like titties. They're pretty. Big titties, little titties, all the titties." I took another sip of my wine.

"I'm game," Brady said without arguing, shrugging at Daniel.

Sliding my hand a little higher on his thigh, I rubbed the tip of his cock through his jeans with my pinky. He looked down at my hand then over at me.

The server chose that moment to return with another round of drinks. I polished off my wine and handed it to Brady to pass along, not stopping teasing him with my finger.

"Here we go," she said, and set the full glass of chard down in front of me, reaching over Brady to do it. Her eyes didn't miss what I was doing, either. She froze for a moment, shifted her weight onto her other foot, and set a beer in front of him and another in front of Daniel.

"Last one for me, please. Switch to Coke after this."

Without looking from my hand, she nodded. "Sure."

Finally, she snapped out of it, turned and walked away. Brady started laughing before I did.

"What's going on?"

"I'm touching Brady inappropriately. I don't think our waitress has ever seen someone do that in public before." I grinned proudly.

"Damn it!" He slid his empty beer away.

"What?"

"I knew I should have gone with paper."

"You never could beat me." Brady held up his bottle for a toast. Daniel clinked his and took a sip of his fresh one.

"You have your phone?" He was cute and deserved a treat.

"Yes?"

"Put it below the table and take a picture."

"What?"

"Trust me," I said with a nod.

In the time it took him to pull his phone out of his pocket and open his camera, I had fished Brady's cock out through his zipper one-handedly. I also hiked up the front of my skirt with the other and spread my legs.

Daniel put the phone down by his crotch, and without looking, started snapping a few pictures. I stroked Brady's cock and diddled my clit to give him a show.

"Now look."

He pulled the phone up and flipped through the pictures, his eyes widening as a small smile crossed his lips.

"Take a vid," I whispered across the table.

When he was done fumbling through the controls, he lowered the phone and the light came on, illuminating beneath the table. While there was no one close enough to notice, I needed to be quick. Leaning over, I sucked Brady into my mouth while I slipped a finger in my pussy, pulling it out and rubbing the moisture all over my lips as I ground my fingers against my clit. I moaned into that suck and Brady hissed in pleasure.

Not wanting an end to the show, I pulled my lips back up his length and let his tip pop free of my mouth before turning toward the camera and smiling. When I sat back up, Daniel pulled the phone above the table and hit play.

It had done an incredible job capturing the sounds I'd made sucking Brady's cock, and you could even hear the little *pop* at the end. I'd been gently stroking Brady while Daniel watched the show.

"You like?"

He tore his eyes from the screen of his phone, and he nodded slowly. I could taste and smell the lust pouring from him.

"You want a taste?"

He nodded.

"Drop your knife."

"Pardon?"

I reached across the table, and his eyes followed my movements as I gently pushed the knife off the edge. It hit the bench beside him and bounced under. "You better get that, don't you think?"

"I should…"

He had to tilt on his side to get under the heavily lacquered wood and then dropped to his knees. I spread my legs and felt his tongue slide up between my folds and trail lazily across my clit. I tilted my head back in pleasure and had a wicked thought. Leaning forward, I lowered my head and whispered, "I didn't mean me." I gently shook Brady's cock in Daniel's direction.

There was a quiet moan under the table.

Jackpot.

126

"Is that okay with you, Brady?" I looked over at him for approval.

He seemed to think about it for a moment, then something passed behind his eyes. It felt like a memory, and I was sure it wouldn't have been the first time Daniel had Brady's cock in his mouth. It had probably been years and years, but it had almost definitely happened at one point in all their years of friendship. Finally, Brady shrugged. He was acting almost uninterested, but the smell of lust wafting from him surged.

Letting go of the velvety softness between my fingers, I watched as a hand encircled his girth and pulled it down from its upright position. My eyes darted up in time to see Brady's lips part as his cock was enveloped by his friend's mouth.

"Bring back some memories?"

Brady's eyes widened in shock, and then a blush spread across his cheeks. "How did you?"

"Know?"

"Yes," he hissed, and started breathing heavier.

"Just a hunch. Boys will be boys." I grinned and kissed him.

When I pulled away from that kiss, the waitress was standing a few feet from our table, eyes glued to the show beneath. Her arms were laden with plates of steaming food, but she wasn't moving a muscle, not wanting to break the spell. Finally, I reached down and tapped Daniel's head. "Food's here," I said softly.

There was a muffled squawk as he pulled away and struggled to get back into his seat without banging his head. The waitress stepped closer and started setting our respective meals in front of each of us. Daniel looked up at her and held up his knife. "I dropped my knife. Think I can get a new one?"

"Right away, sir."

∞ ∞ ∞

127

You could tell it was a strip club just by the parking lot. They have a certain feel to them all on their own. The *huge* sign hanging from the building that said *ADULT ENTERTAINMENT* was the other clue.

"The Candy Shoppe?" I chuckled at the name on the gold foiled door as we walked up. *Thirty-minute drive to Salem just to see some titties. They better be real.*

"Yeah. Been a few years, huh?" Brady looked at Daniel.

"My bachelor party, I think."

"Oh, yeah. Well, let's hope this visit is a little better." Brady laughed heartily.

Curiosity got the better of me. "Why? What happened?"

"Samantha," Daniel answered.

"She showed up to your bachelor party?"

"While he was on stage…" Brady could hardly breathe.

"Well, I'll try to make this visit just as memorable. But in a better way." I cupped his bulge beside me as we walked up to the bouncer.

"Twenty apiece. Lady is free."

Twenty bucks for a cover charge wasn't bad. Ginger charged ten, but Full Exposure was a dive. There were three types of strip clubs. Diners, drive-throughs, and dives. Diners were like topless steakhouses. Nudity was used to entice men into coming and spending vast amounts of money on food and drinks. Drive-throughs were like tension relievers. Guys came in to watch a girl strip and then took her to the back for a private show. They were primarily for guys on their way home to a nagging wife and kids to go in and blow off a little steam. And other things. They were the ones who also paid off local law enforcement to stay out of the back rooms. Dives were the nitty-gritty hardcore titty bars. They tried to keep everything above board, but sometimes shit happened. The girls who worked there were the true professionals. Teasing but never pleasing, unless a Ryan walked in, or someone talked them into going home with them. As for the Candy Shoppe, I wouldn't know what category it fell into until we got inside.

After we walked down a long purple hallway, we entered a dive. Nostalgia, lust, and the heavier smells of sex and cigarettes assaulted my nose, making my eyes water and my heart ache. It had been way too long. I almost trounced up to the bar and asked for an application.

You have a dance studio. And kids.

But...sex!

Butt sex?

If I'm lucky.

I ended the conversation with myself and followed Brady and Daniel to one of the round tables by the stage. Daniel pulled out the white leather swivel chair in the middle of the other two and offered it to me. It looked like it was older than I was. *Oh, the stories it could probably tell. I just hope they used an industrial sanitizer.*

"Thank you, sexy," I said, and kissed him on the lips before settling down and taking my jacket off. Brady draped it over the back of my chair and sat on my left. Daniel took the last chair just as a waitress in a neon green thong and high heels slid up to our table. Her outfit and highlights on her skin were glowing in the blacklights above us.

"What can I get you to drink?"

"Beer."

"Beer."

"Bottle of rum."

"We don't serve–"

I cut her off with a hundred-dollar bill I'd fished out of my purse before we got out of the car. I'd heard her argument before.

"Overly inebriated customers. But you seem fine," she finished with a grin.

"You want a glass with ice and some Coke or something?" Brady was staring at me like I'd grown a cock out of my forehead.

"Nope."

He shrugged and looked at the stage. The dancers were between sets and the new performer was busy wiping down the pole before the next song started.

"Everybody, give it up for Jazmin!" The DJ's voice blared over the speakers just before the thumping bass intro to "More Human than Human" began thrumming through our chests. Jazmin reached out and gripped the pole, using it to do a backflip as she expertly wrapped her legs around it and spun around in a perfect arc. She wore the same excited smile I had plastered on my face each and every time I performed. She loved her work.

"Damn," Daniel said, impressed.

"She's good."

"Better than you?" Brady chuckled.

"Nope." It wasn't a lie. Humans just couldn't compete. She was close, though. Good enough to possibly be a cambion or have some diluted supernatural blood running through her veins.

Daniel's hand rested on my bare thigh. Entranced by Jazmin's performance, I reached down and covered his hand with mine and began slowly moving it back and forth over my sensitive skin.

"Your rum," the waitress said, loudly enough to be heard over the music. She put her hand on my shoulder as she leaned over me and set the bottle on the table in front of me. Her exposed skin was warm, I could feel the heat of it as her stomach brushed my shoulder.

"Thank you."

"My pleasure," she answered, letting the hand on my shoulder rub a small circle over my skin.

Jazmin sashayed over to the edge of the stage right in front of our table and danced, slowly working her top over her head sensuously, just as the first teaser song finished and the second started. She was grinning wickedly at Brady as she squatted down and leaned back, supporting herself with one hand against the dancefloor as she pushed her panty covered mound in his direction.

He took the hint and stood up, pulling a dollar out of the wad of small change we had stopped and gotten on the way over. She smiled at him, the corners of her mouth upturning with a promise of gratitude while he pulled the edge of her garter from her thigh and slowly brushed the bill up her leg and tucked it in.

Her ass dropped to the stage floor, and she leaned back, letting her hand slide down over her stomach as she pressed the thin material of her panties between her lips and slid her finger upward, letting it dance over her clit momentarily before she rolled to the customer beside him.

Brady sat down and gave me a blush. "Wow. She's kind of hot."

"Kind of?" I laughed at his description.

"Okay. Really hot."

"You should ask her for a lap dance."

"I'd rather have one from you."

"I think that can be arranged."

His hand found my other thigh, and I cooed at the sensation of just being lovingly stroked.

"You should both get a private dance from the lovely Jazmin."

The voice slithered over us like melted chocolate while the French accent touched places it had no business being. He'd been masking his presence, so I hadn't felt his approach, and I tried very hard not to seem surprised as I looked up and saw him standing over us.

He wasn't overly tall, but his slender waist was exposed just above his jeans and below his cropped T-shirt. A black suit jacket hung open, draping down from his broad shoulders. The meticulously groomed blond goatee twitched as he smiled at me. He wasn't handsome, he was beautiful. Cascades of blond hair fell over his shoulders in soft waves that I wanted to reach out and caress.

"Hi." Daniel and Brady slid their chairs out a little to turn to see him. It might have been better if they ran away. Safer at least. The statuesque creature standing behind me wasn't remotely human.

"Welcome to my club. I hope you enjoy your evening." He paused to stare at the two hands on my thighs, still lightly stroking. A smile caressed his lips. "But I am sure you will."

With that, he was gone, moved on to the next table.

A vampire owning a strip club. Imagine that. I chuckled at the irony. Humans loved to portray vampires as strip bar owners in almost every paranormal romance book and movie in existence. If they ever found out it actually happened... Let's just say that Mr. Vampire would have to triple the size of the Candy Shoppe just to accommodate the human women showing up at his door. I laughed at the irony. And then frowned when I remembered the attacks.

"Let's go," I said to my boys.

"Go? We just got here!" Brady sounded disappointed.

Daniel, however, saw the look in my eye and stood without being asked twice. "Come on, Brade. We'll get a better show at my place," he said with a toothy grin, and offered me his hand.

Chapter 12

"You need to tell Brady." Daniel sighed as the paint roller *snikt* across the surface of the back wall, leaving a thick coat of blue paint.

I was trimming the bottom of the adjacent wall in gray. Once we were done with painting, contractors were coming in to sand and polish the wood floors. That was the extent of my renovations. The rest of the studio was in great shape. Once I'd signed the closing papers, it was surprisingly easy to get the permits and licenses. My secondary instructor was due any day.

I'd called Ginger, the owner of Full Exposure in Orlando, and cleared it with her before extending the offer to Sage. She had been mentioning that she wanted to get out of the game for a while, but had nowhere to go, and no skills to utilize in a normal nine-to-five job. It was the perfect opportunity for her to get out. The apartment above the studio was hers for the taking, too. Plus, with her help, I wouldn't be spending every waking moment at the studio. It might have made sense businesswise to see how busy we would be before I hired somebody, but I had *zero* business sense. If I had to, I could always get a job stripping. Maybe *that* was my plan all along, and I just didn't know it.

"I know. It's not fair to him," I answered Daniel. "How do you think he's going to take it?"

He stopped painting and set the roller down in the tray beside him. "Probably better than finding out his sister was gay."

"That really bothered him?" I looked up and blinked at Daniel in shock.

"That she was gay? No. That he was going to have to compete against her in the dating department? Yes." Daniel smiled and bent down, wiping some paint from my nose. "You're awfully cute, you know. Even when you're all smudged."

I scrunched my face at him and stuck my tongue out, trying to get over the fear that had settled in the pit of my stomach. Just like with Daniel, I didn't *want* to keep what I was a secret from Brady, I was just afraid of how he would feel when he found out.

If we hadn't run into the damn vampire at the Candy Shoppe, I wouldn't have even considered it. Ever. Until the day he noticed I never got any older. But with the vampire attacking people in Bickering, and quite possibly owning a titty bar in Salem... He might be better off knowing than not. He needed to know when to run.

I snarled at the thought of the vampire. I'd moved well outside the city proper. The odds of running into a vampire should have been slim to none. The odds of running into *two* of them were infinitesimally smaller. They were territorial by nature and didn't want another of their kind within a hundred miles of them, unless they were of the same bloodline...

So, either they were one and the same, or one sired the other. Either way, if the attacks didn't stop, I needed to do something about it. I wasn't the supernatural police or anything, but they were in my back yard. It would only be a matter of time until I got dragged into the mess, and the last thing I wanted was to get outed to the humans. I'd already been targeted once. The next time...would be the last.

"Well, this wall is done. Got another trim brush? I'll finish it up so we can get some dinner." Daniel stepped back and admired his handiwork.

"Dinner? What the hell time is it?"

Daniel glanced down at his watch. "Almost five."

"Son of a fucking bitch!" I nearly dumped the paint cup beside me as I got to my feet and tossed the shop keys to Daniel. "Can you lock up? I forgot I was supposed to pick up the kids from soccer."

"Why don't you just text Brady and ask him to bring them over here? Then we can all have dinner together."

"I can't ask him to do that!"

"Why? He's your boyfriend, isn't he?"

"Yes. But–"

"No buts. Text him."

Sighing, I grabbed my phone off the reception desk and did as he suggested. A simple apology and request. I even said please. My phone went off in my hand before I even set it down.

Too late. We're already on our way to your house. Meet us there and we can grab dinner.

I smiled at his response. "Guess I was later than I thought."

"No. Look outside. It's raining. They probably called practice." He pointed at the window.

It wasn't raining, there was a mini hurricane outside. Wind was blowing the rain sideways down the street. We were going to get very wet just running to the car. Wet and cold.

"Shit. Maybe we should do takeout at the house. Feel like Chinese?"

"You weren't going to cook?" He chuckled and grabbed a paintbrush out of the pack. "Let's finish this up and head out. That way, we won't have to rush to finish in the morning before the flooring people come."

"Good idea." I sent one quick text to Brady, letting him know we would meet them shortly and got down on my knees, grabbing the brush, determined to finish.

Daniel was a much faster painter than I was. Or could ever hope to be. He had the whole wall trimmed in top to bottom by the time I finished the lower half of the wall that I was doing.

"Show off."

135

"Nope. Just hungry." He grinned at me and took all the painting supplies into the back.

We managed to get to the cars relatively dry. There was a break in the squalls as soon as we walked outside. "That was lucky."

As soon as we started driving, it started again. I followed Daniel's Jeep with my SUV and had a hard time seeing his taillights through the deluge. Takeout was definitely an awesome idea. What should have taken us ten minutes to get home, took us almost twenty.

As soon as we pulled onto our street, I knew something was wrong. When the cop car came into view, parked out on the street, my heart sank. Daniel swerved into his driveway, and I skidded to a stop behind the cop car, jammed the transmission into park, and ran for the front door, the rain the least of my worries.

"Karl!" I shouted from outside the door, worry and panic the only thing keeping me going as icy fear flooded my veins.

"In the kitchen, Mom!"

That saved me from searching the house. "What happened?"

I stopped just inside the arch to the kitchen. The kids were standing by the police officer, and Brady was sitting on a stool by the counter. He was holding a wet towel to his face and gently dabbing a gash on the side of his head.

"Brady!"

"Don't worry, ma'am. Headwounds bleed a lot, but it's not that deep. EMTs are on the way."

"You guys okay?" I stared at the kids, looking for any sign of injury.

"We're fine, Mom," Ryn answered. A guilty look passed over her face, but she stared nervously at the cop. I'd find out what that was about *after* he left.

The front door banged open, and Daniel ran in just as I was gently lifting the towel from Brady's head. "You okay?"

"Tis but a mere flesh wound, Milady."

"What happened?"

"The kids were unlocking the house when the Bickering Bandit rushed out between the houses and clobbered me. The kids... They uh...saved me, Kara." He flushed in embarrassment.

"Still don't know how they did it," the cop responded in disbelief.

"We told you, Officer. I jumped and grabbed the guy's legs, and Rynnie started beating his face in."

"And neither of you got a good look at him?"

They both shook their heads. "They were dressed all in black and had a hood and mask," Karl answered for his sister.

"Okay. I'm going to call this in. Glad you guys are okay."

"That's it?" Brady sounded pissed.

"Sir, there are seven patrol cars driving through the neighborhood looking for this guy. If he's still in the area, we'll find him."

Brady opened his mouth to say something else, when I "accidentally" dabbed his wound a little too hard.

He hissed as he sucked in some air and pulled back. "Ouch."

"Sorry," I said, trying to sound apologetic.

"Here's my card. If you think of anything else, give me a call," the cop said, and headed for the front door.

"Useless."

Karl and Ryn sighed in relief as soon as the front door closed. Brady narrowed his eyes at them. Something had definitely happened, something they didn't want to say in front of the cop. "Spill it," I told the three of them.

"Mom?" Karl's voice sounded shaky and unsure.

"Is there anything you want to tell me, Kara?" Brady shifted his attention from them to me.

"Like?" I went with the confused approach out of habit. Daniel had been right. I needed to tell Brady what I was, no matter the consequences.

"Kara..." Daniel's voice spoke volumes.

137

I sighed in apprehension. "You might want to sit down for this."

"I am sitting. Sitting and bleeding. Kara, your kids *saved* me. They didn't just stop the guy—they were beating the shit out of him."

"Self-defense lessons?"

"With claws, *Kara*."

Oh.

"Mom?"

"Okay. Family meeting time. Anybody want coffee?"

"Kara!" Daniel shook his head and pushed me toward the stool on the other side of Brady.

"Fine!" I sighed and sat. "I'm not human."

Brady started to roll his eyes and then stopped, staring at the kids' hands. "What do you mean?"

"She's a demon," Karl answered for me.

Gasping, I looked up in shock at him, and he blushed, leaning back against the counter. "You knew?"

They both nodded.

"Your father?"

"Told us a long time ago. He said to let you have your secret," Ryn gave me a small smile. "But we thought it wouldn't affect us. Daddy told us we would just be a little different, because we were half human."

"Well, normally that's true. I guess under duress, you can," I said apologetically.

Daniel opened the fridge and pulled out a couple of beers, handing one to Brady. "You knew?"

Daniel nodded. "We were attacked in front of the school. Kara saved me."

Moment of truth time. "I was planning on telling you, but not like this." I nodded toward the towel in his hand.

He set it down and cranked open the beer, taking a long drink and not looking at any of us.

"Is she telling the truth?"

Daniel knew he was talking to him. "Yes. We were actually discussing it right before we left the studio. She's terrified of you not wanting her because she's a demon."

"Well, I can't picture myself ever *not* wanting her. Little pissed off that I was left out of the knowing club."

"Sorry," I said remorsefully, looking down at my hands in my lap as a tear slid down my cheek.

"Don't feel bad, Coach. Technically we were in the club, too. She just didn't know that we knew." Karl grinned at him.

"So. A demon?" Brady finally looked at me. I nodded and lowered my eyes back to my hands, wanting to be *anywhere* other than right there, having *that* discussion. "I should totally be freaking out right now, shouldn't I?"

"You're not?" I asked him without looking. It wasn't until his fingertips gently touched my chin and lifted my head, I finally meet his eyes. *Some big bad demon I am. Crying like a human.*

"How can I be afraid of you?"

Oh, my sweet summer child... His challenge made me feel a little better, and I gave a little choked sob and smiled at him.

"What?"

"You just think I'm hot. If you saw the *real* me, you'd shit bricks."

"I doubt that." He looked at me doubtfully and then shifted his gaze to Daniel. "Have you seen her?"

"Nope."

"Aren't you curious?"

"Nope."

He looked at the kids. They were shaking their heads.

"Really? I'm the only one who wants to see?"

"Well, too bad. I'm not showing you. It fucking hurts."

"It does?"

I nodded.

"Well, what do you look like?" He wasn't going to let it go. I could hear it in his voice.

"Kids, go in the other room for a minute."

"Mom?"

"What, Rynnie?"

139

"I think we should see." She held up one hand and her nail hardened and slid out from the tip of her finger. She winced in pain, but kept it there for a moment before letting it slide back in. She had way more control than I ever expected her to have, not that I even remotely had an inkling she *could* change. Cambions who exhibited demonic traits were the rarest of the rare.

"I think maybe you're right. What about you, boy child? Can you?" I motioned at his hand.

He shook his head.

"Be thankful. Mom wasn't kidding when she said it hurts."

"Is it that bad?" Brady looked worried.

"Worse. Ever had a hangnail?" Ryn scoffed.

"Yeah?"

"Now picture your whole fingertip being a hang nail."

"And picture your whole body being a hangnail," I answered with a chuckle.

"Never mind. I don't want to see."

"What?" I was shocked.

"Well, I don't want you to hurt." He frowned at me, and that earned him all the brownie points in the world.

"It's okay. How much do you want to see? All of it? Wings? Horns?"

"What?" He shook his head and chugged the rest of his beer.

"Yes. I can shift parts of me like Rynnie did, or you can see the whole shebang."

"Seriously, Kara. You don't have to. I trust you."

"No." I shook my head and stood up. "All of you were right. I should have told you everything from the start," I paused to look at my kids. "Especially you. You all know what I am, let me show you *who* I am."

Something clicked inside me. It had taken me the better part of my marriage to build up the nerve to let Ryan see me in my full demonic form. He had taken it in stride and got sort of lost in introspection for a few days, but he was still my Ryan and never once shied away from my touch. Not once. If Daniel and Brady knew what I was but never saw it...it wouldn't feel real between us. Stepping back from the counter, I closed my eyes and called my demonic form.

And then I was afraid. Afraid to open my eyes. Afraid to see the look of utter horror on all their faces, even my kids. The fear seized me to my core, and I almost started hyperventilating. All I could do was shift in the spot I was standing, listening to the sandpaper rustle of my skin as I squirmed.

"Holy shit!" Karl's voice broke the moment. He didn't sound disgusted. He used his excited voice.

I opened my eyes.

Brady had stood and moved away, but I was pretty sure it was so he could take in the whole picture. I flapped a wing nervously, and curled it around me. His shy smile was enough.

Daniel was blinking rapidly, trying to tell if I was real or not.

Ryn kept looking from me to her hand, trying to picture what she would look like shifted.

And Karl just stood there grinning at me like a fool.

"Well?"

"You should totally go like that for Halloween! You'd win *all* the costume contests!"

"Thanks, Karl." I rolled my eyes.

"You look amazing, Mom." Ryn smiled and gave me a thumbs up.

Brady looked like he wanted to reach out and touch something. I offered him a wingtip. He gently pinched the membrane between his fingers and let them slide over the smoothest skin on my body. "You're still hot. How can you be hot?" He blinked rapidly, not understanding. I was a succubus. If I shifted on top of him while we were fucking, he wouldn't have batted an eyelash. Without the power of sex, though, he should have been at least a little bit scared.

It was Daniel I couldn't read at all. His face had turned into a stone mask, and he was breathing a little heavier than usual. "Daniel?"

He held up a hand, needing a moment.

A little hurt, I backed up another footstep and wrapped my wings around me. It had suddenly gotten frigid in the room. "I'll shift back…"

"No. Wait a moment. I'm just still getting used to it. May I?" He took a step closer.

"Yes."

He walked around me and let his fingers slide from my shoulder down my back, stopping just short of the junction of my tail above my ass. He lightly touched the tips of both wings and then let his hands glide down the first metacarpals of each wing. I shuddered in pleasure. Daniel leaned in and put his lips next to my ear. "Brady's right. You're still beautiful."

Only then, did I start breathing again.

Chapter 13

"Here you go, Karen. Two-dozen freshly baked chocolate chip cookies."

She looked up at me over the long white plastic folding table, mountains of baked goods piled around her. "Kara?"

"Yes?"

"Freshly baked?"

I glanced down at the clear plastic containers housing the cookies, back to her, and nodded. "Yes."

"By whom?"

"I'm assuming somebody in the bakery department. Don't worry, it looked very sanitary. They were even wearing those hair net thingies."

She closed her eyes, took a deep breath, and I swear I saw her lips moving as she appeared to count from one to ten. "There's still a price tag on the container, Kara," she said calmly after finishing counting.

"Want me to take it off?"

"No! Kara, the whole point of a bake sale is to sell *homemade* goodies! We can't sell store bought items!"

"Why not?"

"Because, next to homemade cookies, those are garbage!"

"Oh... I'm sorry, *Karen*. Are you telling me my cookies aren't good enough?"

"No, Kara. They're not!" She *humphed*, quite perturbed. It was the first time I'd ever seen her angry with me.

"Well, it's not like I can bake. I mean, seriously, did you want somebody to die?"

"Then why did you volunteer?"

"The whole service hours clause of the tuition. You kicked me off the fucking haunted house committee, and I was reminded by Principal Marshall that I needed to have twenty hours in by the end of the first semester. I figured this was a good way to knock out five or six…"

"Hours? For buying Oreos? And I kicked you off the committee because you made me." She pouted, and I could tell she was remembering the noogie I had given her for volunteering me in the first place. It was her fault. Death would have been better than doing *anything* with Marissa.

"Those cookies you are ragging on so savagely have *macadamia* nuts in them. Have you ever had a macadamia nut?"

"Yes. Quite often. I'm sorry, Kara, but if you want service hours, get your ass on this side of the table and help with the bake sale." She snarled at me for emphasis.

In her natural habitat, the Karen was quite formidable. She would have made an excellent demon. "Fine. But you're adding extra hours for the fucking cookies."

"That's the spirit!"

She had the audacity to grin at me. Sighing, I walked around the edge of the table and squeezed between her and the wall, taking up my post beside her. "What do I do?"

"See this mountain of crap? Spread it open over the two tables we have for the bake sale while I finish getting the change bin sorted."

"Fine. Where should I put my cookies?" I swear to fuck, she looked at the garbage can before shrugging. *Cookie snob.*

"Wherever. Just make it look pretty and organized. There's some tablecloths at the end." She pointed two tables down at the stack of orange sitting precariously on the edge.

And with that, I was relegated to busboy on my first day of voluntary slavery. "Need help with that?"

I grinned at Brady, the day having taken a complete one-eighty in one sentence. "What are you doing here?"

"I work here, remember?"

"Shouldn't you be teaching the kids the finer points of winning their next soccer match?"

"Not today. It's the craft fair. This is how Brentworth Academy pays for the Fall Festival expenses without diving into the tuition reserves, and why you're peddling baked goods."

"They really drag in that much money selling brownies and doilies?"

"Wait 'til you see how much they charge for said items..." He winced as he grabbed one end of the tablecloth and helped me stretch it over the pristine white plastic table.

"Well, I'd buy the whole damn table of crap if it got me out of volunteering." I held up my arm. "Look! I'm getting a rash."

"Oh, come on. It's not that bad. Want me to help?"

I looked over at Karen, busily counting cash. "You'd do that?" I blinked innocently at Brady.

"Hmmm. Spending time with the hottest woman at the school while being surrounded by baked goods? Sounds like a dream to me." He flashed an award-winning smile.

"I'd like that." I put my hands behind me, leaned over, and gave him a chaste kiss on his cheek. "A lot."

"Then consider me yours for the next two hours."

"Karen, if my boyfriend volunteers, I get double the hours, right?"

She looked over and rolled her eyes but nodded. "Fine."

"Sweet." I pumped my fist and started transferring the mountain of baked goods to the covered table. We still needed to cover the other one before we could start arranging everything for sale. What would have taken me three-and-a-half hours to do, the two of us knocked out in ten minutes. It was a good thing, too. As soon as we were done, the doors to the gymnasium opened, and the Twenty-

Fifth Annual Brentworth Academy Craft Fair started. I tried to contain my excitement.

My phone dinged.

Pulling it out of back pocket, I smiled when I saw the message.

Coffee?

Yes, please, I answered.

Brady want some?

I glanced up from my phone, looking for Daniel. *Where are you?*

Drive thru at Dunkin'?

How did you know I was with Brady?

Tell you when I get there lol.

It took him ten minutes, and he walked right around the backside of the table, handing me a coffee as he passed. Brady walked over from the end and got his.

"Hey, sexy. You here to sling some brownies?"

"I'd be honored," he answered with a smile.

"Karen!"

She looked up from the cash box after breaking a fifty for the woman who had bought a dozen cupcakes. It wasn't that hard when we were charging four bucks apiece. She took her two dollars and plate of diabetes to the waiting gaggle of crotch goblins in a semi-circle behind her. "What?"

"Triple hours." I grinned at her, and she rolled her eyes.

"Dream on, Kara. His kids go here. His hours go to him."

Daniel blushed and smiled at me apologetically.

"Damnit." I moved a little closer to him. "So, how did you know I was with Brady?"

He flushed and pointed at one of the craft booths across the gym. His ex-wife was hawking her wares. The slut.

"Lemme guess, she immediately texted you to tell her I was cheating on you."

"Close. She texted me a picture of you kissing him on the cheek and told me you were cheating on me."

I chuckled. "And what did you tell her?"

"That you had initiated us both into a sex cult. We meet on Thursdays, and our robes would be ready by the end of the week."

I laughed. "Part of me wishes you weren't kidding. I would have had a lot of fun playing along with that. We could have made a fake initiation video and sent it to her."

Daniel nearly spit his coffee.

"So, what did you really tell her?"

"The truth."

"And that is?"

"That we are both dating you."

"And what did she say?"

"Absolutely nothing. But judging from the look she's giving you right now, I'd say she is having a fit of jealousy."

Instead of turning around to look at her, I kissed Daniel on the mouth. Forcefully. "Thanks for the coffee." Then I meandered down to the end of the table where Brady was being accosted by three blondes wanting cookies and nookies. Of course, I grabbed his ass in front of them. "Need any help?"

He smiled at me gratefully, having successfully marked my territory in front of the other soccer moms. "Tell Karen we're gonna run out of baked goods soon."

I surveyed the damage to the tables. He was right. "Holy shit. Is it like this every year?"

He looked rather uncomfortable.

"What is it?"

"If there were guys buying all the brownies...I would think it was you."

"The sharks are circling the fresh meat," I answered, finally understanding.

He shrugged. I loved that about him. He was hotter than a balor's balls, but he didn't get it. To him, he was just average.

"Does that make you mad?"

"Not as long as you don't put your dick in any of them." I grinned.

"Why would I?" He leaned over and kissed me.

"You're going to wreck business," I chided, and kissed him back.

"Mrs. Dell and Coach Drake, please set a better example for the children," Principal Marshall said disgustedly as he walked by.

"You want us to teach sex ed?"

He either didn't hear me or ignored me.

"Well, I'm gonna go flirt with Daniel, make his ex jealous, and let Karen know we're going to have to close early."

"Dinner after?"

"Love to."

Daniel's line was just as long, if not longer, than Brady's. I stood beside him for a moment until I caught Samantha watching us, and then I caressed his ass, licked his ear, and then walked over to Karen.

"Bad news, boss. We're almost out of drugs. The junkies are gonna start shanking us dealers if we don't close up shop and get out of town."

She surveyed the remaining stock. "They even bought your cookies," she said in disbelief.

"I'm telling you. Macadamia nuts, Karen. Mac-a-dam-i-a nuts."

"Damn it."

"What's the matter? I thought you would be happy!"

"People bought too much."

"Uhhhh…"

"Well, they get a discount when they buy more. We're gonna be short of our goal."

"How much?"

She looked down at the cash box. "About three hundred bucks."

I laughed and grabbed my purse from under the table, opened it and fished out three hundred dollars. "Here."

"Kara! This isn't a donation-based drive. I can't take your money. There are rules. Brentworth Academy *guarantees* that it will never reach out to parents for monetary donations. Goods and services, but never money." She looked at me like I had offered to pay her for sex.

"What's the difference between buying three hundred dollars' worth of cookies and just giving you three hundred bucks?"

"Nothing. You're not supposed to buy the baked goods, remember?"

"Oh, yeah." I frowned for a moment and then came up with a brilliant plan. "What if it was donated?"

"Pardon?"

"Let's say a bakery donated more baked goods. Would that be good enough?"

"Yes?"

"Hang on." I walked outside and hid behind a tree with my smart phone. When I went back in, Karen was staring at me suspiciously. "What?"

"I'm almost afraid to ask what you did."

"Got a local bakery to donate five hundred dollars' worth of baked goods."

"Uh. How?"

"By donating five hundred dollars to Uber Eats. They deliver, you know."

She opened her mouthed, closed it, and opened it again, but nothing came out. She repeated the process until I stuck my finger in her mouth. "Kara, while not exactly *breaking* the rules, that's most certainly bending the hell out of them."

"That's what I do." I grinned.

"Thank you," she mouthed the words. If she had said it out loud, she most certainly would have recognized my almost illicit contribution.

Twenty minutes later, we were restocked and ready to rock out with our cocks out. Figuratively. Karen and I were cockless, and if the guys did it, they would definitely have gotten arrested, and I would have had to beat some serious mom ass.

"Hi, Kara." Brady's sister smiled as she walked up to the table.

"Coach Drake." I leaned forward over the table, putting my hands between the cookies and cupcakes for support.

"That's my brother."

"Other Coach Drake."

"Ouch."

"Sexy Coach Drake?"

"Better, but how about if you just call me Alana."

"When would you like me to call you?" I grinned and offered her a cookie. On the house. With macadamia nuts. It was one of three left.

"Whenever you want." She bit into the cookie and gave me a sexy smile. "Ohh. Macadamia nuts!" She stared at the cookie and grinned at it in satisfaction.

"Told you," I mumbled to Karen over my shoulder.

"Fuck your nuts." Alana and I turned and stared at a blushing Karen. "Oops. That didn't come out right."

"Well, I need to get going. Thanks, Kara." Alana stifled a little chuckle.

"My pleasure," I said sultrily, watching her ass as she walked away and waved at her brother.

"Kara?"

I turned my attention to a solemn looking Karen, dismally staring at the change box. "What?"

She lifted her head slowly and looked over at me. "Why?"

"Was I flirting with her?"

She shook her head. "Why does everybody flirt with *you*?"

"Cuz I'm sexy."

"I'm not?"

I saw where our conversation was heading. In the completely opposite direction I'd been *thinking*. I'd been expecting her to be disgusted that I'd been flirting with another *woman*, but it was because of all the attention I'd

150

been getting. It wasn't her fault she was mortal and I was a literal sex demon.

"Karen?"

She blinked at me with doe-like eyes and a chicken butt haircut. "Yes?" She was on the verge of tears.

"You need to ask yourself a serious question."

"What?"

"Are you happy?"

"Happy?"

"Yes. Do you like who you are and the way your life has turned out? Or do you want more?"

"More?"

I squatted down beside her and put my hand on her knee. "Karen, you're hot, but you're a frump. You have made being a mother into your entire reason for existence."

"What's wrong with that?"

"Abso-fucking-lutely *nothing*. *If* you're happy with that."

"I thought I was. Until I met you." She blushed and looked away.

"And now?"

"I want more."

"And that is the first step on the road to recovery. If it's for the right reason."

"Huh?"

"Do you want more because you're jealous of me?"

She shook her head as her eyes widened. "Don't get me wrong!" She held up her hands. "I am jealous of you; anybody in their right mind would be. But it's not that. I thought I *had* to devote everything I was, am, and will be into being a mother. Then I saw you, and you're like the *opposite* of everything I am. No offense."

"None taken."

"But what it all boils down to, is that you're amazing in everything you do, and you still focus on yourself."

"I'm just a horrible mother."

"See? That's just it, Kara. You're not. What defines a mother is not who she is, but who her kids are. Kara, your kids are fucking amazing."

"That was their father."

"I know you think so, but I see so much of you in them, it's scary. They're strong, brilliant, and so self-sufficient that there is no way they learned how to be all that from their father. That is all you, sweetie."

"Tell you what. I'll make you a deal."

"What?"

"I'll teach you to be more like me, if you teach me to be a little more like you. Deal?"

She grinned. "Deal." She held out her hand, and I grabbed it. Instead of shaking it, I brought the back of her hand to my lips and kissed it. She melted in her chair.

"Lesson one. Don't be normal."

"Got it."

Chapter 14

I rubbed my forehead, trying vainly to get rid of the headache that had formed directly above and behind my eyes. Somehow, I had gotten roped into having dinner with everybody but the kids. We had dropped them off at my house with a crisp hundred-dollar bill and orders to stuff themselves with pizza. The rest of us were having "adult fun night," as Karen called it. It involved dinner at TGI Fridays and copious amounts of adult beverages that had more sugar than booze.

When I looked up, everyone was staring at me expectantly.

"I'm sorry, what?"

Alana leaned in and whispered, "When is the studio going to be open?"

"Oh! Our first class should be Wednesday. Just waiting for my friend to get here."

"Friend?" Karen tilted her head.

"Sage. She worked with me at Full Exposure. She's going to teach on the nights that I can't."

"And you're only offering pole dancing classes?" Rick, Karen's husband asked excitedly. Karen slapped him in the arm.

"Yes. You're coming to the first class, Karen." I ordered her. It was her idea that set my whole plan in motion.

"You betcha. So are Cindy and Allison."

I winced. They were nice enough, but their voices managed to travel through their nasal cavity as it left their

153

voice box. I'd dubbed them the Muppet Twins. For various reasons, but that was the primary one.

"Are you going to be teaching that night?" Alana asked, and gave me a shy smile.

"Sage and I both are."

"I might have to drop by and check it out. Listen to your membership spiel."

I chuckled throatily and took another sip of my Purple Something-or-other. "You definitely should. I'll give you the VIP tour."

She gave me a dreamy look and reached for her glass, nearly spilling it. Brady rolled his eyes from the other side of her. He'd been doing that since she'd sat in his chair as soon as he pulled it out from the table. "I'd like that."

"Will there be any guys taking the classes?" Rick, Karen's husband, seemed a little worried or eager. I couldn't tell. He just wasn't his usual quiet self.

"Honestly, I have no idea. It's usually a woman dominated pastime, but I wouldn't say no to teaching a man."

"Why? Are you interested?" Daniel asked him.

Rick shrugged and took a drink. Then the waitress *finally* brought our food. The conversation was muted while we settled into our plates. I'd ordered spicy chicken over rice, and it smelled amazing. "I don't know. Maybe? I'd have to see."

"Come with me on Wednesday. You can watch or join in," Karen gave him a little nudge with her shoulder.

"I will."

"I might, too." Daniel sounded a little excited.

"Well, if you're going, I'm going." Brady chuckled and popped a rib in his mouth.

The nagging headache turned into a piercing one. While I appreciated the support, I had a feeling it was going to be too much, too fast.

"Why don't you guys wait a bit, and let Kara get it up and running first, before you inundate her with..." Alana trailed off.

"Dicks?" Her brother answered helpfully.

"Yeah. Those."

Rick blushed and mumbled an apology.

"No, Rick. You can come if you're really interested. In fact, it might be better if all of you came," I acquiesced reluctantly. "God knows there probably won't be anybody else there. Might be nice to start off with a full class."

I swear, Brady stuck his tongue out at his sister.

On the edges of my senses, I felt a presence. Quickly, I pulled every iota of lust and power into myself as I masked my presence. Alana shivered and blinked at me in surprise, almost like she had felt it. She rubbed her arm, the one closest to me, shook her head, and started back in on her meal. I'd have to be careful around her in the future, she seemed a little sensitive.

As much as I wanted to turn around and look for the source, I didn't. Exercising patience, I was rewarded for once. The owner of The Candy Shoppe walked by our table and was seated with his date at the booth closest to us. I recognized him in an instant, just as I felt his vampiric power wash over me. Karen was openmouthed staring at him. The round table we were seated at made kicking her in the shin, impossible.

"So, which one of you is dating Kara?" Rick asked between scooping up a forkful of food and shoving it in his mouth.

"We both are," Daniel answered right away.

Rick nearly dropped his fork. "What?"

"We both are," Brady reiterated, almost daring him to have an issue with it.

"Wow. That's kind of cool."

All of us stared at him in surprise. He blushed and continued eating. "Didn't I tell you that?" Karen tried to play it off like she had and failed miserably. At least to me.

"No. You left that part out. I knew Daniel and Brady were friends, but I didn't know they were both dating Kara."

"You're okay with that?"

"Why wouldn't I be?" He seemed genuinely confused. If Karen played her cards right, she might end up with a boyfriend or two of her own. I couldn't have been prouder.

"No reason. Just another thing on the things we've never talked about list." She blushed at the rest of the table.

"Might want to move that one to the things we should talk about list." I chuckled and took a sip of my drink, until I felt a pair of eyes studying me.

Looking over Karen's shoulder, I saw the vampire gazing at me thoughtfully. Not wanting to seem suspicious, I gave him a wink. He shook his head and continued conversing with his date.

It was clear that he recognized me, but I wasn't sure if it was from the strip club the other night or the attack outside the school. I leaned a little closer and whispered to Daniel. "Do you know her?"

"Who?"

"The woman with the blond guy?"

I nodded toward the table and caught the vampire staring at us. I'd forgotten I wasn't the only one in the restaurant with supernatural hearing.

Daniel tried to be subtle and took a quick glance, pretending to look out the window behind them. "No? Should I?"

"Just wondering."

"What are you two whispering about?" Alana asked a little too loudly.

"Daniel asked me what he should wear to his first pole dancing class. I told him the only acceptable thing was a Speedo."

She looked at Daniel and her lip curled, not a sneer, but certainly in distaste. "Please don't listen to her. It is *never* acceptable for men to wear banana hammocks."

"Don't worry. I could tell she was joking, and I don't even own one." He rolled his eyes.

"I can let you borrow one of mine," Rick answered helpfully.

Alana gagged. I just pushed the rest of my food away. Rick wasn't a bad looking guy... Just not someone one wants to picture in a Speedo at dinner.

"So, what should I wear?"

"Get some stretchy pants. Yoga would be best."

"Wear a banana hammock under it though. No free balling. They can get transparent if stretched," Alana added helpfully.

"I'll keep that in mind." Daniel took another bite of food.

"Excuse me, do I know you from somewhere?" The French accent caressed me right in the pleasure sensors. He was using his vampire charms on me, just like he had moved from his table to behind me without my noticing.

"Yes. We met at your club the other night," I answered.

"Ahhh, yes."

"We did?" Daniel seemed confused.

"Yes. He is the owner of The Candy Shoppe."

"Oh!" He blushed.

"You guys went to a strip club?" Alana asked her brother.

"Yep."

"You didn't invite me?"

"We weren't planning on going. It just happened."

Alana *huffed.*

The vampire squatted down beside my chair. "I am Michel." I loved the French pronunciation of Michael. It was just like saying Michelle, but it just seemed so much sexier on a man.

"Kara." I offered him my hand, and he drew it to his lips, gently grazing the skin on the back of my hand.

"Did I overhear you correctly? You are opening a dance studio?"

"You have good ears, Michel."

"As I am sure you do, too." He stared at me levelly. The jig was up. He knew I wasn't human, and that was his subtle way of letting me know just that.

"Yes, I am. I used to be an exotic dancer. I'm going to be offering dance classes at the studio I just bought."

"*Magnifique!* I might send some of the newer dancers for lessons… You would not happen to have a business card?"

"No. Not yet. Having some made this week."

"If I give you one of mine, would you contact me?"

"Of course." Vampire or not, I'd take his money. Then I'd kill him when I confirmed he was the one attacking people. More specifically, me.

He fished one out of his jacket pocket and set it on the table beside me. "I look forward to hearing from you." He slid his fingers over my arm and went back to his seat.

"Uh. What just happened?" Daniel looked at me confusedly. I'd fill him in when we were alone.

"I'll tell you later."

∞ ∞ ∞

"So, what was all that about?"

I was scrunched in the front seat of Brady's car, sandwiched between him and Daniel and loving every moment of it.

"He's the one who owns The Candy Shoppe," I reiterated.

"Yeah, we know. And he wants to send his new dancers to your studio for training. I meant, why was he all over you like cheap French perfume?"

"He's a vampire. That's what they do…"

"He's a what?" Daniel turned to look at me fully, a feat in the narrow truck.

"Vampire? Sexy? Fangs? Blah blah blah?"

"I know what a vampire is, Kara. Don't you think he might have been the one that attacked us?"

"Yep. That's why I'm going to get closer to him."

"How close?" Brady shifted slightly in the driver's seat, not taking his eyes of the road.

"Close enough to find out if he's been munching on the neighbors."

They both got silent after that, until we pulled into Daniel's driveway. "Kara…"

Here we go. "Yes, Daniel?"

"Be careful." He nodded once for emphasis and popped the door open on the truck.

"What he said," Brady reiterated, and opened his door. They left me sitting there in shock.

I slid out, and Daniel closed the door while Brady walked around the truck. "That's it? You're not going to try and talk me out of it and tell me what a horrible fucking idea it is?"

They both shook their heads. "Would you listen?" Daniel chuckled.

"No." I scoffed.

"Didn't see much point in arguing. You're the supernatural one. We're the humans in this relationship. If you think you can handle it, then we just have to trust you. Please don't be wrong."

"I'm not."

"Then there's nothing to worry about," Brady added, and headed for Daniel's front door.

We followed, Daniel getting ahead to open the door with the keypad. I was jealous, our door still used keys. "That's neat. I want one."

"I'll put one in for you this weekend," Brady offered. "It's easy. I did Daniel's."

I turned at the sound of crunching tires behind us. Another car pulled into the driveway. One I didn't recognize. "You have company."

From the look on his face, it had to have been his ex-wife. Nobody could possibly have that look for any reason other than walking the green mile. "What's she doing here?" He stopped and looked at us. "Go ahead, I'll see what she wants."

Brady nodded and walked inside. Me, not so much. I stepped into the shadows and darkened my skin, fading

159

into the blackness. I wasn't spying, I was being a witness and keeping an eye on the obviously crazy bitch.

"Sam?"

"Hello, Daniel." Her voice echoed the sneer I was sure was plastered on her face. The streetlights were reflecting on her windshield, hiding her face from view.

"What can I do for you?"

I was very grateful for my preternatural hearing.

"I see Brady is here."

"Yes?"

"What about your whore? Is she here?"

"Goodbye, Sam." He turned and walked away from her.

"Dan, wait! You were supposed to give me an answer…"

"I already did. It was no, remember?"

"You said you were going to think about it!"

"No. You told me to think about it."

"Did you?"

"No. I didn't see the point. I'd already given you the only answer you'd ever get."

"Please?" The angry, condescending tone to her voice vanished.

Daniel's sigh sounded more tired than exasperated. "Sam, I loved you with all of my heart. You stomped on it and left me. Now, I'm happy for the first time in two years, and you want me to take you back? When hell freezes over!"

"Oh, it's okay for your slut to bang other guys, but when I do it, I'm a horrible person?"

"Kara didn't hide it. She talked to me about it before Brady. You could learn a *lot* from her, and I'm not just talking about relationships, Sam. You're self-centered, egotistical, maniacal, untrustworthy, and a thousand other things."

"But I love you."

"No. You might have at one point, but those days are *long* passed. Go home, Sam. I'll mail out your check on

Friday." He turned again and headed toward the front door, ignoring her sobs and then angry shouts.

Instead of sneaking inside and pretending I didn't see anything, I lightened my skin and stepped from the shadows. He gasped when he saw me standing there, but smiled when he realized I'd been watching. "You worried about monsters or ex-wives?"

"Both. Especially when there isn't much distinction between the two." I winked at him to let him know I was kidding.

"You were looking out for me, right? You weren't being a nosy girlfriend?"

"Me? Nah. Perish the thought. Rampant vampire roaming the neighborhoods. Just wanted to make sure you were safe. That, and I don't trust your ex."

"That makes two of us." He opened the door, and we walked inside his house. Brady had a beer and a glass of wine waiting for us.

"So, what did the ex-hag want?" Brady set the remote down and stood up, joining us in the kitchen.

"She's still a hag," Daniel answered with a chuckle.

"How come you didn't tell me she wanted to get back together?" I narrowed my eyes at him.

"Would you have told you?"

"Good point."

"Really? What happened to Mr. Dreamcoach?" I assumed Brady was talking about Samantha's personal trainer, since technically, he was the dream coach.

Daniel shrugged. "Beats the hell out of me. I didn't ask or care."

I *tinked* my glass against the neck of his beer bottle. "To us, then," I said, and raised my glass.

"Does that include Alana?" Daniel shot me a shit-eating grin.

"Do you want it to?"

"Doesn't matter. Do *you* want it to?"

I just smiled into my wine glass. Things were definitely getting interesting between all of us. I just hoped

161

Brady could handle it. It was his sister, after all. Most guys didn't like *anybody* dating their sisters. I could only imagine what it would be like to have your *girlfriend* do it. "Maybe." I left it at that.

"Well, there's been something I've been meaning to discuss with the both of you." Daniel coughed to clear his throat.

"What?" Brady tilted his head, a little bit of worry etching subtle sexy lines around his eyes.

Daniel opened his mouth and closed it a few times, at a loss as where to start.

"Spill it." I elbowed him in the ribs.

"Since we're both dating Kara, why don't you move in here? It's a friggin' *five*-bedroom house. The kids will still have their rooms for the weekends they're here…"

Brady held up his hand. "Dan, I appreciate it, but when I got divorced, my sister got a bigger house so I could move in with her. The rent is a lot more, and I couldn't just dump all that on her."

"Ah. Okay. Just thought I would offer."

"I appreciate it." Brady grinned and smiled at his friend.

"You guys could bunk here, and your sister could move in with me." I grinned at him and chuckled. I'd meant it as a joke, but I kind of liked the idea. My chuckle deepened.

They were staring at me like I'd lost my ever-loving mind.

"You and your sister move in here. I'll live with Kara." Daniel grinned at Brady.

"Oh, hell no. You move in with Alana, I'll take your house, and Kara can sneak over here at night."

"Your sister *hates* guys."

"She doesn't hate them. She just doesn't find them attractive."

"Plus, she's scary. Why the hell should I go move in with her and let you have all the fun?"

"Exactly."

"Girls, girls. Stop fighting. You're both pretty." I leaned over and kissed each of them on the cheek.

That shut them up. For a moment. "Why don't you both move in here?" Daniel looked up at Brady.

"Huh?"

"You and Alana. Move in here. I have five bedrooms."

"Because one of those is your office. I'm not bunking in the same room as my sister. No way in hell."

"I'll move my office to the basement. I need more room anyway."

"I vote for that idea." I grinned mercilessly. "Like having a smorgasbord next door."

"You're serious?" Brady narrowed his eyes in suspicion.

"You guys are renting, and you *gotta* be coming up on the end of your lease. You got divorced the same month I did."

"Yeah, we're supposed to renew next month."

"So, don't. Move in here."

"How much?"

"How much what?"

"Rent?"

"None. The house is paid for, and I bought out Sam's half."

"Then let us pay for the utilities."

"Half the utilities."

"All of them, except for what you claim for your business."

"Deal." Daniel grinned and held out his hand to shake on it.

"Oh, hell no. Let me talk to Alana first."

"Want me to?" I volunteered helpfully.

"You stay out of this," they said simultaneously.

"Sheesh. Well, I'm going to go check on the kids and go to bed. Night, boys." I gave them each a kiss and headed for the door.

Chapter 15

Strip bars in the early afternoon were a lot different than strip bars at night. They were less crowded, quieter, brighter. Which wasn't a good thing. With the lights on, you could see how disgustingly dirty they usually were.

The Candy Shoppe was cleaner than most I'd ever seen, but I wouldn't rely on the five-second rule if I ever dropped a piece of candy.

The music moderately thrummed as one of the older dancers took the stage. I headed for the bar and sat down. "What can I get you?"

The bartender wore a black button-down long-sleeved shirt with the cuffs rolled halfway up his muscular forearms. "Rum."

"And Coke?"

"Rum."

"You got it," he answered with a chuckle. He grabbed a tumbler, put a scoop of ice in it, and poured a rather generous amount of Bacardi over it. "Ten."

I fished out a twenty and set it down on the bar in front of me. He gave me my change in ones. "Is Michel around?"

"You have an appointment?"

"No. I thought I would surprise him."

"It's a little early for him to show up, but I'll let him know you're here, miss…"

"Kara."

He picked up his phone from behind the bar and sent him a message. I turned around to watch the dancer while I waited. At least for an answer.

The music was soft enough that I heard the bartender's phone *bleep*. He picked it back up, and his eyes widened in surprise. "He'll be here in ten minutes. Drinks are on the house." He opened the register and tried to hand me the rest of my money back from the twenty.

"Keep it."

"Thanks." He stuffed it in the tip jar.

The sets were longer during the day. The second dancer had just taken the stage when Michel entered through the front entrance, his presence a sweeping coolness that settled over the club.

"Kara, I am surprised to see you."

"Good to see you again," I lied. Okay, not really. He was damn pleasant to look at. Especially in the floofy white shirt that was only halfway buttoned up.

"Care to step into my office?"

"Is it safe to sit?"

"Avoid the couch." A dreamy look passed over his face, and a small smile lifted the corner of his mouth.

"Will do."

He offered me his hand and I took it, letting the coolness of his skin calm my nerves a little. As soon as I'd sensed his presence, I'd been on edge. Not like he was a predator and I was prey. More like, I was a predator and stumbled into his territory, and a big pissing match was about to go down.

He opened a red wooden door at the back of the club, and I braced myself for cheesy, but gasped at elegant. A rosewood desk sat in front of the back wall, brown leather chairs in front of it. A matching leather throne, for lack of a better word, sat behind it. To the side were video monitors mounted to the paneled wall. The infamous couch threatened to block the entrance as the L-shape filled the rest of the wall.

"Have a seat." He motioned to one of the leather chairs in front of the desk as he walked around and took his throne.

"Thank you."

166

"You must be eager to bring in some business to your studio."

"Pardon?"

"Is that not why you are here? To offer your services to my dancers?"

"Oh. Yeah."

His eyes narrowed. "Let us cut to the chase. I know you are not human. I can feel your power. If you were a vampire, you would already be dead. What is it you really want, Kara?"

I decided to opt for the truth. "The other night, my human and I were attacked by a vampire. I just dropped by to let you know if it was you, I will kill you."

"Could you?" He wasn't being challenging, merely curious.

"Easily."

"You see, Kara? That is the thing about being a predator. Every so often, you are reminded that you are not the deadliest one around." He smiled at me. "Fortunately, it was not me who attacked you or your mate."

"But you just said if I were a vampire, you would have killed me. Are you telling me there is another in the area, and you're allowing them to attack people?"

His smile vanished. "You are sure it was a vampire?"

"Not a hundred percent, but one has to ask oneself, what are the odds that three different types of monsters settled in the same suburban town?"

He nodded. "Slim to none."

"Exactly."

"So, where does that leave us?"

"Either you are lying to me to save your hide, or the odds really just weren't in our favor."

He leaned forward and rubbed his chin with his fingers before settling his head on his hand. "Then we are unlucky. For I am not lying."

"I wish I could believe that."

"So, where does that leave us?"

"At a very precarious place. I'll take you for your word, for now. Either the attacks will stop, and I'll be happy you heeded my warning. Or they keep happening, and I catch the real culprit, or I catch you and kill you."

"Then I have nothing to worry about." He smiled, almost as if he were enjoying my threats.

"Let us hope so."

"Now, shall we get down to business?"

"Fine."

"I get a lot of new dancers. Up until now, they had always formed sort of a mentorship program with the more experienced members of my dancers. It has worked well for years, but honestly, the girls coming in for work..."

"Millennials are killing the stripping industry?" I laughed.

"To put it succinctly... Yes. Yes, they are."

"And you want me to train them?" I blinked at his audacity.

"My dancers train the newer ones out of generosity. I would rather pay you."

Sighing, I nodded. It was more than I wanted, but with Sage's help, it might be quite lucrative. Strip clubs went through dancers rather quickly, for a multitude of reasons. Business might actually be pretty steady just from Michel.

"Now, the only question that remains is your qualifications."

"Well, I attended Julliard..."

"Truly?"

"No. I'm a fucking stripper. From my ass to my nose. I've been employed for forty years, and I'm..." I almost let loose with what I was. It would probably be better to keep him guessing. "Really fucking good at it."

"Would you prove it?"

"Pardon?"

"I am about to make a very solid investment in your company. All I ask is you put your money where your mouth is. Show me."

"Here?"

He pointed at the door behind me.

"Fine."

We left his office, him leading the way, and I was surprised at how much the club had filled in the short time we'd spent behind the closed door. The excess illumination had been toned down, and the music had increased in volume. Apparently, inversely proportionate to the age of the dancer on the stage. She looked like she might have been the daughter of the dancer performing when I walked in.

"Michel?"

He stopped to look at me over his shoulder. "*Oui?*"

"I'm not wearing any panties."

"Since you are not an employee of the club, we shall call this amateur hour. I am not responsible for what happens when others take the stage."

"Fine by me," I answered his challenge.

His grin told me he had been expecting me to back down, but happy I hadn't. He nodded and headed for the DJ booth, pushing the pimple-ridden youth out of the way and turning up the volume. "Ladies and gentlemen, the Candy Shoppe has a special guest star for you this evening. May I introduce you to Kara!"

Still rather early, the applause was underwhelming, but I strode out to the middle of the stage anyway. Putting my hands behind my back, I leaned back against the pole and looked at Michel over my shoulder. An epic cover of "Paint it Black" pounded out of the speakers. Closing my eyes, I reached above my head, grabbed the pole, and swung my legs up above me.

The crowd actually cheered at my brief acrobatic display. Since that was what I wanted to showcase, that's what I focused on. Gripping the brass between my legs, I let go with my hands and used the upper half of my body to swing my head behind me, twisting the pole as I circled around the stage, arching my back.

Coming back around, I grabbed the pole beneath me and let myself drop, stopping just before I touched the floor. From there, I went into a handstand and spread my legs. My ass was toward the audience, and my loose skirt billowed around my thighs as it dropped down around me. That's when the real cheering started as a few of the patrons surged toward the stage, offering me dollars to come closer.

The rest of the song became a blur as the beat throbbed in tune with the blood in my veins. Ignoring everyone around me, I focused on the art of the dance and used every acrobatic trick in my repertoire. I landed on the stage and fell back against it, spreading my legs and offering everyone a view of my excitement at the exact moment the song crashed to a stop.

"Give it up for Kara!"

And they did. Bills rained down beside me. Some larger than the usual singles that usually were offered after a performance. Picking myself up off the floor, I collected what was closest to me, leaving the rest for the next dancer.

"Holy shit," she said as I passed her.

"Thanks." I gave her a small smile as I headed for the stairs. The amount of lust in the club was almost overwhelming as I drank it all in.

"You were more than magnificent." Michel's voice caressed me in places it had no business being.

"More than magnificent?"

"Perfect." He offered his hands to help me down the three steep steps.

"Thank you."

∞ ∞ ∞

"Are you ready to do this?"

"You bet your ass!" Sage squealed in the passenger seat next to me as I pulled into the parking lot of the studio. "Seriously, Kara. I can't thank you enough for doing this. It's like a dream come true."

"Say that after you see the tiny ass apartment over it."

"It could be a shoe box, and it would beat my last place. Every time a jet took off, I swore it was going to come plowing through my wall. And don't even get me started on the crackheads next door."

"Well, you're in the burbs now, bitch. Nothing but craft beers and beards as far as the eye can see."

"First thing I'm gonna buy is a friggin' jacket. It's freezing."

"This is actually warm. Buy a really thick jacket. Can't have you freezing your titties off."

Shutting off the engine, we got out and walked around to the front. Once we were inside, she gasped and smiled as she twirled around and took in the hardwood floors, gleaming brass poles, shades on the front windows, newly replaced acoustic ceiling tiles, and fresh coat of paint.

"Silhouettes?" She motioned to the name splashed across the back wall.

"Silhouette Dance Studio, to be exact, but Silhouettes for short."

"Pretty name, but why?"

"Accident, actually. See the blinds on the front window?"

She nodded.

"When they're closed, the lighting ended up being perfect. You can't see the dancers, just their shadows on the front window."

"That's kind of awesome."

"And free advertising." I grinned.

"As long as nobody falls..."

"Yeah. Watch Karen. She's cute, but has all the coordination of a five-legged giraffe."

"How cute?"

"Very." I wiggled my eyebrows at her.

"So, you seeing anybody?" She grinned at me and put her hands behind her back, leaning against the wall behind her.

"Yep. You'll meet them tonight."

"Them?"

It was my turn to grin. "Stay away from the two hot guys and the sister…"

"Holy shit, Kara." She stared at me open-mouthed. "You finally over Ryan?" She wasn't being insensitive. In fact, she whispered the question.

"No. I never will be. But it was time to move on."

She nodded. "I'm happy for you."

"Thanks. Go get cleaned up. Class starts in thirty."

She grabbed her bag from the floor and headed up the stairs. I thought about giving her the tour, but she'd find everything on her own. It was her place, I decided to let her enjoy it. I needed to get all the membership forms out and the iPad register up and running anyway.

Stepping behind the counter, I sat on the swivel stool and grabbed the folder with all the forms I'd be needing and powered up everything else. Turning on some music, I had just turned it up a tad, when the bell over the door chimed.

"Love what you've done with the place." Brady's sister walked through the door, took one look around and smiled at me shyly.

"Alana! Congrats. You're my first customer."

"So, where do I sign up?" She set an exercise bag down by the wall and walked over to the counter.

"Right here, but tonight's class is complimentary. Sign up after if you like it."

"I'm sure I will." She grinned saucily and leaned over the counter, giving me a small kiss hello on the cheek. "There was only one car in the lot, I thought your new instructor would be here?"

"She is. Her car is parked at my house loaded up with all her stuff. We took my car."

"Oh, is she staying at your place?"

I wasn't sure, but I thought I detected a note of jealousy in her voice. "Nope. I gave her the apartment upstairs." I pointed up. "She's moving in after class."

"Oh. Good."

"Why is that good, Alana?" I knew the answer, I could smell it on her, but I wanted to hear her say it.

She blushed. "Because."

"Why. Tell me why, Alana."

"Because, I like you."

I grinned at her. "See? That wasn't so hard, was it?"

She was practically hyperventilating. "Speak for yourself."

I crooked my finger at her. "Come here."

She walked around the counter, cautiously and approaching me slowly. "What?"

"So, you have no problem with me dating your brother and his best friend, but you don't want me to see other women?"

She shook her head.

I stretched, standing, she was a little taller than me on my stool, and I gently kissed her on the chin, just below her bottom lip. "I'm good with that."

"With what?"

"Not seeing other women. I find them attractive, but there is just something about you. Probably the same thing I see in your brother. Do you want to date me, Alana?" I traced her jaw with my lips after whispering in her ear. She shivered in front of me, her legs giving out slightly.

"Yes."

"Why? I'm not a very good person." In fact, I wasn't a person at all.

"You're beautiful."

"So, you're just attracted to me."

"You didn't let me finish. You're confident. You can be sweet, but you're stoic. You see everything around you and you're above it all. I love the way you smile evilly when you think nobody is looking. I absolutely adore the way you sm...sm..." She trailed off, unable to finish her sentence.

"Smell?"

She nodded. I touched her hips lightly with the tips of my fingers, letting them slide over the small patch of

173

exposed skin between her leggings and her top. She shivered even harder, leaning forward and practically begging me to touch her more. Alana might have a dominating personality, but not in a relationship. She was pure bottom.

I let my lust leak out a little more, and she mewled as she inhaled, letting her face move a little closer to mine. "Do you want me, Alana?"

She pulled back and nodded shyly. "More than I've ever wanted anybody in my life," she whispered back.

Just as I was about to kiss her, the bell over the door chimed again and Karen and her friends walked in. Shocked, Alana dropped low and slipped under the counter. "What are you doing?" I whispered my question.

She pleaded with me only using her eyes. Everybody knew she was a lesbian, but she didn't want to get caught in a precarious position. I patted her on the head in sympathy.

"Hello, ladies. Welcome to Silhouettes." I grinned at them, not getting up from my seat.

"Oh my *God*, Kara. I absolutely love the place!" Karen squealed and headed right up to the counter, gripping my hands in glee. I was forced to turn my stool toward Alana in her hidey hole.

"Hi, Kara," Cindy and Allison both said from a safe distance by the door. Out of all the other parents in the neighborhood, they were the nicest. That wasn't saying much. I didn't ever see us hanging out if Karen wasn't around, but they were tolerable.

"Hey. Welcome to my studio. Do you guys have any experience?"

They both nodded.

"We all used to go to the one that was here before they closed down. I'm so excited! Where do I sign up?" Karen was rubbing her hands together excitedly.

"Well, let's get through this first class. See if you like your instructor, and then we'll talk."

"Did I hear my name?" Sage walked back out into the studio, smiling at the three girls.

174

"Everyone, this is Sage. We used to work together."

They started talking excitedly when I felt a pair of hands touch my knees and gently spread my legs apart. Glancing down, all I could see of Alana under the counter was said hands and her knees as she settled herself on the floor in front of me.

Leaning as close to the counter as possible, I whispered, "What are you doing?"

Her soft, almost musical laughter was all I heard in response.

I leaned over the counter and put my chin on my hand, feigning interest as Sage introduced herself and struck up a conversation with our first students. I managed not to gasp as Alana's fingertips started making slow circles over my spandex covered mound.

Distracted, I didn't notice Karen break away from the pack and lean against the counter in front of me until she spoke my name.

"You okay?"

"Yep. Just a little distracted," I managed to stammer as I uncrossed my eyes.

"Are you going to be showing us any of your moves tonight?"

I started to answer her, stopped, and started again three times before I finally managed a breathy, "No."

I blinked as the back of her fingers pressed against my forehead. "You look flushed, but you're not running a fever."

"I told you, I'm fine." Alana's lips pressed against me, kissing my lips gently beneath the countertop. I wanted to push her away. Or half of me did. The other half wanted to pull her closer and trap her with my thighs. Normally, I wouldn't have batted an eyelash, but she didn't want to get caught, and I didn't want to shock my first customers on the very first night. "Y-y-you better get over there. Sage is starting, and you don't want to p-p-piss off your t-teacher."

"You're sure you're okay?"

"F-fine," I managed to stammer as Alana's lips were replaced with the tip of her finger as she trailed it up through the narrow channel on the front of my yoga-pants.

"Okay. I'll be right over there if you need me. She waved over her shoulder at me as she walked away.

I put my elbows on the counter and held up my head. Alana must have heard Karen. As soon as she was gone, she spread my legs further and started nibbling at my flesh through my pants. Her teeth, her lips, the warmth of her breath were almost too much to handle, and I focused on breathing and the pleasure that was assaulting me.

The bell over the door chimed once more, and in walked Brady and Daniel. I managed a weak smile and motioned toward the class that had already started.

"Sorry we're late," Daniel said to Sage as he and Brady took two of the empty poles behind Karen and her cohorts.

"Is that Daniel and my brother?" Alana whispered beneath me.

I sat up and looked down at her grinning mischievously from between my thighs. "Yes…"

Her grin widened and took on a wicked curve. She reached around me and started pulling the back of my yoga pants down. She wasn't going to get very far with me sitting on the stool. "Lift your butt up?"

"No." I laughed at her absurdity.

"Awww. Come on. Nobody will see you."

"No. But they might hear me…"

"It will be fun. And hot."

"And wet. No."

"Please," she whispered, practically begging.

It was the please that did it. I could hear the desire and want in that simple word. I could also tell it was the last time she was going to ask. With a sigh, I put my feet on the ground and lifted myself up off the stool like I was adjusting myself. It was quick enough for her to slip my pants over my ass, and she pulled them down over my knees as I sat back down. The chair was quite cold, but I had a feeling it wouldn't be for long.

176

"Happy?" I ran my fingers through her hair as I leaned on the counter with one elbow.

"You have no idea..." She slipped one of my shoes off and tugged my one pant leg over my foot, rendering me practically naked from the waist down. Hopefully, nobody would be needing me in the near future. There was no way I was getting them back on without being spotted. The excitement of the situation only heightened my desire.

Karen slipped from the pole and landed on her feet. The soft screech of fear drew my attention toward the class as Alana spread my legs and kissed the hair above my lips, trailing her lips over my hood and gently suckling me into her mouth. I wanted to ask Karen if she was okay, but it came out as a muted groan. The class turned around and stared at me. Even Sage cocked an eyebrow in my direction. "Are you okay?" I managed to stammer concernedly at Karen.

"Yeah. I'm fine. You?"

I nodded and smiled as Alana let go of me and let her tongue travel my groove. I put my feet behind her back and used my legs to pull her against me. "Fuuuck," I whispered as everyone turned around, continuing with their stripperfication.

"Did you like that?" Alana slid her hands over my thighs and used her thumbs to pull me apart.

"What do you think?"

"I think you did." She chuckled and let the tip of her tongue dip inside me. "You taste fucking amazing."

I couldn't even formulate a response as she tackled the task at hand. Groaning as softly as possible, I leaned back against the stool and pushed myself forward in the seat as she made love to me with her mouth. I used my fingertips to comb through her short blonde hair as she lapped away. When the tip of her finger trailed through my wetness and circled my entrance, my eyes widened in fear and anticipation. "Don't you dare," I warned.

"You don't like it?"

"Too much," I looked up to see if anyone had heard my overly loud response. They were focused on Sage, but she was looking at me, a knowing smile on her lips as she continued with her instruction.

My admission was enough for Alana to slip her finger inside. My hips began bucking involuntarily as she clamped her mouth over my clit and teased me again with her tongue. I gripped the counter with my hands and let the orgasm sweep through me like a freight train. I bit my lip, trying not scream her name, convulsing as silently as possible.

Which, apparently, wasn't as quiet as I thought. Six sets of eyes were staring at me as I pushed myself back into my seat and tried to compose myself, while Alana chuckled softly as she tried to dress me from her perch and plant little kisses over my thighs.

Chapter 16

"Thanks for covering for me," I said with more than a little bit of embarrassment in my voice.

"No problem, Boss." Sage grinned from the passenger seat. "So, that was the sister?"

"Yep."

After everyone had turned around to see what my cry of ecstasy was for, I played it off as having twisted my back and was in pain, but I didn't think anybody bought it. As soon as Alana had my pants back up, I walked around the counter, wincing in pain. It was a stellar performance on my part, but pain and pleasure are distinctly different noises. Usually.

Sage, on the other hand, walked around the counter and sat down before I could stop her, giving me a knowing smile and blocking anybody from seeing Alana tucked away in her hiding spot. Only after everybody had left, did she finally come out and refuse to look Sage in the eye.

To me, she apologized and tried to run out of the studio before I stopped her, kissed her, and told her to meet me after class on Friday for a date. Then she was all smiles and elbows, grinning as she tripped over herself to get out of the studio.

"She was gorgeous," Sage said with a smile.

"She is. Looks just like her brother."

"Isn't that going to get a little weird, dating both siblings?"

"Well, it's not like I'm going to do it at the same time."

"Them, you mean."

"That's just gross. No. Plus, Alana doesn't like men, so it's not like I'm going to invite her to party with me and Daniel, either."

"As I said, things are going to get a little weird. Did you talk to Daniel and Brady about it?"

"Of course. Beforehand."

"Before mouth, you mean."

I laughed and slapped Sage in the arm as I pulled into the drive thru of the one Dunkin' Donuts on the way back to my house. "Coffee?"

"Cream and sugar."

"You gonna be okay moving in by yourself tonight?"

"You saw my car. It's books and clothes. I think I'll manage. Thanks for furnishing the apartment above."

"My pleasure. Don't worry, I'm going to work you to the bone. Especially with all the noob strippers Michel is going to be sending our way."

"Stripper Academy. Whoda thunkit?"

"That sounds way better than Silhouettes," I answered with a chuckle. "Plus, the shock factor might have gone over a little better with the soccer moms. Made 'em feel a little bit naughty."

"They do crave everything outside of the mundane. They have their world. We have ours. You always want what you don't have."

"Like a normal life?" I elbowed her in the ribs and ordered our coffee through the staticky speaker. I hoped they could hear me better than I could hear them.

She grinned and nodded.

"Normal is overrated."

"Says the girl who had everything." She hadn't meant anything by it, but her past tense hit home and my heart ached. My face must have darkened. "Oh, shit. I'm sorry, Kara. I didn't mean it like *that*."

"I know."

She reached over and put her hand on my arm, flashing me an apologetic look.

"Don't worry, Sage. It's all good."

Her eyes drifted to the side, like she was pondering something. "Think I should drop the stage name? I've gone legit now."

"Up to you. I know your name is Chrissy, but you'll always be Sage to me."

"Yeah."

"Plus, there might be thirty Chrissies and Christinas in your classes. Easier if you stand out."

"True story," she agreed.

We pulled up to the window, and I paid for the coffees that the bored looking blonde teen handed to me while she ran my card. I was chugging scalding hot goodness when she handed it back to me along with the receipt.

"Never understood how you could chug that shit. It's too hot for me to even sip."

I was about to open my mouth to make up some excuse, when my phone dinged in the center console between us. I had one of those moments you get when you knew something was wrong before you got the news. My hand shook as I slowed down and pulled into one of the parking spots by the exit and grabbed my phone.

Mom HELP

I slammed the car into reverse and squealed the tires, backing out of the space while hitting the call button on Karl's text. I didn't breathe, and I was pretty sure my heart didn't beat until he picked up on the third ring.

"Mom?"

"Where are you?"

"At the park by the house. McGuinness."

"What's wrong?" I swerved through traffic and yanked the wheel to turn onto Brickham Road, stomping on the gas as we hit the straightaway.

"Rynnie..."

"Is she hurt?"

"No. She um..."

"Karl. If you don't tell me what the fuck happened in the next three seconds..."

"She uh. Just get here. I don't know what to tell you."

181

"She's not hurt?"

"No."

"Are you?"

"No."

"Good. That's all that matters."

"The cops might not see it that way."

Fuck. "Be there in two minutes." I ended the call and stuffed the phone back in the console.

"Everything okay?"

"The kids are in some sort of trouble."

"Need help?"

Images of my daughter with fangs and claws flitted through my red hazed brain. "No. They're at the park, and I have to drive by the house to get there. I'll slow down enough for you to jump."

"Okay. But if you need me, call."

"Deal."

True to my word, I slowed down enough for her to get out of the still moving vehicle. As worried as I was about the kids, I probably slowed more than I needed to. I might suck as a parent, but I was a good friend. She didn't even fall.

It took less than a minute to get to the park at the end of our street. It was really easy to spot with the three police cars, firetruck, and ambulance parked around it. The flashing red, blue, and white lights were very illuminating and patriotic. I skidded to a stop by one of the squad cars parked away from the others.

"What the hell are you doing, lady?" A cop was walking around his patrol car to give me shit.

"My kids called. They're at the park."

He crooked his finger at me and motioned for me to follow him to his car as I slid out the door of my SUV. "Can I check on my kids first?"

"No."

"Listen, Officer…"

"O'Malley."

182

"My kids called and said something was wrong. While I appreciate that you have a job you think you need to do, I'm checking on my fucking kids first." I started to walk away.

He decided to stop me. "Look, lady–"

He was on his back on the ground looking up at me in complete shock before he even felt my hand grab a fistful of blue polyester and swing him over my shoulder.

I knelt beside his head. "Kids first. Talk later."

He blinked and nodded in understanding.

When I stood up and resumed my journey toward the throng of people in the middle of the park, the other two officers had their weapons drawn and trained on me. They must have seen my pseudo judo cop flop and felt I was a lethal force worthy threat. All five-and-a-half feet of me. I put up my hands and kept walking. Toward my kids. Who were being questioned by another officer without the presence of a parent or guardian.

He blinked at me in surprise when he noticed me, looking up over Rynnie's shoulder. Then he saw his partners trailing behind me, shouting at me to get on the ground with my hands behind my head. His hand moved toward his gun, but he didn't draw it.

"Mom?" Karl actually ran over to me and threw his arms around me.

The cop he'd been talking to held up his hand to the other two behind me. The tension that had been at my back the whole walk eased minutely. "Mrs. Dell?"

"Yes," I answered without looking up at him. "What the hell happened, Karl?"

"That's precisely what I was trying to find out. One of the kids they were with stopped breathing."

"So, you were questioning my children without a lawyer or me present? My *fifteen*-year-old children?" I shot him a death glare.

"You seem to be under the assumption that your kids were in trouble. They're not. I was just asking them if any drugs were involved to help the other kid." He narrowed his eyes angrily.

"Karl. Answer him."

"I already did."

I turned to the cop. "You have your answer. I'd like to speak to my children now, please."

"If you tell me why two of my colleagues have their weapons drawn and another is hobbling toward us." He tilted his head and cocked an eyebrow at me.

"He told me I couldn't see my children. I put him on the ground." I cocked an eyebrow back at him, daring him to arrest me.

"Talk to your kids, Mrs. Dell. Then you and I are going to have a chat." He motioned Ryn toward me and gave another hand signal to the other cops before walking over to the paramedics.

I put a hand on both of my kids' shoulders. "What the hell happened?"

"We were um…" Karl paused to think of an excuse.

I looked at Rynnie. "What happened?"

"We were at the park with Jason and Mandy."

"Who are?"

"They live on the other side of Karen's. Jason is in our class, and Mandy is a year older."

"And what where you doing?" I had a feeling I already knew the answer.

"Kissing. That's *it*. I swear!"

Yep. "And Jason stopped breathing," Karl supplied helpfully.

"Yes!"

I sighed, nodding in understanding and hugging her to my chest. "You're coming into your power. Did you feel more alive after you kissed him?" I whispered the words into her ear.

"Yes," she whispered back.

"You fed from him. I don't mind that you were fooling around, but you need to be careful. Is the boy going to be okay?"

184

She nodded as she pulled away. "Karl performed CPR until the ambulance came. That kept him alive until they could hit him with those electrical paddle thingies."

"Defibrillator," I supplied.

"Yeah. That."

"Thankfully." I stepped closer to my offspring, pretending to look over their shoulders at the EMTs working on the Jason boy. "No drugs were involved. You don't know what happened to him," I whispered to the two of them to set their stories straight. I felt bad for the boy, but with him surrounded by paramedics, there was no way I could get close enough to him to slip him some life force back. Especially after assaulting a police officer.

Instead, I waved the cop back over. "Is he going to be okay?" I nodded toward Jason on the gurney.

The cop shrugged. "I don't know."

"Kids, go sit on the swings."

They nodded and wandered the short distance to the newish looking wood structure with swings dangling from one of the crosspieces.

I gave the cop a once over, finally seeing the man instead of the badge. Truth be told, he looked like a male stripper in a cop uniform. Nobody should be that buff. I could almost see his abs *under* his bulletproof vest. His hair was short, like most policemen, but it wasn't a flat-top, thankfully. I definitely would have liked to meet him under better circumstances. "Sorry about before. I was worried about the kids."

"Understandable. But you assaulted a police officer."

"Who was more worried about throwing his power around and keeping me from my children than actually worried about what was going on. Right before two other officers drew their weapons on an unarmed woman trying to get to her children. Who were being questioned by the police without a lawyer or guardian present. Should I call the evening news now, or wait until I get home? Unless *I'm* under arrest, then I would like my lawyer present at the station when I get there."

"Seems like you've had a few brushes with the law."

"I'm a stripper. Of course, I have."

"You've been arrested?"

"No. They were my biggest clients. They're very chatty when they get lap dances."

Good cop chuckled. Bad cop limped up to us with his handcuffs out. "You're under arrest for assaulting a police officer, bitch!"

I looked at good cop.

"Thompson. Did you try to stop this woman from getting to her possibly injured children?"

"Of course, I did! The little junkies gave something to Marissa's kid!"

He was on the ground again with a chest full of angry stripper mom snarling in his face before he blinked again. Good cop had his arms around me and was yanking me off of him when the other two surrounded us with their guns drawn.

"Mrs. Dell! Calm down!"

"Fuck him, fuck you, and fuck them. He called my kids junkies! Gimme my fucking phone, I'm calling the fucking news station!" I let good cop drag me off O'douchebag but broke his grip on me with my arms. He made a surprised sound and let me go before pushing the guns of the surrounding officers toward the ground.

"Everybody, calm down!" He turned and made calming motions toward me and put himself between all of us. When I made a huffing noise and pretended to inspect my nails, he turned to the cop on the ground. "You get in your car and get your ass back to the station. I'll deal with you when I get there."

"Are you fucking kidding me, Lieutenant? She assaulted me twice!"

Good cop didn't say a word, just pointed at the cop car sitting next to my SUV. "You two, take the girl and see if you can find the boy's mother," he said with little room for argument.

When they holstered their weapons and walked toward the ambulances, he finally turned back to me and let out the breath he'd been holding.

"I though you said cops liked you."

"They do. When I'm mostly naked."

He couldn't help it. His eyes flicked down over my body and he smiled. "I'm sure they do. Look, Mrs. Dell. I'm sorry for my officer's behavior. He's dating the boy's mother. It's why I had him away from the scene when you stumbled across it. Would you like to file a complaint?"

"No. But tell Officer O'Malley, next time he comes between me and my kids, I'll put him *in* the ground instead of *on* it. Got it?"

He sighed. "While I appreciate you not filing a complaint... Please don't threaten the lives of my officers in front of me. Or at all," he added thoughtfully. Thankfully, he was making light of the situation instead of being a dick about it.

"Fine." I laughed it off like I'd been joking.

He pulled out a notebook. "Take your kids and go home. Do you have a phone number I can reach you at if I need anything else?"

"Like what?" I narrowed my eyes suspiciously. He was hot as fuck, but I didn't trust cops. At all. I'd given too many of them lap dances. They were very handsy.

"In case they find drugs in the boy's system. Or, God forbid, he doesn't make it and we need to continue our investigation. A detective might want to talk to your kids again. With you present, of course."

I took the notebook from him and jotted down my phone number before tucking it back in his shirt pocket. "There. Are we free to go?"

"Of course."

"See you, Lieutenant."

"Have a good evening, Mrs. Dell."

I motioned toward the car to the kids and started walking. They caught up. Halfway across the park, my phone started ringing. I pulled it out of my pocket and saw

187

an unknown number flashing off the screen. Turning around, I looked at the lieutenant holding his phone up to his ear.

"Just checking," he said loud enough for me to hear, and shut off his phone.

Chapter 17

"It wasn't your fault. Hell, it's more *my* fault than yours, Rynnie." I reached over the counter and ran my hand over her head, soothingly. Or at least I hoped it felt that way to her.

"You should have seen his eyes, Mom. He was panicking, and I couldn't stop. I felt whatever was inside him pouring into me, and I *liked* it. Now I want to throw up." She started sobbing and put her forehead down on her arm.

I looked at her brother helplessly.

"Ryn… I'm sure you'll learn to control it."

"I don't want to. I'm never kissing another boy again as long as I live."

"I should have warned you. You are unique, Ryn. Most cambions don't exhibit *any* characteristics of their dam. You shouldn't have been able to change. To steal the essence of a human is…unheard of. I am truly sorry."

"Why Ryn? How come none of this is happening to me?" Karl almost sounded disappointed.

"Because you might be a true cambion. Or because boys develop later than girls. You be careful, too. Let me know if you start to grow scales in strange places."

"Scales?" He looked horrified and covered his crotch with his hands.

"Kidding, boy child."

"That's not funny."

"Yeah, it was." Ryn was giggle sobbing. Still upset but taking pleasure in her brother's discomfort.

"Well, starting tomorrow," I paused, and ruffled Ryn's hair. "You and I are going to start working on controlling your powers."

"Okay."

"Get to bed, the both of you."

They nodded and headed upstairs, Karl moving a little faster than his still upset sister. "Night, Mom," Ryn said with a small, sad smile.

"Night, Child."

"Love you."

I repeated the words without thinking. Only when she was out of sight, did I clutch my chest with my left hand, an unfamiliar ache ripping through my heart. "I love you." Words I had spoken less than a dozen times in my entire existence.

"I need to fuck something." The words made me feel a little less...*dirty*.

Grabbing my phone off the counter, I dialed Daniel.

"Kara?" He picked up the phone on the first ring, sounding worried.

"Can you come over?"

"Everything okay?"

No. I just told my child I love her. "Rough night."

"Be right there."

The phone clicked dead, and a minute later, there was a soft rapping noise on the front door. I threw the latch and opened it. Daniel and Brady were both standing there in gray jogging pants and slippers, rubbing their bare arms against the cold. I paused to enjoy the show.

"Can we come in, or are you waiting for our nipples to shatter first?" Brady gave me an imploring look.

Shaking my head to break the spell, I stepped out of the way and let them in. "You're staying at Daniel's already?"

"After class, we watched the game, and I was one too many beers into the wind to drive home."

"Lucky me." I grinned and motioned toward the kitchen. "Coffee?"

"It's twelve o'clock at night," Daniel answered incredulously.

"I'll have a cup," Brady said with a huff.

I put three cups up to brew, and Daniel reluctantly took one. "Let me guess, I'm going to need my energy."

"I made it with Red Bull instead of water." I laughed to let him know I was kidding. If I was going to add anything to his coffee, it would be Viagra. He didn't need an erection that lasted four hours, I did.

"I only half think you're kidding."

"So, what happened?" Brady's curiosity got the better of him.

"Let's just say that my daughter is a little more like her mother than is good for the neighbor boys."

"And girls?" Brady grinned at me.

"If that was a cheap shot at me dating your sister..."

"It was."

"I thought you were okay with it?"

"I am. Doesn't mean I'm not going to tease you, or her, about it." He took a sip of his coffee, smiling over the rim.

"You're a shit."

"Big one."

Daniel was hiding his smile and trying not to laugh by hiding his mouth behind his hand. "Guess that explains the noise in class tonight."

"Don't blame me. I am innocent."

"A regular saint."

I hissed and gave him an evil look. Then my phone started ringing. Sighing, I grabbed it off the counter and saw the lieutenant's number flashing on the screen. I hadn't memorized it, or anything like that, but it was fresh enough in my memory for me to recognize it. "Lieutenant?"

"Mrs. Dell?"

"Yes?"

"Your dance studio is on fire."

∞ ∞ ∞

191

The three of us spilled out of my SUV onto the wet street as the fire department battled the blaze burning angrily through the bottom floor of the studio. The walls and wood floors giving it ample fuel.

"Fuuuuck," I screamed, my breath fogging in the cold air, even with the heat from my dreams going up in smoke.

The lieutenant made a beeline from his police SUV toward me. "There's somebody trapped on the second floor."

"Sage! Why didn't she get out the fire escape?" I started running toward the building, but the lieutenant stopped me with a hand on my arm.

"Mrs. Dell! It's over a thousand degrees in there! Your friend is just waiting on fire rescue to get the ladder truck here from another station. This is the third fire tonight."

"Is she okay?"

"She's in the bathroom, in the tub with the water running. The firemen had her open the window and stuff a wet towel under the door. She's okay for now."

The building started to creak.

The metal struts in the walls were giving. Gasping, I tore my gaze from the lieutenant's chiseled features and shrieked in horror as the front of the studio shifted. It didn't collapse, but it was enough for the plate windows in the front to shatter and a few of the surrounding bricks get pulverized into rubble.

The grinding didn't stop as the building settled on the remaining brick. "Fuck this."

Ignoring the shouts of protest from the lieutenant, I charged at the building, wishing I could shift in plain view, but as a human, I jumped through the shattered front, ignored the flames as they licked my skin, and headed for the stairs in the back. It reminded me of Hell. The heat was blistering my skin, and I smiled as the familiar pain sent a shiver down my spine. Safe in the flames, I changed. The blistering heat turned into a gentle summer breeze as I marched through the flames and took the stairs two at a time.

One thing was for certain, Sage was going to need a new place to live. Her apartment, and everything in it, was already ash. As was the center of the floor over the studio. Luckily, the bathroom she was in was in the corner of the building and still safe for a few more minutes. I was under the vague impression that the lieutenant was blowing smoke up my ass about the direness of her situation.

Winging over the hole in the floor, my clawed feet settled on the ember covered wood outside the blistered white paint of the two inches of wood keeping Sage alive. Kicking out with a demonic foot, the door shattered. The fire roared as air was sucked through the newly created portal. Flames danced at my back, rushing toward the source of fuel, but I blocked their ingress with my wings until it balanced out. I took one step inside the bathroom and shifted, Sage unseen behind the drawn wet plastic curtain.

"Sage!" Her hand was hanging over the edge of the tub.

I pulled back the curtain fearing the worst, but she blinked up at me under the spray of water.

"Kara?" Her voice was raspy. Even tucked in the bathroom, she had breathed in an ungodly amount of smoke.

"Hang tight." I reached up and tore the curtain from the rod, covering her with it, and wrapping her up in it as best as I could when I scooped her up in my arms.

She thrashed against my chest, but her words were unintelligible through the plastic over the cacophony of burning building.

Not daring to shift again, I walked out of the bathroom and dropped through the gaping wound in the floor down to the studio. Giving a war cry, I charged toward the front and jumped through the window and flipped us over the rubble, tumbling out into the street at the feet of the firemen and angry looking police officer.

Giving him a thumbs up, I closed my eyes and let my head fall back against the cold concrete.

193

"–the fuck were...thinking? You...have died. Get...EMTs over here! You...them soaked..." The lieutenant's voice was fading in and out as the sound of my pulse drowned him out.

A cooling spray of water washed over us. The familiar flames disappeared as my clothes were doused. I started to calm and then shiver as the wetness mixed with the cold air of the Massachusetts fall. I would be fine in a few minutes, but if I jumped up and told everybody I was fine, they wouldn't have believed me anyway. I lay there as they loaded Sage and me up on separate stretchers.

"Are you okay?" Daniel whispered in my ear.

I nodded and gave him a knowing look. He sighed in relief and squeezed my arm before his features crumbled in despair.

"It's okay, Daniel. It's just a building."

"I know. But you worked so hard."

"We did. But we can rebuild it."

He nodded as the EMTs pushed him out of the way and wheeled me toward the ambulance. I pushed away the respirator and snarled when he tried to put it back.

When I was loaded, they started to shut the doors, but were stopped by the lieutenant as he slipped inside. He plopped down on the seat next to my gurney and let out the breath he'd been holding.

"That was the bravest thing I've ever seen," he said, and treated me to a disdainful look. "And also the dumbest. She would have been fine until the ladder truck got there."

"You're full of shit. The floor was about to give out, and the window in the bathroom was too small for *her* to fit through, let alone a big burly fire fighter."

"I know. But I'm supposed to say stuff like that to keep people like you from doing stupid shit like that." He crossed his arms over his chest and cocked an eyebrow at me.

"But people like me rarely listen to people like you. I did what I had to do. She's my friend."

"And I'm sure she's going to be very grateful. I don't have to lie to you anymore. If you hadn't done what you did, she'd be dead."

I sat up and flashed him a smile, resting on my elbows behind me. "Which is why I did it. Damn, I stink." I sniffed the air, grimacing at the smell of burnt clothes and hair. At least I wouldn't have to shave my legs any time soon. The pink flesh was already healing visibly through the holes that had burned through. I'd be good as new by the time we got to the hospital. If I could have slowed down the process, I would have. But it wasn't an ability I could control. The only thing that would slow it was holy water, and asking to stop by a church probably would have set off more questions than my miraculous healing. Either way, there was going to be questions I needed to start coming up with excuses for.

The lieutenant narrowed his eyes at my legs, stared, got up and ripped open one of the holes in my leggings. "How are you not burned to a crisp?"

The EMT in the back with us, who had been ignoring us for the most part, actually protested. "Take it easy! She's probably in shock and covered in first degree burns. Back off, Lieutenant."

"Do her legs look burned to you?" He motioned at my legs.

The EMT moved down, and I felt his eyes travel over them from ankle to thigh. Gently, he trailed a finger over the pink flesh. "That's not possible."

I decided to play dumb. "What's not?"

"You're not even blistered…"

"Of course not. The firemen doused me with water, and I didn't stop running the whole time."

"Lady, your pants were melted to your legs."

"I was wearing lotion?"

"Made out of asbestos?" He blinked at me like I was an idiot. My plan was working.

I just shrugged, leaned back, and closed my eyes. If I pretended to sleep, I wouldn't have to answer any more questions I had to pretend I didn't know the answers to.

Just as the sirens were getting on my nerves, we pulled in front of the emergency room. I was whisked inside and put into the room next to Sage. How they could call it a room with curtained walls, I didn't know, but at least it gave me the opportunity to get up and check on her when nobody was looking.

"Kara?" Her voice was two octaves below mine and sounded like she had mistaken insulation for cotton candy.

"Shhh. You're going to be fine. Don't talk."

"Thanks."

I just nodded and rubbed my knuckles gently across her cheek around the oxygen mask plastered firmly to her face. "Get some rest. I'm sorry about all your stuff."

"I was too tired to unpack the car. Being lazy finally paid off. All I lost was some clothes and a toothbrush," she croaked, and gave me a plastic covered smile.

"We'll go shopping when you get out of here. My treat."

She nodded, knowing better than to argue.

"But your studio…"

"Can be rebuilt. I had a hefty insurance policy on it. We'll be fine."

"Ahem. Actually, I need to talk to you about that."

I turned and glared at the lieutenant, who had been eavesdropping. "I'll talk to you later," I told Sage, and gently touched her shoulder, going back to my room. "What about?" I closed the curtain after the lieutenant followed me.

"On the record. Do you have any idea how the fire started?"

"No."

"I'd ask you if you had a beef with your friend, if I didn't watch you rush into a burning building to save her."

"You think *I* started the fire?"

He sat down on the green plastic chair next to my bed and rubbed his face with his hands. "You did just mention a hefty insurance policy."

"I just bought the freaking building and poured my life into it. Of course, I did. I'm not stupid."

"Maybe business wasn't as good as you'd hoped?"

"After being open for a *day*? Come on, Lieutenant. You know you're barking up the wrong tree. Why do you even think this is arson to begin with? Maybe it was just faulty wiring?"

"Three empty gas cans behind the studio was a pretty solid clue."

"Oh. Yeah. I could see how you might have drawn that conclusion. Were there any prints?"

"The building is still on fire, Mrs. Dell. Stuff like that is going to have to wait."

"Kara."

"What?"

"My name. Call me Kara. Mrs. Dell is kind of stuffy Lieutenant…"

"Grindel."

"Like the monster from Beowulf?"

"I think that was Grendel."

"Close enough."

He sighed. "Josh. Just call me Josh."

Grinning at him, I hopped back up on my bed. If we were going to have an unpleasant conversation, at least I could be comfortable.

He just shook his head at my acrobatics. "You're sure you're human?"

I blinked in surprise. "Whaaat?"

"I'm kidding. But you should be burned to a crisp and unable to move. Hopping up on a hospital gurney should be a little more difficult than you're making it look."

"Strippers are very…flexible."

"Of course, they are."

"I could give you a demonstration some time…"

His cheeks matched the color of my freshly healed legs before he turned around and darted through the curtain.

"Huh. That wasn't a no."

Chapter 18

Waking up sandwiched between Daniel and Brady was the absolute highlight of my existence since we'd moved to Bickering. I was nuzzling Daniel's shoulder and Brady's arm was draped over the two of us.

"Good morning," Daniel said with a smile, and kissed the top of my head.

"Yes. Yes, it is." I groaned lazily and pushed my ass back against Brady's hardness. His soft snores spoke volumes. He was still sound asleep, but his hips were grinding himself against me out of pure instinct. It didn't get any more primal than that.

I was content with the grinding and the warmth, but Daniel slid his hand over my hip and grabbed a handful of flesh, pulling my cheeks apart and exposing my wetness to Brady's probing. He didn't slip in, but the tip of him slid over my moist lips and then pulled back, rubbing me in just the right way.

I cooed and pressed my forehead to Daniel's.

"Is he inside you?"

"No."

"He's always had terrible aim." He laughed softly, brought his hand back over my hip, and ran his fingers through my pubic hair, exploring on his own and trying to get to my clit between my thighs.

"Feeling left out?" I lifted my leg and opened the gates for him.

"No. Just trying to help."

I gasped as he reached between my legs and guided Brady inside me. "Fuck."

"He is now." He smiled at me and let his lips graze mine in a gentle kiss.

Brady found a sleep rhythm and started grunting in pleasure. His arm slipped between Daniel and I, and pulled me against him as Daniel returned his fingers to my enlarged clit and began tracing lazy gentle wet circles over it. Closing my eyes, my moans matched Brady's as I gripped Daniel's cock in my hand and began stroking. Officially, the best morning ever.

"This is so hot, I'm not going to last long," Daniel whispered, and kissed me again.

I grinned as I pulled away from the kiss. "Get on your knees and feed me my breakfast."

"What do you want to eat?"

"Sausage and cream." I tugged on him roughly.

"Your wish is my command. And pleasure."

Slowly, he pulled away and did as I asked, moving quietly. I was practically drooling by the time the head of his cock reached my waiting lips. My hand returned to his cock and pulled him to me as I sucked him into my mouth and ran my tongue over his sensitive head. Brady's hand shifted to my hip, and he snaked the other one beneath me, gripping me firmly around my waist as he picked up the pace of his thrusting.

"Good morning," he said with a chuckle.

Popping Daniel from my mouth, I answered, "It is now," and resumed my ministrations. Lust filled the room, and I sucked it in with every bob of my head and thrust of Brady inside me. Breathing through my nose, I was gasping for breath when I felt the familiar tingle in my favorite place. Letting out a groan as my own orgasm raced through me, I tilted my head back and let Daniel slide free as he started ejaculating in my open mouth.

"Holy fuck, that's hot." Brady slammed himself against me, and I felt his cock throbbing as he emptied himself inside me as the three of us rode it out together.

Brady was the first to pull free. I let go of Daniel and rolled on my back, smiling at the ceiling and utterly content. Brady's hand slid over my chest and squeezed my breast, pulling me toward him. My eyebrows rose as he kissed me, covered in Daniel's cum, without even pausing to consider it. Hot, wet, and salty kisses might have just become my new favorite as he devoured my mouth.

I started whimpering into that kiss when Daniel parted my legs, and his lips devoured me below.

Breaking the kiss, my head ground the pillow as my back arched off the bed. "What is going on with you two?"

"A little agreement between gentlemen." Brady rested his head back on his pillow and watched me in the throes of ecstasy.

"What kind of agreement?"

"Well. We both agreed that our lady should always be super clean. So, we agreed to always clean up after ourselves or each other."

"Holy fuckballs, that's a good agreement." My hips started bucking as Daniel's tongue invaded me.

"We thought you would like it." Brady sucked my nipple between his lips and grazed the tip with his teeth.

"Don't nibble. Bite."

He sucked more of me into his mouth and closed his teeth down on my flesh as he pinched the other between his thumb and finger. Pain and pleasure melted together, and became this extraordinary *thing* that smothered me before it exploded inside me. I screamed their names as my voice took on a demonic timbre while I came and came and came. Finally, I couldn't take any more and gently pushed their heads away simultaneously.

"Wow."

They were both grinning at me like idiots. Beautiful, loving, gorgeous idiots. My fools.

∞ ∞ ∞

"Fuck." A tear actually rolled down my cheek.

"Maybe the inside looks better than the outside?" Karen tried to peek inside through the blackened remains of the window. "Nope." She sighed and stepped back, giving me a sad look. She saw my tears and hugged me on the street in front of Silhouettes.

"What are you going to do?"

"Rebuild. I just… I just got the fucking place opened, and now it's going to be *months* before I get this place fixed back up."

"It might take that long to get the insurance money."

"You're a regular ray of fucking sunshine, Karen."

"Oh, sweetie. I'm sorry. I'm just letting you know what to expect. That's what friends are for."

"Sugar coat that shit."

"I will."

I kicked a piece of broken window toward the ruined building. "Maybe I should just buy another building and fix that one. Then just recoup my losses with the insurance money."

"But then you'll be fucked if your insurance claims fraud."

"God damn it, Karen."

"Sorry. Come on, I'll buy you a coffee while we think about it." She gripped my arm and headed us back up the street toward the Dunkin' on the corner.

"You said if the insurance claims fraud. Just out of curiosity, why?"

"Oh, it's all over town that three gas cans were found behind the studio. Most people are saying arson, but I've heard the fraud word a couple times, too. I wouldn't worry. I know you didn't torch your own place."

"Really? News travels that fast here?"

"Half the neighborhood dates cops. Is married to cops. Or just has a side cop. They like the handcuffs."

The image of a hunky lieutenant flashed through my mind, and I grinned. Then another one of him cuffed to the headboard of my bed. "Yeah. I can see that."

202

She pulled the door open with her free hand and pushed me inside the warm, coffee scented corner of heaven. "Usual?"

"Yeah. Thanks," I answered.

"Grab us a table."

"'Kay."

I meandered through the crowded restaurant until I found a relatively clean table and plopped my ass down, rubbing my eyebrows in hopes of easing the tension headache I'd developed.

Yes. Demons get headaches. We're usually better at giving than getting, but it still happens.

"You look like you could use something a little stronger than coffee."

Blinking in surprise, I looked up. I recognized his voice, but it was still a shock to see the Lieutenant Grindel standing over me, a half-donut in one hand and a thermal mug of coffee in the other.

He saw me staring at his breakfast. "Not one donut joke, or I'll arrest you."

"On what charge?"

"Unlicensed stereotypes."

"It's not a stereotype if it's true. Sit?"

He nodded, giving me an uncertain smile as he set his coffee down and pulled out the chair. "Come to survey the damage?"

"That I didn't cause? Yes."

He sighed and took a bite of his sour cream donut, washing it down with a swig of coffee. "For the record, I never thought you did. But I had to ask."

"Fair enough."

"Oh. Who's this?"

"Karen, meet Lieutenant Grendel."

"Grindel." He shook his head and turned, offering Karen his hand until he saw her overburdened with coffee and a bag of donuts. "Here." He took the two hot cups of coffee and set them on the table.

"Thank you, Officer." She smiled at him, sitting down in the chair next to me and sliding one of the coffees in front of me. "There's your devil's brew."

"Devil's brew?" The lieutenant cocked an eyebrow.

"She drinks that shit black. Like some sort of monster. Doesn't appreciate the finer points of cream and sugar."

"I like cream. Just not in my coffee." I grinned at Josh from across my lid as I took a long swallow.

He almost spit his. Karen just stared at me with her hand in the bag of donuts.

"What? It's delicious on raspberries."

"That's where you were going with this? Really?" Karen shot me a dubious look.

"You've never had jizzberries?" I grinned at her and watched the color drain from her face. Mission accomplished.

Lieutenant Grindel was rubbing the tension headache from his forehead. "I was glad I ran into you," he muttered.

"Was?" I chuckled. "Were you happy to see me, or was it business?"

"Business, I'm afraid. The fire inspector is definitely ruling it arson. Know anybody who would want to torch your place?"

"Hmmm. Boyfriend's ex. An angry soccer mom. Parents of my daughter's boyfriend. The one cashier at the grocery store I called a cunt because she smashed my bread. The principal's secretary, the president of the HOA's wife, the bitch in the flower shop across the street. Oh! And my second-grade teacher. But she's dead, so I don't think it was her. Unless she crawled up from the pits of hell...but no. That seems a long way to go just for a little payback. It was only her cat. She got another."

He looked imploringly at Karen for a little help before turning his attention back at me. "Kara, this isn't a joke. Somebody set fire to your studio. I want to catch them, and you're making jokes."

"I'm not!"

"She isn't?" He looked back at Karen.

Karen shook her head. "Most women tend to find Kara a little…"

"Over the top?"

"Let's go with that."

"So, no men on your list of possible suspects?"

"Oh, no. Men adore me."

"I'm sure they do." He laughed and took another sip of his coffee.

"Do you?"

He blinked. "Do I what?"

"Adore me?" I smiled cheekily and took another sip of my coffee.

"I have to go. Text me a list of names when you have a moment. I'll look into them." He quickly pushed his seat back and practically scrambled out of the donut shop.

"I think he likes you."

"Well, he hasn't shot me. Yet."

Karen handed me a donut. "Do you really think it was one of them?"

I took the offered treat and nibbled a sliver out of the cruller, thinking about each and every one of them before shaking my head. "No. I don't. They might key my car or try to fuck one of my boyfriends, but I don't think any one of them is capable of lighting a match."

"Who do *you* think did it?"

"Probably the same person who's been attacking people. The Bickering Bandit, or whatever they're calling them."

"Them, not him?"

"No. I had a run in with them. I couldn't tell if they were male or female."

"Wait. What?"

"Daniel and I were attacked, but…uh…Daniel scared them off."

"Oh my God. Why didn't you tell me?"

"It was no big deal. Neither of us were hurt, and the bandit took off. Case closed."

"Is it? Did you let the lieutenant know?"

"Kinda slipped my mind until now."

"You think they're pissed because they couldn't get to you?"

I shrugged and finished the last of my donut. There was just something about French crullers. Sweet, not too sweet. And it was like eating corrugated air. You could pack away five or six of them before you noticed it.

"Well, be careful. And don't go anywhere alone."

"I'll be fine. Same goes to you."

"Oh. I have pepper spray and a taser in my purse." She reached into the bag on the table, and I heard the crackle of electricity. "Let those bastards try anything with me."

I opened my mouth to warn her, but I stopped myself. There was no way to tell her without raising her suspicion. I liked Karen, but she was the last person in the universe I would share my secret with. It would get around faster than if I showed up at the next PTA meeting with wings, horns, and a tail. Instead, I just covered her hand with mine. "Be careful, Karen. I mean it."

"I will."

"Good."

Chapter 19

"Hey, beautiful." I smiled at Alana and stepped out of the door to let her into the house. She blushed and ducked inside.

"I just heard, are you okay?"

"Yeah. My clothes were toasted, but I was fine."

"What about Sage?"

"Just got off the phone with her. She's doing fine, and they should release her sometime tomorrow. They're just worried about all the smoke she inhaled." I sighed, more than a little worried about my friend. She was going to be fine physically, but she had taken the destruction of the studio worse than I. She had been looking forward to a new start and getting out on her own. Now she was jobless, but not homeless. She was going to stay in our spare bedroom until the studio was fixed. I needed to make it happen sooner rather than later. That decision had drastically changed our date plans. I'd planned something romantic, but I had a feeling Alana wouldn't be *too* disappointed.

"So, where are we going?" I added a touch of clairvoyant aptitude to Alana's repertoire.

"It's a surprise," I answered with a small laugh.

"Why am I afraid?" She wrapped her arms around my waist and leaned down for a soft kiss. She smelled like strawberries, and I melted into her embrace, running my hands up her back.

"Because you know me," I said as I pulled away from her kiss. "We better stop, or we'll never make it to dinner."

"I'm good with that."

"But we'll miss all the fun."

"That's what I'm afraid of."

"Missing the fun?"

"No. Your idea of it." She slapped my butt as she headed for the front door. I couldn't help but grin as her skirt covered ass swayed seductively down my hallway.

Once we got in her car, she revved the engine of her late model Camry. Probably to keep the engine from sputtering out. "Want me to drive?"

"What? Don't like my teachermobile?"

"Do you?"

A sad look crossed her face, and she shook her head. "No."

"Me neither. Come on, let's take my car. You can drive."

Without turning the key, she let go of the gas and shut the engine off all on its own. "Okay," she said embarrassedly.

Squeezing her knee in sympathy, I smiled and got out of the deathtrap as fast as I could. "I'ma smack your brother for letting you drive that heap."

"There's something wrong with the fuel injectors. It was an eight-hundred-dollar fix that neither one of us could afford."

"Ouch. Well, once you guys move in with Daniel, the money you save on rent can start going toward a new car. Or repairs. Or whatever." Reaching in my purse, I pulled out my keys and tossed them to Alana.

"Are you *really* sure you're okay with us moving in with Daniel?" Her mouth frowned in concern.

"Are you kidding me? Hmm. Let me think about that for a minute. Yes. I'm really good with it." I grinned at her as we got into the SUV.

"Nice ride."

"Thanks."

"So, where we headed?"

"Do you like steak?"

"Only meat I'll willingly put in my mouth," she said with a musical giggle.

"If you're trying to make my panties wet, I'm not wearing any."

She stopped short in the driveway, the tires giving a short chirp. "Seriously?"

I nodded.

She slammed the car into park, lifted herself off her seat and shimmied her silk panties down over her feet. I caught a brief glance at her small patch of blonde hair before she pulled her skirt back down almost to her knees. She handed me her panties, leaned over, and whispered, "Now we match."

She put her panties in my hand, their warmth turning me on almost as much as the lust that came with them.

"Let's eat," she said sultrily, and put the Escalade back into reverse.

"Not while you're driving. I don't want my car wrecked."

We pulled into the parking lot of the steak house closest to our final destination. "Are you sure about this place? Seems kind of pricey." She stared at the entrance over the dashboard.

"Yep. C'mon. Let's eat."

It was pricey, but busy. But then again, the people of Bickering weren't hurting for money for the most part. We got a booth for two and put in our drink order. Alana tried to order a Coke because she was driving, but I shook my head at her and ordered a second glass of wine. "We can call a cab if we have to. This is a date. You're supposed to be having fun."

She blushed and nodded to the waitress.

"Be right back with your drinks. Do you want an appetizer?"

"No thanks."

She nodded at me, closed her book, and headed toward the bar. I had slid into the same side of the booth as Alana, and she leaned against me when we were alone. "Thanks."

"For what?"

"Taking me on a date. I can't tell you the last time I've been on one."

"Why? You're beautiful. I would think the girls would have been lining up to take you everywhere."

"Welcome to Massachusetts," she said with a huff of disgust.

"What? We're not in the bible belt. I would think same sex relationships wouldn't be a problem."

She shook her head. "This is the burbs, Kara. Everyone is married or divorced and looking for their next opponent. The few flings I've had were always with married women wanting a little excitement in their lives. And always ended when they wanted to include their husbands."

"Oh." I let my fingers glide over her cheek. "Is this your way of telling me not to suggest Daniel in our play?"

She chuckled, and lifted her head from my shoulder. "No. I didn't think you would. You're…different from most of the people around town. But yes. Don't. I'd rather you just break it off with me now, if that was your plan. Daniel and my brother have been friends forever, and he's definitely in the brother category. And the has a penis category. Sorry."

"I never had any intention. But I'm glad you told me in case *he* ever got any ideas." I kissed her slowly. Until the clank of glasses broke it. The waitress gave us a shy smile and pulled her order book back out. "Are you ready to order? Or did you need a few…minutes."

"I'm ready." I was actually starving.

"Me, too."

"Prime rib, medium rare."

"And for you?"

"I'll have the same, but medium well."

"I'll have those right out and bring you some more drinks."

She nervously took our menus and scampered off. She might have been old enough to serve drinks, but I doubted

210

she could order them. "I think we make her nervous." Alana returned her head to my shoulder.

"I think she's jealous of me."

"Ha! I doubt that. We're probably the first women she's ever seen openly…"

"Openly what?"

"Into each other." She tilted her head and kissed my shoulder.

My hand snaked its way into her lap, and I gently rubbed her thigh. "I am."

"You are what?"

"Into you. Definitely."

She leaned up and kissed me. When she pulled away, the eyes of the people at the tables around us were openly staring. "Oops." She sat up and put an inch of space between us.

"Fuck them." I scooted closer to her and held her hand under the table.

We were saved by our waitress setting our food in front of us. We ate in silence, but the warmth of our smiles was more than enough. The food was fantastic, but the company was better.

"Did you guys save room for dessert?"

"Nope. We've got that covered." I winked at her and smiled when she blushed.

"I'll bring your check." She smiled and took our empty plates.

"You're gonna kill that poor innocent girl."

I chuckled and smiled at her when she brought our bill. "Thanks."

She nodded and scurried away again quickly.

When I opened the bill, she hadn't charged us for the wine and put a smiley face next to her 'You are a beautiful couple' note. Laughing softly, I showed the note to Alana before I stuffed more than enough cash into the black leather book and set it on the table. "Ready?"

"For what?"

"It's a surprise."

211

"As long as there isn't a bunch of guys dancing in G-strings. I'm up for anything."

"Nope. No guys." I took her arm and headed toward the Candy Shoppe.

She stopped us at the door, looked at the sign in wild eyed amazement and flashed me a grin. "You're taking me to a strip club?"

"Yep." I smiled back at her, but I was filled more with relief than happiness. I hadn't been too sure how she would feel about going to a titty bar on the first date.

"Woah. I haven't been to one in…years."

"I'm kinda surprised you have."

"College. It's how I found out girls were way hotter than guys. That, and my roommate. We spent a lot of time at the one by the college."

Sighing, I walked in and raised my voice over the throb of the music. "I miss working."

"Dance for me sometime?" She bumped my hip with her own.

"Definitely."

We made our way to the exact table Brady, Daniel, and I had sat at the last time we were there. "Welcome back," the same waitress said as she put a couple of cocktail napkins down on the table in front of us. "What can I get you?"

"Bottle of champagne."

She blinked in surprise. "Are you sure?"

"Yes, please. And let Michel know that Kara is here, if he has a moment?"

Instead of answering, she nodded and headed for the bar. I used the moment to look around and smiled at Alana, who was enraptured with the dancer on the stage.

"She's hot," I whispered into her ear.

She nodded and blushed as she gave me a shy smile. "She is. Not as hot as you, but still hot."

That earned her a kiss. "You're already getting into my non-existent panties. No need to butter me up."

"I don't know. A little butter might be fun."

212

I flashed her a toothy grin. Alana was like that. Shy and demure, but still playful when it counted most.

"Kara. A pleasure to see you again. What can I do for you?"

Michel stood behind us and spoke at a normal volume, knowing full well I would be able to hear him even over the cacophony of the club. "Have a minute?"

"For you, of course."

"I'll be right back, Alana. Watch my drink."

She nodded and turned her attention back to the stage. At least she was distracted while I did a little business. Michel led me through the crowded club to his ornate wooden office door, ushering me inside and closing the door behind us. "I heard about your studio. You have my sympathies."

"Which is precisely why I came to see you."

"If it is for a loan…"

I shook my head, nipping that in the bud before the silence became awkward. "No."

"Then what can I do for you?"

"I need a *contractor*."

"And what makes you think I know one?" He hadn't missed the inflection in my voice. He knew exactly what I was after, and it wasn't a burly guy in plaid.

"You're a vampire who owns a strip club in the suburbs of Boston. I'm pretty sure you didn't get where you are through permits, bank loans, and inspections. I had a heavy blow dealt to me. I want to recoup what I had and give it some protection."

"*Contractors* are not cheap. And someone may notice."

"Like who?"

"Whomever set fire to your building."

"I don't care. I'm going to have guards around the place once it's fixed. They won't get a second blow in."

He sighed heavily and rubbed the stubble on his chin.

"Fine. I shall have them meet you at the proposed location tomorrow evening. Will that suffice?"

I cranked out a smile for him. "I would be indebted to you."

"That is one place you do not want to be, *chère*."

"Fine. You will have my *gratitude*."

"Something tells me, that is exactly where I want to be." He smiled at me and stood up, offering me his hand. "Enjoy the rest of your evening. And your companion."

"Oh, I will." I chuckled softly and left him sitting there. I had a hot date waiting.

And she wasn't alone.

One guy with a beard and a leather vest had taken my seat. His less intelligent looking friend had taken the seat on the other side of a *very* uncomfortable looking Alana.

"Do not hurt them, *chère*." Michel's voice caressed the back of my neck as I strode purposely in their direction.

"No promises."

"Signal my bouncers if you require assistance."

I waved at him over my shoulder just before I got back to the table. "Excuse me. You're in my seat."

"Well, looky here. Another one, Vinnie. Looks like you get to have this one." He reached over and patted Alana on the leg. "What's your name, sweetheart?"

"You can call me her girlfriend."

"No shit. Dykes?" He looked at Alana and back to me. "Pretty sure my friend and I can change your minds."

"Sweetie, it's because of pieces of shit like you that we prefer the company of each other. Please leave."

"You got a problem?"

"Yes." I sat down at the last empty seat and put my elbow on the table. "You see, I *love* eating pussy."

"I ain't got a problem with that, as long as I can watch."

"That's great. But the problem is, if I were to eat two *greasy* pussies like you and your friend, I would get heartburn. So, run along, douche nugget."

His face went from intrigued to angry with each word I said. By the time he understood what I was saying, he had reached apoplectic. "You fucking cu–"

He didn't get to finish his sentence before I slapped him out of his chair. He hit the floor with a roar of surprise, and I winced when I realized he had put his open mouth on the disgusting floor of the strip club. Personally, I would rather have licked the floor of a movie theater. Or a subway car.

He was getting up on his hands and knees when I kicked him in his very exposed ass and smiled when he slid forward at least five feet across the slick polished concrete. He was going to need *two* showers. I was pretty sure that was his quota for the year.

"Leave, Vinnie." I didn't even look at his larger friend.

Apparently, I'd been wrong about his friend. He had more brain cells than his buddy. He got up and left the table in a big old hurry. I looked up just in time to see Michel give me a small salute from across the room.

"How did you do that?" Alana sounded more in awe than afraid, so at least I had that going for me.

"Guys like that piss me off. Adrenalin," I lied smoothly. I needed to tell Alana what I was before we got too serious, but it wasn't the time or the place. "Sorry about that."

"Sorry? Thank *you.* I asked them to leave at least twenty times. They didn't believe I was here with somebody. They were sure I was a dancer."

"I can see why. You have a dancer's body."

"Volleyball."

"Want to get out of here?"

She just smiled and nodded. I stood up and offered her my hand. She reached out to take it, when I saw a wave of horror cross her features as she opened her mouth to scream. Normally, the odds of a human sneaking up behind me were slim to none. However, I relied on my hearing and subtle changes in the air currents around me to sense danger. There was nothing supernatural or magical about it. Standing in the middle of a strip club with giant speakers, cheering, bottles clanking, and people shouting, my senses were more than a little dulled. If it weren't for the change in

215

my date's expression, I would have taken the knife in the back. It wouldn't have killed me, but there would have been a lot of blood and explaining to do. As soon as I realized the danger, I dropped to the ground just as the blade traveled over my head.

But the damage was already done. Demons have many instincts. The most dangerous one we possessed, however, was survival. I'd been attacked with a weapon. The dimwitted human was dead, he just didn't know it yet.

Crouched on the ground, my left arm shot into the air and grabbed his arm just in front of his elbow. With a twist of my wrist, the joint snapped, and the knife went flying into the group of guys standing by the wall sipping beer and watching the show. From there, I stood and brought my right hand straight up, and just before it got close to the soft underside of his chin, my hand shifted into a demonic claw. I curled my fingers into a fist, all but one finger. The claw pierced his flesh, impeded by his tongue, and pierced the roof his mouth. Stopping just short of killing him, I turned to face him and drank in the fear wafting from him, thicker than the combined lust of the club.

"You couldn't stop. You just had to show me how big of a man you were. And then, when I showed you how very small you were, you couldn't live with that, could you? You had to be bigger and badder. And now look where we are." Exerting a bit more pressure, I lifted him up onto the tips of his toes as he struggled not to let my talon pierce the last inch into his brain.

"I would let this be a lesson, but I can tell no matter how many times you are taught, you wouldn't learn. So, I'm going to finish you right here and now. Goodbye, human," I snarled, and started to drive my finger into his brain. Until Alana's hand rested gently on my arm.

"Don't. Please."

I felt the heat leave my eyes as I turned to look at Alana's sweet face. "Why?"

"Because you're not a killer."

I almost argued with her, until I saw the look she was giving me. Imploring. Pleading. Letting my hand shift, I lowered douche nugget to the floor and pulled my normal looking finger from his wound with a wet squelch, letting him drop to the floor at my feet.

"Come on, let's go home."

Chapter 20

The police had different plans for me.

The only thing we had going for us is that we weren't in Bickering. A lieutenant was glowering at me, but he wore a Salem PD uniform, and was nowhere near as good looking as Grendel.

Even though Michel had given his account of the events that had occurred in the club and told them I'd only been defending myself, I was still handcuffed, and the only warm part of my body was my ass as I leaned against the running squad car.

"We're going to find the weapon, you know."

No, you're not. "Good luck."

"Did he stiff you on a blowjob or something?"

"Seriously. Go fuck yourself. I told you what happened, you donut sucking, coffee slurping, fat sack of shit." Probably not the wisest thing to say to a police officer, but I was about three seconds away from snapping the cuffs and putting my hand through his belly and pulling his nuts through the hole. I found that thought much more sexually appealing than unleashing my lust on him.

"Fuck you, whore."

That earned him a headbutt, and me a nightstick from another officer to the side of the head. Totally worth it. "You couldn't get laid in a morgue, you fat fuck."

The officer who smacked me in the head accidentally laughed, then coughed to cover his amusement before he pissed off the lieutenant.

"Put her in a cell," The lieutenant snarled at Mr. Giggles.

"On what charge?" I snarled.

"Resisting arrest."

"Good luck with that. I'm already in cuffs, fuckhead."

"Oh, I'm sure I can come up with any number of charges. Including prostitution and attempted murder."

The two people who had walked up behind the incredibly stupid lieutenant blinked in surprise and coughed to let him know they were there.

"What the fuck do you want?" The lieutenant growled and turned around angrily, stopped, and backed up until he stood beside me. I debated swinging my legs around his neck and choking him out, but I probably would have gotten shot before it happened. Plus, he might have liked it. "Chief?"

"Lieutenant." He shouldered the man aside and stepped beside me, checking the rapidly healing lump on the side of my head. "Are you okay?" The chief was graying, but didn't appear to be that old. He was certainly younger than me, but I aged better.

"I'll live."

"As your attorney, I advise you not to say another word, Ms. Dell." The other well-dressed gentleman moved a little closer.

"My attorney?"

"Well, technically, I am on retainer to Michel, but he has put you under his blanket of protection."

If Michel gets me out of this mess, that ain't the only blanket I'm going to be under. I giggled at the thought. The chief pulled a set of handcuff keys out of his pocket and motioned to my wrists, unlocking the steel restraints with practiced ease. "On behalf of the Salem PD, I offer you our humble apologies for the actions of our former lieutenant."

"Chief?" The fucktard was practically shaking behind his boss.

He spun and rounded on the man. "You are suspended pending an investigation." Then he put his finger in the man's face, put his mouth next to the lieutenant's ear, and began a litany of hushed angry whispers. His eyes widened with each of the chief's words, until the man couldn't take any more and started fighting back the tears.

"What just happened?" I whispered the question to my new lawyer.

"The knife you knocked out of the assailant's hand hit the chief's son in the leg. He's the one over there in the ambulance getting bandaged up. You got lucky. He told his dad *exactly* what happened. Looks like my services weren't even needed. Daddy doesn't want any of this in the papers, but better safe than sorry." He pulled out a card from the pocket of his wool trench coat and handed it to me. "Pleased to meet you. Call me if you have any more problems."

"Oh, I will. Thank you..." I paused to look at his card, "Mr. Davies."

"Call me Joseph."

"Thanks, Joseph."

He nodded and headed for the club, presumably to let Michel know what transpired. I grinned at the lieutenant, saluted Officer Giggles, and went to find my girlfriend. I found her leaning against my SUV, crying and talking to Daniel and Brady.

"Hey, kids."

"Kara!" Alana became a blonde blur as she practically tackled me, kissing my face. Brady and Daniel were chuckling at her exuberance, but I could see the tension ease from their faces.

"What happened?" Brady's voice cracked.

"Wrong place, wrong cop. I was screwed six ways from Sunday until the chief and my lawyer showed up."

"You have a lawyer already?" Daniel couldn't hide his surprise.

"Apparently."

"Well, come on. Let's get you home. You can tell us what happened in the bar when we get there. My sister tried, but she was a little hard to understand through the wracking sobs."

"Come on, Kitten. Let's go home."

221

∞ ∞ ∞

"So, how much is this going to cost me?"

The demiurge stroked his long goatee and adjusted his glasses as he surveyed the damage to my studio. "Kara...this won't be cheap."

I sighed, fearing those exact words. In the human realm, I was comfortable. Upper middle to lower upper class as far as finances were concerned. I would have been more comfortable if I didn't buy a second house and the dance studio. However, the demiurge wasn't interested in human finances. They dealt in power. "How much?"

The demon pulled out a calculator from his finely tailored suit. I thought he was going to start crunching numbers right there on the sidewalk, but little puffs of smoke shot from each key as he punched in figures. He was calculating how much magic it would take to renovate my studio. When he was done, he whistled and shook his head sadly at me.

Without a word, he put the palm of his right hand against my forehead. His power swirled inside me, into my depths. It wasn't unpleasant, but it wasn't exactly foreplay, either. When he finished, he patted me on the head. "More than you can spare, little one. I am sorry." He turned and started to leave.

"More than I have on me."

He stopped in his tracks and looked over his shoulder as a couple walking down the sidewalk gave him a wide berth. To them, he probably looked like a well-dressed businessman. To me, he had long, spiky purple hair and a grin that split his face from ear to ear, filled with pointed yellow teeth. That grin was on full display, pleased at my words. "You have a hoard?"

"What the fuck kind of demon would I be if I didn't?"

"A normal one. For one as young as you are to have accrued power and not squandered it is unusual."

222

The truth was, I had delved into it. Going without eating for so long, I hadn't had a chance. But I'd only skimmed a bit off the top to survive and keep the dreams at bay. My unwillingness to take any more had been my motivation to get out of bed and actually do something with my life. "How much more do you need?"

"Double what you have. Half to fuel the magic and the other half as payment."

It was doable. About half my hoard, but he didn't need to know that. "Deal." I held out my hand to seal it.

He looked down at my palm, and I could tell he was regretting his quote. He should have asked for more. With a sigh and a roll of his eyes, he put his hand over mine and drew a dagger from the air and plunged it through them. I could feel his blood mingle with mine, and a flair of power blasted the dagger from existence. It was much more elegant than a file folder full of documents that needed to be signed.

"Payment up front, little one."

I motioned for him to follow me into the alley between the buildings. Even decrepit, the studio was mine and tied to my power. It was one of three places on earth, and one in hell, that I could access my funds, for lack of a better word. Letting the index finger of my right hand extend into a clawed talon, I etched a rune into the brick and plunged my hand inside. The power followed it out, and I shut it off when I had enough swirling in my hand.

The demiurge licked his lips and stared at the glowing red mist. "Exactly as it looked before."

"Yes, yes. I shall turn back time and make it as it once was."

I held out the ball of power to him.

He grabbed it with both hands and drew it to his chest, his head swaying in ecstasy as he shoved it through his gray pinstriped suit. He stood quietly as he made my power his own. When he finally opened his eyes, they were alit with purple fire. "The rest?"

I debated trying to hold out until the work was complete, but he had demanded payment up front. With little else to do, I offered him my neck.

Wrapping me in long, spindly arms, he enveloped me in his darkness and pierced my flesh with his wicked teeth. I hissed in pain, and then in pleasure, as he drank his full, leaving me weak.

"Enough," he bellowed, and licked my blood from his lips before releasing me. "Go. I shall set your spells and tomorrow, your precious building will be whole."

And hopefully, everyone in the neighborhood will buy my story about night contractors. It was a gamble, but I wanted everything back to normal. And once I had accrued enough lust to fill what he had taken, I was going to ward the place to within an inch of its life. I had done my home the minute I had power to spend. I should have done the studio, too.

"Thank you."

"Go."

I left him in the alley and ducked back out into the sunlight, shielding my eyes and putting my sunglasses back on.

"Please tell me that wasn't a drug deal."

I squeaked and spun, almost slashing the lieutenant, *my* lieutenant, across the chest with my claws. "You scared the fuckjuice out of me. Jeez, Grendel."

"Josh *Grindel*. We've been over this. Were you dealing drugs in that alley?"

"Uh. No. Why? You want some?"

He shook his head, and the smallest of smiles graced the farthest corners of his mouth. But he didn't take the bait and frowned. "Then who was he?"

"Who?"

"Gangly guy?"

"My contractor."

"In an Armani suit?"

"He's kind of pricey. But he gets the job done *quickly*."

"How quick?"

"He has a team coming in tonight. I might be open very soon."

"Huh. How much does he charge? I have a wall I need to replace in my garage. The hot water heater blew." He started toward the alley, but I stopped him with an outstretched hand.

"Trust me. You can't afford him."

He narrowed his eyes at me. "Please tell me you didn't fuck him as payment."

The lieutenant sounded *angry*. Much angrier than he should have sounded. Almost like he was *jealous*. That, I could work with. "I'll pretend you didn't just call me a whore. But to answer your question, no. I didn't." I wasn't disgusted, but I pretended to be and stomped off. It was the only thing I could think of to get him to stop asking questions I couldn't answer.

"Kara. Wait." It was his turn to stop me with an outstretched hand. "Sorry. It was the only thing that popped into my head when you said I couldn't afford it." He paused after he finished talking, staring at his hand on my arm and not removing it.

"So, you called me a whore, but I guess I should be flattered you would think a fuck from me would be worth an entire building." I grinned at him.

"That's not what I meant!" He finally released his grip, but looked like he wanted to touch me some more.

"You don't think my fucks are worth it?" I took a step closer and looked him in the eye as I smiled at him sultrily.

"I'm sure they are but–" He flushed bright pink and turned away, took a few steps, stopped, spun on his heel, and walked back over to me. It was almost comical. "Can we start this conversation over?"

"No fucks?"

"No fucks."

"Good. Cuz I'm fresh out of fucks to give. Buy me a coffee?"

"Sure." He smiled and motioned for me to lead the way to the Dunkin' down the street.

"You sure do patrol this neighborhood a lot. It's because of the donuts, isn't it? Don't lie."

"No. I was hoping to run into you again."

"Oh?" I grinned up at him and slid my arm around his.

"Yeah. I wanted to ask you what the ever-loving fuck happened last night." He looked down at me wrapped around his arm, but didn't say anything.

My face fell. "Heard about that, did you?"

"Uh, yeah. A couple of my officers moonlight there as bouncers."

"They can do that?"

"As long as they're not on duty."

"It's a long story."

"It takes a while for the coffee to cool. We'll have time."

He opened the door, and we got our coffee, taking a table not far from the one we had sat at the day before. I sat down and popped the lid off, taking a drink to clear my thoughts as far as what and how much to tell him. He had done the same, but instead of taking a sip, he dunked half his donut into his steaming mug of coffee.

"Huh."

"What?" He carefully took a bite of the donut, and I snickered as part of it flopped off the end and splashed back into his drink.

"The place is called Dunkin' Donuts, but I think you may be the first person I've ever seen actually *dunk* his fucking donut."

"Nah. Tons of people do it. It's how they got their name."

We looked around, and I snickered at the utter lack of dunking.

"Shut up. It's good. You should try it."

"Not a huge fan of donuts. 'Cept crullers. Those are tasty."

He pulled one out of the bag and offered it to me.

"Fine." I took it and ripped a piece of it off and popped it into my mouth.

"You didn't dunk."

Sighing, I ripped off another piece and tried it. The universe exploded as two distinctly different flavors blended into something new, something better, something splendid. It was as if the creator had made the two glorious things to be brought together in harmonious ecstasy. "Holy shit."

"Told ya."

"Yeah. Yeah. You're brilliant. Let me enjoy this without you gloating."

"I don't gloat."

I cocked an eyebrow at him as I shoved another soggy piece into my donut hole.

"Sometimes. Maybe. So, talk. What happened last night?"

Sighing, I shoved the rest of it in my mouth. I washed the soggy mass down with another drink before folding my hands on the table. "I was on a date last night. The contractor you saw does some work for Michel, he owns the Candy Shoppe. I went there to get his number, and I figured Alana would enjoy some after dinner entertainment."

"Who's Alana?"

"My date."

"You were on a date...with a woman? At a strip club?" I could practically smell the smoke as his brain hastily painted the scene in his head.

"Yes. She's actually the sister of one of my boyfriends, but I like her, too."

"One of your boyfriends? How many people are you dating?" He didn't sound accusatory, just took another sip of coffee like it wasn't the weirdest thing he'd ever heard.

"Three. Including Alana."

"So, you're bisexual, or it was just kind of a play date?"

"Date date. But she's a lesbian, so don't get any mighty ideas, Jack."

"Josh."

"Figure of speech."

"You're under the assumption that I'm interested in dating you." He hid his smile behind his coffee cup, taking a sip and staring at me intently.

"Aren't you?" It would have been news to me. I'd been flirting hardcore, stopping just short of handing him a business card that said, 'Fuck me.'

"Seems kind of dangerous to me."

I nodded appreciatively. He wasn't wrong. "Only sometimes. Like when we get attacked by the Bickering Bandit or my studio goes up on flames."

"Or you get attacked by a rambunctious pair of sexually frustrated Neanderthals at a titty bar."

"Yeah. That, too. One of your officers told you what happened, apparently. Why am I retelling the tale?"

"I wanted to hear it from the source."

"You just wanted to stare at my ass again."

"Maybe," he said with a laugh.

"Okay. So, these guys start horning in on Alana while I'm talking to Michel. They didn't like it when I came back and kicked them out of my seat."

"Two girls at a strip club probably sounded like a wet dream come true."

"But they didn't understand the word no."

He nodded, sadly. "Most guys don't. You should see some of the calls we get."

"I can imagine." I patted his hand, not liking the sad look in his eye. Grendel had seen some shit. "So, anyway, I kick them to the curb, literally, and the nastier one of the two tried to slice me open with a knife. I knocked it out of his hand and karate chopped him in the throat."

"Stabbed him in the chin."

"I'm telling the story."

"What did you use?"

We were venturing into dangerous waters. If I said a weapon, I was admitting to a crime. If I told him I used my fingers, he might call the local insane asylum and have me committed. "My nail. I just meant to jab him in the gullet, but my acrylics split his pasty neck sack like a haggis."

228

"Haggis?"

"Scottish dish involving beef and stomach. Kinda gross. Smells worse."

"So, you shoved your finger into his neck. Then what happened?" Even though he sounded sincere, he still gave me a dubious look.

"All hell broke loose. Their lieutenant, who is much uglier than you and smells like beans and whiskey, thought I shanked him with something and accused me of being a prostitute."

"Clive Owens. He's a dick."

"A demoted dick."

Grendel's eyes widened in surprise. "How did that happen?"

"The knife actually hit the Chief of Police's kid in the leg. Junior told daddy what really happened, and I got roughed up by Clive. Things did not end well for him."

"Wait, did you say you were attacked by the bandit?" His eyes narrowed in suspicion as my previous words suddenly registered.

"Yep. Twice. Well, me once and then my kids another time. Meant to tell you about that after our conversation at the hospital, but I forgot."

"That's kind of important. Were you hurt? Why didn't I see your name on any of the police reports?"

"Because...uh...I didn't call you guys when I got attacked. But you might have seen Brady Drake and my kids on the other."

"Why the fuck didn't you call?"

"My date scared him away."

"Your date?" He laughed out loud, not bothering to hide the fact he was calling bullshit on my tale.

"Yes. Daniel can be very growly and snarly when someone attacks me with a knife."

Grendel paused, kind of stared off into neverland, and sipped his still too hot coffee. "Well. One thing is for certain."

"What?"

"You are most definitely trouble."

"No. It just follows me around like a lost puppy. Or a cop."

Chapter 21

"That was good, right?"

Karen rubbed the bridge of her nose and shook her head, clearly exasperated with my lack of soccer knowledge. "No, Kara. That was not good. It means the opposing team gets a penalty kick."

"But Karl already kicked that boy with the ball. Wouldn't getting kicked again be too much of a penalty?"

She growled in frustration. "Your kids have been playing soccer for *how* long? Don't you know what a penalty kick is?"

"Maaaybe."

"Your son kicked the other player instead of the ball. It was an accident, but it's still a penalty. The boy he hit gets to take a penalty kick. That means he gets to try and make a goal."

"Well, it's a good thing that kid sucks."

Karen stared at me like I had grown an extra head.

"What?"

"We don't say other peoples' kids suck."

"Even when they do?"

"Especially then."

"This game is weird."

Karen patted me on the leg and joined the other parents in the communal boo.

"I can't say they suck, but we can boo?"

"We're not booing the player. We're booing the shit call. Karl didn't do it on purpose, but he still made contact with the player."

"Like I said, this game is weird. I'm going to get a drink." Lifting myself off the lawn chair, I adjusted my sunglasses before slipping between the couple standing behind us and heading for the concession stand. I'd finished my water bottle filled with vodka, and the hour we'd spent sitting in the sun had left my mouth feeling like the floor of the seventh level of hell. I was parched.

And of course, there was a line. Forty-two people long. All waiting to get hot dogs, popcorn, and pretzels. Unfortunately, the soccer field was set in the middle of one of the less posh residential neighborhoods. There wasn't a convenience store in sight. Steeling my nerves, I got at the back of the line and silently vowed to bring a cooler with me to the next game.

"Yeah. I don't know what she did to my son. I'm assuming the little tramp drugged his drink or something. She looks exactly like her mother, and probably figured that would be the only way Jason would kiss her."

I recognized the voice before I recognized the boy's name and realized she was talking about my daughter. Marissa was five people ahead of me in line and talking to two of her cronies, not caring in the slightest who overheard her. She must not have realized I was behind her. Just as I hadn't realized her kids were friends with mine. Or that the bitch lived that close to me.

"The whore is just lucky I don't press charges for her daughter assaulting my son."

If I had an ounce of power left to my name, I would have breathed a cloud of lust in front of me and gotten the four people between us to scamper off in the nearby woods to bang their brains out. I could picture Marissa's face as I stepped up behind her. Unfortunately, my tanks were bone dry.

"Did you hear? Connie saw her and the girls' soccer coach sucking face at a restaurant. I knew she was a carpet muncher. You can just tell by looking at her. She's probably only banging Daniel for his money." I didn't recognize either of the two women standing beside

232

Marissa, but I'd remember their faces in the future. They just ended up on the shit list. When that list was in the possession of a demon, things had a tendency to not go so well.

"What a whore," Marissa chimed in. "But then again, she's probably got to get it when and where she can. Beggars can't be choosers. Coach Drake isn't exactly the poster child of feminine beauty. She looks like her brother with tits."

Enough was enough. She had insulted me. I could live with that. She had somewhat insulted my daughter by saying she looked like me. I had refrained from gutting her like the pig that she was. But then she had gone and attacked one of the sweetest, most generous people I had ever met. I was about to rain down the fires of hell upon her.

Unfortunately, I couldn't get caught. So, I seethed. I seethed in demonic fury as I pictured pushing the four people between us out of the way and ripping out her throat. And I stayed that way. Even when they got their food and turned around, I quickly pulled a miasma of misdirection around me. They walked past me without batting an eyelash.

I debated following them, but my thirst outweighed my need for revenge. If I let it stew, it would be all that much sweeter anyway. I settled for ordering two Sprites, chugging the first, and taking the second back to my seat. I made it hallway there when I saw my arch-nemesis break away from the crowd and slip into one of the two blue and teal portable latrines. The indicator on the door slid from vacant to occupied, and my frown turned into a smile. The gods of luck had descended to earth and kissed me gently and lovingly, wrapping me in the arms of fortune.

Dropping my Sprite into a nearby trash can, I circled around the latrines looking for witnesses. Everybody was concentrating on the second half of the game. A cheer rose up, and even the people at the concession stand moved to the field to see what had transpired. I prayed Karl had redeemed his earlier indiscretion and scored another point for our team as I put my back against the dusty plastic.

"This one's occupied," Marissa's annoyed voice sounded from inside, muffled through the vents by the roof.

"Oh, so sorry," I said a few octaves higher than I usually spoke, disguising my voice as I circled around to the front. Letting her escape wasn't an option. I called a flame to my hand, and it sputtered with my depleted power, but hopefully I could get it hot enough to melt a little bit of plastic.

"What's that smell?" Her voice didn't sound panicked, yet. Merely worried.

"I had Taco Bell. Sorry."

"Ew. Gross."

Staring at the flame, I poured what little I had left into it until it burned blue, almost white, and shoved my palm against the seam between the door and wall, fusing them together in a ripple of molten plastic.

"What the fuck is burning?" We had officially entered panic mode. She hit the door full force, panties probably still around her ankles.

I didn't have much time until her muffled screams drew the attention of the rest of the field. With every ounce of strength I possessed, I pushed the port-a-potty over. Giggling maniacally, I ran as it fell onto its back. Only when I reached the relative safety of a copse of pine trees by the parking lot, did I turn to survey my handy work.

My mouth fell open in shock. The blue water had exploded out of the only opening, the one Marissa had been sitting on, and pushed her through the plastic white roof, completely separating it from the rest of the structure. Lying there in an azure pool, Marissa screamed and sputtered, desperately trying to pull her panties and leggings up as she fervently struggled to breathe. Then she rolled over on her knees and vomited. Not that I blamed her, I probably would have, too. I hightailed it back to my seat.

"What took you so long?" Karen turned an gave me a suspicious look as I dropped into the seat next to her.

"Huge line."

"I thought you were getting a drink."

"I did. Chugged it before I got back here."

"Why do you look nervous?"

"I was worried about the score. Are we still winning?"

"Yep. Karl got another goal just a few minutes ago. Is that screaming?" She sat up straight in her seat and looked behind us. In fact, most of the other parents were doing the same.

"Sounds like it," I answered, and turned to look while I plastered a look of concern on my face. "Coming from the parking lot?" I even got out of my chair and started walking in that direction, a masterful performance on my part.

"Sounds like it's coming from by the concession stands." Karen hurried past me, a throng of parents in our wake.

And so the mob bore witness to my handiwork, arriving just in time to see Marissa Smurf finally drag her leggings over her ample ass and stare at us in anger and horror.

"Marissa?" I made her voice a question. "Are you okay? What happened?"

Her eyes locked on to me, seething in hatred. "As if you don't know, you fucking cunt."

A few of the parents gasped and covered the ears of the children that were present.

Marissa didn't care.

Marissa was *pissed.*

"You don't think *I* did this? How the hell am I going to push an entire latrine over by myself?"

A few of the parents nodded in agreement. It was simple physics.

"Especially with you in it. I mean, come on. Let's be reasonable."

Her eyes narrowed even more. Which was quite comical with her blue-dyed eyelids. "I don't know *how* you did it, but I *know* you did it."

"Well, I was with Karen the whole time. You must be mistaken. Plus, why would I have a reason to do something like this to you? I mean it's not like you were insulting my daughter or Coach Drake, right?"

The crowd had seemed a little skeptical. But that quickly shifted to disbelief. Everybody loved the Drakes. Some more than others. Not as much as I did, or with as much tongue, but they were beloved. "What?"

"I mean, I might have done *something* like this if I heard you call her a carpet muncher, or something equally as derogatory. But luckily, I was nowhere near you when you were spouting off at the pie hole. Things *could* have gotten ugly. And red instead of blue."

The crowd might have missed my thinly veiled threat, but Marissa didn't. She quietly stood up, calmly wiped as much liquid from her face and arms as she could, and stormed off in the direction of her SUV.

"Please tell me you didn't do it," Karen whispered in my ear.

I just patted her arm and headed back to the game to grab my chair. I'd wait out the rest of the game in my vehicle. There was no way I was giving the Bitch of Bickering another chance to slash *my* tires.

∞ ∞ ∞

It is done. The demiurge's thought flittered through my brain like a gentle caress much later in the morning than I was expecting. The damage must have been more extensive than he thought. He'd given me the impression that it would have been completed overnight. The connection between us tore apart with a gasp of pain from me, and then my hand started hurting where he had driven the dagger through our flesh.

"You okay?" Daniel reached over the kitchen counter and rubbed my hand worriedly.

"Yeah. The studio just finished. Feel like getting a coffee?"

He smiled and nodded. "I'd love to."

I walked over to the stairs. "Sage!"

She leaned over the banister. "What?"

"Meet us at the studio."

"Huh?"

"It's fixed."

"No fucking way." She wasn't excited, she was skeptical.

"I told you the contractor I hired was magical." If she only knew I'd meant it literally.

"I'll meet you there!" Excitement had finally surpassed her skepticism.

"You want the coffee?"

"Please!"

"Come on, Daniel." I gave him a smile and reached for his hand.

We got in the car and headed downtown. After the game, I had run home and taken a shower to wash the sweat off. He had shown up shortly after. It was nice spending some time with him alone. Lately, he and Brady had been attached at the hip. I snickered at the thought.

Daniel whistled as we passed the studio on the way to Dunkin'. "Holy shit. You can't even tell there was ever a fire. It looks exactly the same."

"Yeah. He turned back time on the building itself."

"Well, shit. I'll just hire him to fix the house next time something breaks."

"Yeah. You wouldn't be able to pay for his services."

Daniel frowned at me, and I realized how it sounded. Shaking my head, I put my hand on his knee. "Demons like that have no need for human currency. I had to give him more than half of my accumulated power."

"Lust?"

"For lack of a better word. I eat lust, I can use lust, but inside me, it is just raw unadulterated power. I gave him all I had in me and half of what I had in…storage? The bank?"

"Power banks?"

"Something like that. I can stash it in Hell."

"Wait. Hell is real?" he asked at the exact moment the girl working at Dunkin' asked our order over the static filled speaker.

"Three coffees. One black, and two with cream and sugar."

She gave our total, and we pulled up to the window. I paid and got our coffees, and then pulled away before I started answering. "It's real, but not like you imagine. You don't just end up there when you die, no matter how much of a bastard you were in life."

"Oh, thank God."

That earned him a laugh. "Yeah. Cuz you're a total asshole." I rolled my eyes.

"Hey. I was raised Catholic. Divorce and premarital sex are sins."

I coughed and laughed at the same time. Thankfully, I hadn't been taking a sip of coffee. "Not to mention what we've got going on."

"Yeah. That, too." He grinned.

We pulled up to the studio and parked right in front. It was my turn to whistle. The demiurge had gone above and beyond. Through the window, I could tell the studio was back to normal. The *outside* of the building, however, looked thirty years younger. The brick wasn't clean, it was perfect. There were no gouges, cracks, or missing bits of mortar. Even the corners were crisp and straight. Hopefully, nobody would notice.

"It looks amazing."

"Yeah," I answered a little nervously, taking a gulp of coffee and wishing I'd had the sense to bring something stronger to put into it.

Unlocking the front door, we went inside. The same overachievement on the outside was present inside, too. I just hadn't been able to see it through the glass. The wood floor was immaculate, the patches in the walls were gone, and the poles were gleaming. It was beautiful.

"What's wrong?"

"He did too good of a job. Everything looks new."

"That's a good thing, Kara."

"How?"

"Contractors. Everything is supposed to be new. It was a replacement, not a repair."

"Which would work inside, but not the outside. The stone and brick look new. There's no way I'm going to pass that off as a nighttime of work."

"Sweetie, there isn't a contractor on earth that could have repaired this in a night. My suggestion is that you hang up some tarps in the window and stay closed for a week or two."

I nodded. Daniel was pretty fucking smart. "Good idea. Is there a hardware store close?"

"There's one three blocks down on Olive," a voice answered from behind us. A voice I recognized in an instant.

Fuuuck.

"Hey, Grendel," I said and turned slowly, schooling the panic off my face.

"Mrs. Dell," he answered, and let the door close behind him as he walked around the studio, checking out the repairs.

"What brings you to my humble studio?"

"I'd be lying if I said this was a social call." He didn't turn to answer me, just kept studying the walls, windows, and floor. He even ran his fingers over several of the surfaces.

"Well, do I pass my building inspection?"

He sighed and stopped by the counter, leaning against it while crossing his arms and staring at the two of us. He pointed at the window. "See the sub shop across the street?"

I leaned back to get a better view. There was indeed, a sub shop across the street. Rosetti's Subs. I hadn't noticed until he pointed it out. "Yep. You hungry?"

"Nah. See the second floor of the building?"

I had to bend over and tilt my head to see it, but it was there. Most of the older buildings in the original part of downtown had second floors. Just like the studio. Some of them were offices, and some were apartments. "Yep. I see it."

"Did I ever mention I live there? Own the building and rent out the bottom floor to pay the mortgage."

"That's smart."

"Yes. I basically live there for free. My parents left it to me before they passed."

"I'm sorry for your loss." I gulped, having a feeling I knew where he was going with his tale.

"Want to know the best thing of living across the street?"

"Watching all the hot women pole dancing in the window?"

"You had blinds."

"You get to keep tabs on your favorite miscreant?"

"That, too. But something else."

"Yoga pants. Every guy loves yoga pants."

"No, Kara. I loved the fact that I could watch your so-called contractors as they busily restored your property to its former grandeur. Want to know how many contractors it took to do this marvelous of a job?"

I sighed and shrugged.

"Exactly *none*. Not a fucking one. Nobody showed up last night, and yet at various points in the night, the building started reshaping itself. Care to explain that?"

"Elves?"

"Nope. Didn't see anybody with pointed ears."

"They're tiny. Since the shoe repair market crashed, they've had to adapt and overcome. They formed a union. Building Restoration Elves, I believe they're called now. I

240

mean cobbler sounds like a dessert anyway, so it's probably for the best."

"Various points during the night? Sounds like you were dozing off and missed all the work, Lieutenant," Daniel chimed in helpfully.

"That's what I thought at first, too. So, I set up my phone to record when I wasn't watching. Want to see the video? It's kind of cool. I did the whole time-lapse thingy." He hit play and held the phone up for us to see.

Sure enough, the building regenerated all on its lonesome. At least there wasn't a demiurge in the picture. *That* would have been impossible to explain. Not that the rest was any easier.

"Nanites," I lied smoothly.

"Nanites?"

"Yep. Leetle tiny robots," I answered in my best Gru impersonation. "That guy you saw me with yesterday is a scientist. They're not available for public use yet, but he's a friend of a friend. No contractors or materials needed. That's why he charges so much."

Grendel started looking around the studio and nervously pulled away from the counter. "Is that safe?"

He bought it. Guess it's a more logical explanation than magic. "Should be. Though we are keeping the studio closed for a few days, just to be sure."

"Good. Don't need anybody getting munched on by tiny robots. Maybe you guys should get out of here, too." He kept glancing around the walls and floors the whole time he was speaking. I would have bet money on his dreams not being very pleasant for the next few weeks.

"Thanks, Grendel."

"Will you friggin' call me Josh. Or Grindel. I'm not a monster."

"Meh. I kind of always thought Grendel was the good guy and Beowulf was a drunk bully."

"He ate villagers."

"They probably deserved it."

241

Chapter 22

"A movie?"

Brady nodded, grinning. "Come on. It will be fun."

I looked at Daniel for backup. He just shrugged and nodded. I was officially outnumbered. "Fine, but I get to pick it."

"They only have one."

I should have known something was up when they insisted we take Brady's truck with the large bench seat that spanned the entire width of the truck. He drove, I sat in the middle, and Daniel got the window. It wasn't entirely unpleasant, and I got to keep my hands warm on their thighs as we drove. And drove. And drove. Thirty minutes and two stiff cocks later, we pulled into a run-down drive-in on the edge of some town I didn't know existed on the outskirts of Boston.

"Holy shit. You guys have an actual drive-in?"

Brady pulled up to the kiosk and paid. The attendant slipped a ticket under the wiper and waved us in. "Yep. Only one in the area. They show classic movies, too. Anybody want popcorn?" Brady opened his door and stood outside, letting the cold air in while he waited for an answer.

"Get a large, we can share. And some drinks," Daniel answered, and reached over to dial the radio to the frequency listed on the post that held the speakers.

"Fancy," I said with a stifled giggle.

Brady's door shut, and I sighed, snuggling up against Daniel for a little more warmth. "You okay?"

"Just cold."

"You look a little run down."

I smiled and nodded. Hopefully, after our date, I would have a little more fuel in the tanks. At least enough to not look so rundown. After the lieutenant had left and we had gotten Sage settled in her apartment, we hung tarps over the windows in hopes that the Bickering Bandit would assume the place was still under construction and not worth burning again.

The greatest thing about Sage was that she had walked into the place, took one look around and whistled. That was the extent of her shock. She hadn't asked one question, bless her little heart. "So, what movie are we watching?"

"You didn't see the sign when we pulled in?"

"No."

"Army of Darkness."

"What's it about?"

"Demons." He grinned.

I groaned.

Daniel's phone dinged, and he looked at the message. "Be right back. He needs help carrying stuff."

"Want me to go?"

"Nah. Stay here where it's warm. I'll be right back."

"But I'll miss you." I smiled, kissed him, and gave him a little rub. Sipping his lust, I laughed as he pulled away, adjusted his pants, and headed for the concession stand.

Alone, I put my feet up on the bench seat and hugged my knees. Not in fear, but to stay fucking warm. My ass was frozen to the vinyl seat of the truck. I was about ten seconds away from death, when the two of them slid into the truck and scrunched me in their warmth, a bucket of popcorn in each of their laps.

"Thank t-t-the creator. I nearly froze to death."

"Why didn't you start the truck and turn on the heat?"

I stared blankly at Brady for a moment. "Because I didn't think of it," I answered honestly.

"Silly demon," he answered with a laugh, and handed me a cup that was warm.

"What's this?"

"Coffee. I figured you'd want something warm. You can share my Coke if you get thirsty."

"I *flove* you."

"Flove?"

"Fucking love. It's a word. Look it up."

It got *eerily* quiet in the truck.

"What?" I turned my head back and forth between to see what was wrong.

"You love me?"

"You brought me coffee." Panic seized my heart. I'd meant it as a joke because he had gotten me coffee, not because I wanted to declare anything about how I might feel about him. Sighing, I continued. "I meant it as a joke, to say how appreciative I was about you bringing me coffee."

"Oh." He frowned a little, barely noticeable, but I felt it more than I heard it.

"Look. Both of you. I was married for fifteen years, and I could count the number of times I dropped the L-word on one finger. It's just not in my…nature. I might not be able to express how I feel about you, but I'll try. I'd take a bullet for you. How's that? I'd *definitely* take a bullet for you. Close enough?"

"But a bullet won't kill you."

"No, but it would hurt like a son of a bitch. That's how much I care about you." I kissed both of them, *hard*.

The truck immediately warmed as they started breathing again. Human males were ridiculously easy to please, and I smiled as I picked my coffee back up.

"Fine. We'd take a bullet for you, too," Brady whispered, and kissed my shoulder.

"Fifty-cal." Daniel did the same.

"When does the movie start?" I gulped down some of the warm brew, trying to think about anything except for the nagging feeling in my gut that I had somehow betrayed Ryan by getting a little mushy.

And I swear on everything that is unholy, I felt him slap the back of my head and tell me to quit being stupid. I smiled and leaned against Daniel, putting my leg over Brady's lap. He seemed to wince when I hit the popcorn bucket.

I reached over and grabbed a handful of popcorn as the opening credits started rolling. Right after that, the movie exploded into action and I sat up, thoroughly enjoying both the acting and cinematography. The demons were cheesy looking, but it was part of the movie's charm. I started cheering for the demons as I alternated snagging popcorn from both of their buckets.

Thirty minutes in, my fingers grazed silky smooth skin and rigid flesh. Blinking in surprise, I peered into Daniel's bucket. Sure enough, the head of his cock was just above the level of the popcorn. Brady started laughing. Cocking an eyebrow at him, I looked into his finding the same result. The both of them had cut holes into the bottoms of the buckets and somehow managed to insert their hard-ons inside. I giggled and ate more popcorn, grazing their flesh teasingly as I did.

"There is a flaw in your plan," I said softly as I continued to watch the movie.

"What's that?" Brady was the one brave enough to ask.

"I fucking love popcorn."

"What's wrong with that?"

"Your cocks are gonna taste like it." I made chomping motions in the air at the screen, not looking at them as I did it.

Their gulps were audible, and I chuckled as I stroked them inside the buckets. Quickly, they started moaning and forgot about the movie and my threats.

"Butter makes good lube. But I knew that."

"Kara?"

"Yes, Daniel?"

"I'm getting close…"

I snickered and let go of both of them inside the buckets. Using both hands, I worked the popcorn container up and over Daniel's salty rod. He winced a couple of times, but it wasn't my fault. He should have made the hole

246

bigger. Glancing at the SUV next to us, I grinned at the guy in the driver's seat who had been watching us instead of the movie. I shifted my knees onto the seat and lowered my head slowly into Daniel's lap and took him into my mouth.

He leaned back against the seat, and I felt Brady's hand slip under my skirt, gently rubbing my hip as I serviced his friend.

Brady turned in his seat and gently lifted the back of my skirt up and over my ass. Half-expecting him to dive right in, I moaned as his lips slid over the flesh of my cheeks, raising goosebumps over my skin. "So fucking beautiful," he whispered, and let the tip of his tongue touch my clit, give it a little flick, and then slide up between my lips, and he pulled me in for a kiss.

I groaned against Daniel in my mouth, and his hips rose to meet me as he hissed in pleasure.

"You like that?" I asked him, lifting my head and looking out the window. The guy in the driver's seat and his male passenger both had their cocks out and weren't shy about jerking off in front of each other. I smiled and licked my lips, before giving them a knowing wink and taking Daniel back into my mouth. Our spectators were out of my sight, but just knowing they were watching made it all that much hotter.

"Look at the SUV next to us," I mumbled to Daniel around his shaft.

"Holy shit. Should we stop?"

I didn't bite, but I seized him between my teeth.

"I'll take that as a no."

"Smart man," I answered with a giggle, and twirled my tongue around his tip. A bit of semen leaked out. He didn't come, but he was getting closer. "You gonna come in my mouth, Daniel?"

"Do you want me to?"

"No. I want you to come in my pussy."

"Then you better get in my lap."

As he said it, Brady plunged his tongue farther inside me and slipped a finger in my ass. I squealed in delight and pushed back against him as I stroked Daniel in my hand. He grabbed my fist with his and stopped my motions. He was closer than I thought.

"Do you want him to come inside me, Brady?"

He gave a muffled yes, but was unwilling to let me go.

Smiling, I pulled away and turned around in the seat, offering myself to Daniel, who pulled me into his lap. I lay back against him, his cock emerging between my thighs. His hands immediately found my breasts and began kneading them while I reached down between my legs, grabbed him, and let him slide inside me. Thankfully, Brady's truck was huge, and we had plenty of room.

"Oh, God. You feel amazing." I started panting before either of us started moving.

"So do you," he whispered in my ear as he kissed my neck.

I started grinding against him, dripping from being so turned on. I noticed our audience. They had stopped stroking their cocks and were stroking each other's.

I mouthed the words "That's hot" at them through the glass.

Brady crawled over, put his face in my lap, and started suckling my clit as his best friend pierced me. My orgasm was instant, fierce, and lasted seven lifetimes. I couldn't stop coming, and neither could Daniel. As soon as my muscles contracted in blissful agony, I felt him swell inside me, and my wetness tripled as his fluids mixed with mine.

Brady was there to drink it all. He let go of his hold on my clit, and his tongue bathed us both at our junction. When Daniel slipped out from inside me, Brady took him into his mouth and cleaned every last drop.

"Fuck, that is so fucking sexy," I whispered to him, and ran my fingers through his hair. "Fuck me, Brady."

He pulled back to give me room, and I got back on my knees and bent over, offering him my freshly fucked hole. He slipped inside me, groaned, and then pulled it out to rub the wetness over my other entrance.

I grinned over my shoulder. "You want my ass?"

"Fuck yes."

"It's yours."

He stroked my back and slipped the tip inside me. My flesh stretched around him, and I took Daniel's still hard cock back into my mouth and suckled the tip while I got used to the sensation in my ass. The sensation and the girth. Neither of my guys were lacking in the Department of Penetration, but they weren't so massive I couldn't take them in my ass, either. They were absolutely perfect. For me.

"Slow," I warned as he began working himself inside. I mewled with every inch and groaned when I felt his balls against my pussy after what felt like forever.

"So fucking tight."

I giggled until he began to pull back, then I lost the ability to see and think. Slowly, he built up a rhythm, and by the time he had found his pace, I was a jumbling, mumbling idiot with a mouthful of cock. It was the happiest I had been in a very long time.

Brady's movements became choppy as his pleasure began to overwhelm him. "Going to come!"

His words were more than enough to send me over the edge, too. The orgasm was completely different than the one I'd had in Daniel's lap. It wasn't instant, it built and built and built, until it drove over me like a runaway bus slamming into the guardrails. I screamed around Daniel's cock as he erupted into my mouth. I closed my lips, breathed through my nose rapidly, and swallowed everything he had to give. Then we collapsed on each other.

"What are our friends doing?" I asked Daniel.

He glanced over at the vehicle next to us and started laughing, but his cock gave a little twitch of life beside me. "The guy in the passenger seat is blowing the driver. Guess their hands weren't enough."

"That's hot." I started looking around for napkins, found the stack on the dash and used a couple to get rid of some of the evidence of our love making. Tossing the napkin into the empty bucket of popcorn, I grinned. "Let's go home, I need a shower." I rolled onto my back and put my feet up on Brady's lap after he had pulled away and tucked himself back in his pants. Grinning, I realized my empty tanks weren't so empty anymore. If we fooled around in the shower...I would probably have enough juice to ward the studio.

∞ ∞ ∞

My hand stopped glowing against the shining wood floor of the dance studio as the final push of power sealed the ward I'd placed on the entire building. I felt it settle over everything like a finely spun web. Smiling in satisfaction, I stood and dusted off my leggings.

"Kara?"

I squawked. Sage had been sound asleep, I'd checked. Not wanting to waste any power, I hadn't made sure she'd stay that way, and her fearful voice scared the ever-living crap out of me. "Oh, Sage. Don't sneak up on me like that."

"Sorry. What are you doing? Everything okay?"

"Yep. Just thought I saw a scratch on the floor. I was in the neighborhood, and I decided to stop in and double check everything."

"Awww. Your baby is safe. I'm taking good care of her." Sage smiled and leaned against the counter.

"I know you are. Just wanted to admire the shiny new construction," I lied, and gave her a grin.

"Want a drink?"

"Sure. Whatcha got?"

"Rum and Coke."

"I'll have a rum."

She laughed and ran back up the stairs. I waited down in the studio. It only took her a minute to return with a bottle of rum in her hand and two tumblers. She put them on the counter and poured a little in each glass before handing me one and clinking hers against it.

"To a new new beginning," she said with a cute little giggle, and took a swallow. "Ugh. How do you drink this stuff straight?"

"Nobody said you couldn't put Coke in yours."

"I know. But I wanted to be like the big kids."

Judging from her face, she was regretting her decision.

"Burns good." I laughed and walked around the studio, pretending to look at everything, but really just checking the wards for any holes. On a whim, I tore down one of the tarps and raised my glass at Grendel in case he was watching.

"Should I take down the other ones?"

"Sure. The place is safe now."

"Huh?"

Oops. "I mean, I've got the cop across the street watching the place now. If anybody tries anything again, they're gonna be sorry."

"Ahh. Okay. "

My phone dinged in my pocket.

Mom. Someone is outside and trying to get in.

I blinked at the phone and opened up the line to the wards I had on the house. Nothing was setting them off. *Are you sure?*

Yes. The lock keeps twisting, but I'm holding it.

I'll be right there! "Gotta run, Sage. Night!" I slammed the rest of the rum and handed her the glass. "Lock up behind me."

"Will do, Boss."

My kids were in danger. The first thing my brain did was stop working as I ran out the door, got past the studio window, and launched myself into the air. My wings tore free and beat downward, pushing me up above the buildings and into the night sky. It had been pure instinct, but it worked out. I could fly in a straight line a hell of a lot faster than I could get my SUV through the streets of Bickering,

Within minutes, I dropped into the front yard and banished my wings, running for the door and shoving the key into the lock. It wasn't turning. "Karl?"

"Mom?"

"Oh, thank God. I thought they came back." The lock clicked, and the door opened. Grabbing my boy child, I hugged him to my chest and started breathing again. "Where's your sister?"

"On the phone with the police."

"Thank the creator you guys are smarter than your mother."

"Not smarter, but a little more in touch with how the world works. Like how growing children need oxygen to live." He was struggling in my grip, but I assumed it was because he was too embarrassed to hug his mother. I didn't realize I was asphyxiating him.

"Sorry."

"'Sokay. The hug was nice though." He gave me a smile and stepped out of the way to let me in the house. Just as three squad cars skidded to a stop in front of the house. Four police officers poured out of two of the cars, guns drawn. Grendel got out of the third and immediately started canvasing the area. "Are they still here?"

"No. They left before I got here," I called out to him from the door.

"You four, patrol the area. Call me if you see anything out of the ordinary. I'll stay here and make sure they're safe."

"Yes, sir," they replied like a well-oiled military machine, and got into the squad cars. One went the direction they had come from, spotlight shining between the houses, and the other pulled away in the opposite direction. Just as Mr. and Mrs. Donaldson came out their front door and started bitching about the noise and HOA regulations about parties after six PM. I gave them the finger and walked inside the house. I needed some coffee to steel my nerves and keep me from killing the old bastards.

"You okay?" Grendel had entered the house behind me and followed me into the kitchen.

"Been better. Scared the shit out of me."

"Yeah. Nothing worse than having your kids need you and you're not home."

"Speaking from experience?" I knew absolutely nothing about his personal life, other than his parents had died.

"I raised my little sister when my parents died. No kids, though."

"Shame. You'd make a good dad," I said honestly. He just had that feel to him. Some of the same qualities Ryan had. "Coffee?"

"Please. I think I'm going to need some."

"Oh?"

He looked at Karl standing by the door and watching the front yard like a protective gargoyle. Ryn came running down the stairs and tackled me in a hug from behind. "Thank God you're home."

"Yep. All safe now, kiddo. Why don't you go to bed? You have school tomorrow."

"How can I possibly go to an institute of higher learning when I had a near death experience? I think we should stay home tomorrow." She grinned conspiratorially.

My first reaction was to laugh and say, "Okay." But the cop in my kitchen made me think better of it. "Nice try. Get your ass to bed and drag Sir Karl with you."

She looked at Grendel, back at me, gave me a knowing nod and grinned. "Come on, doofus. Mom's being all parental and shit."

Karl gave his sister an annoyed look, but he nodded and followed her up the staircase. With my hearing, I could tell they stopped at the top of the stairs, and I could practically feel them leaning over the banister to hear what we were going to say.

I handed the first mug of coffee to Grendel. He held it in his hand but paused for a moment while I reloaded it with a pod and another mug. When I finally turned to him, he lifted his mug in a dramatic salute. "What's that for?"

"Just returning the toast you gave me from the studio."

Oooh. Shit. "Hahaha. I didn't think you were watching."

He took a swig of coffee and set it down on the counter. "Have any cream?"

"Milk okay? It might not be expired." I chuckled nervously and turned around, trying to concoct a story on how I got to the house so quick. Schooling my face, I set the jug on the counter and grabbed him a spoon out of the drawer.

He checked the date and splashed some of the milk in his mug, slowly stirring it with the spoon. "Boy. You sure got here quick. You must have been driving like a bat out of hell."

Time slowed to a grinding stop as fear seized my chest in a vice. "Yeah. Luckily, all the cops were on their way to my house, or I might have gotten a ticket."

"Whose car did you take? Sage's? Because yours was sitting in front of the studio when I left."

"Yep. She threw her keys at me and told me to go. She's got that little sporty model, and I drive a tank."

"That's funny." He took another sip of coffee. "I didn't see it in the driveway."

"I pulled it into Daniel's garage. I have a clicker."

"Which you took out of your car, to get in her car, and then drive all the way here."

"Yep. She has a leak in her roof. I thought it might rain."

"Because upholstery is more important than kids."

"Sometimes. Depends on if they clean their rooms or not."

"Cut the shit."

"Consider it cut."

"How did you get here, Kara?"

"I flew," I said jokingly.

"At last. I get an honest answer out of you." He set the mug down and crossed his arms, leaning his hip against the countertop.

"Whaaat? Lieutenant... Are you high?"

"I walked out of my building the moment you ran down the road, jumped into the air, and wings sprouted from your back."

My face fell. "Shit."

"Not that I blame you for being careless. I mean, your kids were in danger. So, what are you? Those weren't angel wings I saw. I was hoping you would catch my bat out of hell reference. Demon? Succubus?"

My mouth fell open as I stared at him. He had taken two guesses, and they'd both been right. "How did you know?"

"This is one of the oldest parts of the country. We're literally right next door to Salem. I've seen some shit." He picked up his mug and took another swallow of coffee. "I'll be honest, I kind of figured it out when you ran into a burning building and healed before we got to the hospital. And when I heard you stabbed somebody in the neck. With your *finger*."

"So, now what? You arrest me? Kill me? Call the FBI and have me carted off to Area 51 to be dissected?"

"That would probably be the CIA not the FBI. But no."

"What? Why?"

He sighed and pulled out one of the stools under the counter and sat. "Because you're not evil."

"I'm literally from Hell. Of course, I am."

"No. You're not. Neither is the vampire that owns the strip club. Or the werewolf who owns the convenience store on Elm. Or the elf who takes care of the graveyard. Or the brownie who cleans my apartment. You have two kids. You were married. You own a dance studio. You're not evil. The guy who shoots his wife and his kids and then takes his own life. *He's* evil. The priest that molests hundreds of kids before he gets caught. *He's* evil. The guy

255

who shoots his girlfriend in the head when he finds out she's pregnant. *He's* evil. You? You're just horny."

"I have a tail, too."

"I meant..." He blushed, and I couldn't but help myself. I leaned in and kissed him on his nose. To his credit, he didn't pull back. In fact, he closed his eyes and leaned forward a little, letting his lips touch mine. It wasn't a chaste kiss either, and I found myself returning it. Until his tongue touched mine.

I pulled away. "I know what you meant. And while the thought of this going further sounds pretty fucking amazing, I have a boyfriend. Two of them. And a girlfriend."

"I know. I'm sorry."

"Don't be. It's not that I'm not interested, but it would be evil of me to throw you down on the floor and fuck your brains out without discussing it with them first."

"Does that mean you want to?" He grinned.

"Fuck the hot cop who knows my secret? What better way to make sure it *stays* a secret? But to answer your question honestly... Yes. I do. You might be a big pain in my ass, but I like big pains in my ass. So, what are we going to do about the Bickering Bandit? They're pretty evil, and also not human."

"Are you sure?"

"Um...pretty sure, yeah."

"Well, I'll trust your judgement.

I clutched my heart. "Are you sure you're human?"

"Har har."

Chapter 23

"It's been a whole week without so much as an arson attempt, breaking and entering attempt, or a physical assault. Maybe they're gone?"

I gave Karen an incredulous look as we walked up to the ticketing booth of the Fall Festival. Apparently, the theme was fucking pumpkins. They were *everywhere*. I was going to have horrid nightmares and have to move to Australia where I'd never have to see another one again as long as I lived. Aussies were weird and didn't celebrate Halloween, but they had koalas and other cute shit, so it seemed like a fair trade. And it wasn't like I had to worry about all the stuff that could kill a normal human. Australia sounded better and better.

"Well, this is a festival! Let's have some fun and eat lots of stuff we shouldn't."

"The faces of our enemies?"

"No! God! What? I meant caramel apples and cotton candy."

"Why shouldn't we eat that?"

"Because it will go straight to our asses." Karen glanced down at me, snarled, and mumbled, "Never mind."

Shrugging, I handed the woman behind the plexiglass a fifty and asked for two arm bands for the kids. They were all excited about riding the carnival rides, and I didn't feel like making twenty trips to the booth to buy tickets. The arm bands were expensive, but they could ride as much as their little demonic hearts wanted. Sounded like a good plan to me.

Leaving Karen to bitch about the prices of the rides, I took the bands back to the kids and smiled at Daniel, Brady, and Alana. They were meeting us here, but I didn't expect them to be that quick about it.

"Hey, Beautiful."

I dropped and kicked my leg out, not expecting anybody behind me. Grendel jumped and held up his hands. "Woah!"

"Shit. Sorry, Grendel." I rubbed the bridge of my nose.

Brady and Daniel were stifling laughter. Alana just looked amused. So did the rest of the crowd around us who had just watched me try to leg swipe a law enforcement officer.

"You okay?" Grendel asked, moved closer and let his hand slide over my back.

Turning and pressing my forehead against his chest, I shook my head. "No. It's been too quiet. My nerves are frayed." Looking up at him, I gave him a wan smile. And I hated to admit it, but just seeing him put me a little at ease. It had been a week since he had first let his interest be known. It took me three whole days to build up enough nerve to talk to Brady and Daniel about it. Another two, to ask Alana. Not one of them had batted an eyelash, all of them agreeing that there was more than enough of me to go around. If I didn't know better, I would have thought they were calling me fat.

"Here kids. Have fun." I handed the bracelets to Karl, and they took off without looking back.

Daniel looked around. "Did you ditch Karen?"

"I think she was asking for a manager, so I came back."

"Well, I've got a carnival to patrol. You kids have fun."

"Thanks, Grendel." I gave him a goodbye kiss, smiling because he *finally* accepted his nickname with no more bristling. "Meet me in the haunted house later." I grinned sultrily and pushed him away.

"Should we find the beer tent?"

"Leave it to Alana to be the voice of reason." I gave her a love tap on her ass and grabbed her hand, looking for the familiar red and white striped bastion of sanity.

"There it is," she said, and dragged me toward the middle of the festival.

Apparently, Bickering had a plethora of voices of reason. The beer tent was packed. "You two find a table, we'll grab the beers," I told the boys.

"Wish us luck," Daniel answered, doubt tinging his voice.

"Come on." I pulled Alana along, dodging the crowd until we made it to the end of the line.

"Think they'll find a spot before we get the beer?"

"Think we'll get the beer before we die of dehydration?"

"Good point."

Alana, being taller than me, stood behind me and wrapped her arms around me while we waited. And waited. We drew some curious looks, but I was used to that, even standing by myself.

"Does it bother you? I can let go."

"Does what bother me?" I pretended not to know what she was talking about.

"The stares."

"Nope. Not a bit."

She kissed my neck. "I think that's what I love most about you. You don't give two fucks about anything anybody might think about you."

"Nope. I don't care if they like me, I just want the ones that do to be happy."

"Well, I am."

"Good." I smiled at her over my shoulder. "Does the school care that you like women?"

She sighed. "Brentworth Academy has *many* faults, but that isn't one of them, thankfully. Do you think I would teach at the same school as my *brother* if more schools in the area felt the same way? Boston isn't the most...progressive of places."

"Ever think of doing something other than teaching?"

"Nope. Kind of in our blood. Mom and Dad were teachers."

"Ever thought of teaching college?"

She whistled. "I'd love to, but I'd have to go back to school and get my master's degree. Too much money."

I tossed around the idea of helping her in my head, but my funds were...not the best they'd been in a long time. Maybe once I sold the house in Florida, I could give her a hand. She must have seen my face running calculations. "Would you really want me in a locker full of twenty-year-old girls?"

"I trust you." To be honest, the thought hadn't even crossed my mind. I could feel her heart. I'd trust her in a dressing room full of strippers.

That earned me a full on, over the shoulder kiss.

When I pulled away, the people around us who had been politely making an effort not to stare, gave up and stared. "What?"

At least none of them were drunk enough to actually start anything. "We should probably get more than one beer apiece. I don't want to stand in this line again," Alana whispered in my ear.

There was a grinding of metal, a few screams of terror, and then everything was drowned out by the cacophony of panicking people. Everyone in the beer tent surged out onto the fairgrounds. Greedily, I rubbed my hands together and headed for the front of the line.

"Kara!" Daniel was motioning me toward the exit.

"What is it?"

"The Ferris wheel!"

I shrugged.

"Where are your kids?"

The last ride in the place they would have been on was the Ferris wheel. I actually enjoyed it. It was pleasant being that high without having to beat my wings to get there, but my kids always thought it was boring. They were more into the zippy rides that made you want to puke. "I doubt they're on that. Seriously."

My phone started ringing in my pocket.

I had one of those 'oh shit, something's wrong' moments as I pulled it out of my pocket and answered Rynnie's call. "Where are you?"

"Mom! We're on the Ferris wheel, and it's falling apart!"

Time stopped, or maybe it was just my heart, but I ran for the exit, plowing tables and chairs out of the way as I hit the plastic flap and smacked into the backs of a crowd of people watching in horror as the entire wheel tilted on its axis and the metal groaned like a thousand tortured souls.

I put the phone back to my ear. "Rynnie?"

"I'm here! Mom, it's going to fall!"

"Listen to me, sweetie. Jump. Grab your brother and jump. Call your wings, sweetie. I don't give a fuck if anybody sees. We can move."

"Mom! I can't. I'm too scared. I can't move, Mommy..." Her ability to form coherent words evaporated as she started babbling and crying. The wheel shifted a little bit more, only holding on by the one side still attached. Judging from the sound of shearing metal, it wasn't going to stay that way for long.

I wasn't the only one who had come to that conclusion, either. Everyone in the surrounding area and on the rides in the shadow of the Ferris wheel started screaming and running toward safety. I snarled that none of them were doing anything to help.

"Rynnie, I'm coming, baby. Hang on." Hitting the end call button, I stuffed it back into my pocket, took of my jacket, and handed it to Daniel.

"We're coming with you."

"Not if you can't fly," I answered, and put my hand on his shoulder.

"Kara, you'll be seen."

"Don't care. I'm sorry, but I have to save my kids."

He sighed and nodded as I ran toward the evacuating crowd. Weaving through the onslaught of people, I wasn't quite ready to call my wings and scare the shit out of everybody until I was absolutely certain there was no other way. When it took me two full minutes to make it to the wheel, I almost regretted my decision.

Scanning the lowest seats, I swore a streak of curses that would have burst a nun's ears into flames when I realized they were in one of the highest possible. "Rynnie!"

My voice boomed over the shrieks of the crowd. A moment later, Karl's head leaned over the side, and I saw the relief on his face. I was there, he knew he would be safe no matter what.

I ran for the cracked support brace and stopped short when a pair of very strong human arms encircled my waist. "Kara! Stop!"

"Grendel, you don't want to get in between me and my kids right now."

"I know, but if you start climbing up the side of that thing, the whole fucking thing could come down."

"And if I don't, it could anyway. Let me go. I'll fly up there then."

"And let hundreds of people see you?"

"You think I give a fuck?"

"No. And that worries me. Let's come up with a plan that doesn't get anybody killed or you outed."

"Like what? What the fuck could we possibly do?"

"I have three firetrucks on the way. My buddy at the docks is already on his way with some industrial cables. Two of those trucks are going to brace that thing up, and then the ladder truck will get those kids out. Be patient, please!"

I debated ignoring him and doing what I wanted anyway, but his plan sounded plausible. Crossing my arms, I stomped my foot and gave him a pouty, "Fine."

He heaved a sigh of relief and shook his head. "They're going to be fine, Kara."

"They better be, Grendel."

He put his hand on my shoulder, a brief gesture of comfort, and then started shouting for everybody to clear out of the way. Nobody moved. They had gathered in a Ferris wheel-shaped semicircle some distance away, staring in rapt horror and fascination. Several police cars parted the sea of people, and then Grendel had them push them back and to make a road for the fire engines to get through.

Daniel ran up to me and handed me my phone. "It's Karl."

"Hey, kiddo. How you holding up?"

"Not so good. Rynnie's a mess. What's going on?"

"They're bringing in some big ass firetrucks to pull the wheel the other way while they send up a ladder truck."

"Should we try climbing down?"

"Do you think your sister can?"

There was a moment of silence. "No."

"Then just stay where you are and don't move."

"Tell that to everybody else. They're flailing around."

"Make them stop, Baby."

"They're kids, Mom. It ain't gonna happen."

"Hang on. Stay on the line." I walked over to Grendel, orchestrating the entire operation. When he saw my face, he stopped talking.

"What?"

"Talking to Karl. The kids in the other cars are panicking. You might want to put somebody on a blowhorn and reassure them and tell them to stop flailing around."

He nodded to one of his officers, who ran to the trunk of his car and pulled out a shiny new megaphone. Tuning it on, he pulled the trigger twice and nodded when it squelched loudly. The cop ran over to me and tried to give it to me.

"Oh, hell no. I'm not the most reassuring of people. You do it."

He looked at the lieutenant. Grendel rolled his eyes, took it and pointed it up at the kids stuck on the ride. "Everybody!" The megaphone gave a squeal of feedback, and he tried again a little softer. "Everybody! Kids. I need you to sit very still, okay? Shaking and screaming isn't the best thing to be doing right now. We have some firetrucks coming to get you guys. Everything is going to be fine, but I *really* need you to move as little as possible."

That just caused the screaming to get louder.

I put the phone to my ear. "Karl?"

"That was reassuring. Now they're scrambling over the edges."

He wasn't lying, either. It looked like a third of them thought climbing down two-hundred feet was a better idea. I growled and grabbed the blowhorn from Grendel. "Stop!"

They stopped.

"Sit back down and stay there. Anybody who moves is going to end up a tomato splat on the fucking pavement! Sit your asses down, be still, and we will rescue you in a minute, do you understand?"

There were a few muffled yesses and then silence.

Grendel chuckled as I handed him back the megaphone. "Effective."

All I could do was shrug.

The fire engines showed up and weaved slowly through the part in the crowd. The lieutenant, in conjunction with the very scared looking carnival workers, cleared a path behind the Ferris wheel and started attaching the inch-thick cables that had shown up right after. One flaw in the plan was how to hook them to the center struts almost a hundred feet in the air.

The ladder could go that high, but the weight of the cable was too much for it, and they couldn't brace the ladder against the already unstable ride and pull it up with a winch, either.

"Fuck." Grendel was pissed his plan hadn't worked. I didn't point out that the ladder wouldn't be tall enough to get the kids out of the higher cars, anyway.

"Plan B?"

"Not yet. We'll call you Plan C."

"What's Plan B then?"

"Helicopters."

"Oh, for fuck's sake, Josh. That will blow the whole damn thing over."

"Any ideas?"

"Yes. Let me go the fuck up there and rescue my damn kids."

"What about the others?"

For a moment, I almost said, "I don't give a fuck." Almost. But then I thought about how I would feel if somebody else left my kids to die. I gagged at the emotion that swelled up inside me. "I'll get them down, too." I gulped and fought down the nausea.

He growled in frustration. "There's got to be a way."

"Give me a cable."

"What?"

"Attach one as high as the ladder can go. Then bring it back down, and I'll go up with the second one. When it can't go any higher, I'll climb up the rest of the way."

"They have to be the same height, or it won't work."

"Then send me up for both."

"You won't be able to go any higher, Kara. We're talking thousands of pounds."

"Then we need a thinner cable."

"Anything smaller will snap."

The Ferris wheel groaned behind us. We were out of time. "Grendel. I'm sorry," I said and ran toward it.

"Kara! No!"

We were on the side of the Ferris wheel with the fire trucks. The nearest person, beside the firemen and police, were over a hundred feet away. Even so, there was no way I was going to get away with this without being seen. Especially by the kids and few adults who happened to be on the ride. But we were out of time. I just hoped I could get everyone off before it came crashing down.

I leaped into the air and let my wings burst forth with the usual crackle of bone and the snap of flesh as I flapped down, forcing myself up into the air. Flying up the center column, I didn't stop until I was at the top. Karl and Rynnie

265

stared at me in wonder. As in wondering what the fuck I was doing.

"Mom? What are you doing?"

"Plan C. Come on," I said, and outstretched my arms.

"Take Ryn. You can't carry us both."

"The fuck I can't. Give me your damn hand, Karl."

One wonderful thing about my children was that they listened. Always. Not once in their lives had they been told to, or not to, do something and done it. They both leaned over the edge, and I sighed in relief as I yanked them from the car and slowed the beat of my wings, dangling them beneath me until their feet were on the hard-packed earth below.

They ran toward the firetrucks, but I didn't stop to watch. I didn't want to see the fear on the faces of the emergency workers. Again, I floated up to the highest cars. A blonde teenager was huddled with her younger brother, fear evident on their faces as I hovered in the air beside them.

"Obviously, I'm not here to hurt you. Do you want me to save you?"

They honestly thought about it for a moment before the older one nodded and the little brother reached out for my hand. Again, I lowered them gently to the earth. This time, two of the firemen were waiting with blankets while I launched myself up for the next round. The two teen boys trusted me more than the sister and brother, but I was hot, even though I had wings. Halfway down, we were met by the ladder. Firemen were waiting for me to deliver them, halving the distance I had to travel. One of them even nodded and smiled as I deposited my payload.

When the top was clear, we split up. The ladder went one way while I went the other. We worked in tandem, pulling the kids and adults from the car. Not one of them said anything about my wings or seemed afraid. Probably because the metal of the Ferris wheel was almost in a constant state of rumbling as it slowly tilted farther and farther. At the midpoint of our evacuations, it started wobbling slowly as it started to give way more and more with every sway. We only had a few cars left, but I already knew we weren't going to be in time.

"Climb!" I shouted to the kids in the lower cars as I dropped to the ground and pulled my wings back inside myself. Diving through the metal framing, I emerged from the other side and pushed against the center strut. The wobbling slowed but didn't stop. There was no way in hell I was going to keep it from falling. Not even with all my demonic strength.

Then Karl appeared next to me. And Ryn on the other side. Then Grendel, a few cops, and all the firemen. Then the crowd broke and people started showing up by the dozens. Everywhere there was a place to hold, hands appeared and started pushing against the weight of several tons of steel reaching hundreds of feet into the night sky.

Surprisingly it was enough for the ladder truck to get the rest of the kids to safety. When they were finished, they yelled, "Clear!"

Slowly, hands started letting go as people ran to the sides of the ride.

"Go," I told my kids. For the first fucking time in their lives, they didn't listen.

That's when I noticed the claws and the rippled flesh of demonic skin on their forearms. *Both* of them. Karl was shifting just like his sister. I smiled at Karl, turned to Ryn, and gave her one, too. The braces on the corner of the ride snapped, and the wheel wobbled.

"Run!" They let go and turned to run, but I reached out and grabbed their collars, pushing them through the ride to the other side. I started to go when the platform beneath my feet snapped and dropped out from beneath me. Hanging on to the strut, I rode it backward as the wheel toppled over me, pushing me backward to the ground.

Scrambling around the steel girder I stared in horror as something became very clear. The metal in my hands was rippled and blue. *Somebody* had applied a great amount of heat to it. That's what caused it to break.

"Fuck," I said as I was ripped sideways and smashed into the ground.

The crash that followed seemed to last for hours. Or at least until I lost consciousness.

Chapter 24

The familiar groan of steel rang in my ears like Karen's voice at six in the morning before coffee. I smiled at the sound. It meant I hadn't been ground into demon puree.

My eyes were sealed shut with blood. When I managed to pry them open, the bright sun nearly blinded me. I tried concentrating on the muffled voices around me, but the pain in my everything became the new center of my universe.

The sound of blowtorches, compressors, and the jaws of life lulled me back to sleep. I kept waking and catching flashes of what was happening around me. People were talking to me, asking me questions, but I couldn't understand what they were saying. When I started to finally come to, I realized it wasn't the sun that had blinded me, it was the work lights centered over my crushed body.

"Kara! Mrs. Dell, can you hear me?"

"Yes. Stop fucking shouting. My head hurts."

The EMT chuckled. "I'd ask how you were doing, but it's pretty obvious." He leaned a little closer. "If it wasn't for the wings, I'd be wondering how you were alive. Don't worry, we'll get you out of here."

I nodded and closed my eyes, returning my head to my steel pillow that felt like the most wonderful thing in the world at that moment. "Are my kids okay?"

"Yep. Everybody is. Thanks to you."

"For what?"

"Being the hero we needed."

That was the last thing I wanted, but it sounded better than being set on fire or crucified. Or doused with holy water. It didn't do anything, but it was usually pretty gross. They left that shit sitting out *forever*. People dipping their fingers in it. Yuck.

My diamond plate blanket was finally cut away, and several girders shifted under the release of pressure. The stabbing pain in my stomach got infinitely worse, and I screeched in pain. Two of the EMTs jumped down into my hole and supported my weight. It alleviated *some* of the pain, but not all. I felt like a shish kabob. Lifting my head, I saw why. One of the smaller support rails had gone through my left side and was sticking out my right side. I couldn't heal until I got it out.

Everything else was starting to snap back into place. Even the crushed bones in my legs and pelvis were reknitting themselves. "Pull it out."

"We can't. You're impaled on it, and we can't get to the bottom of it. We're going to have to cut it and then pull you off. Once we do, you're going to lose a lot of blood and probably go back into shock. You stay with me, okay?"

"Just fucking cut it and pull me off. My body will fix the rest."

He started to say something else but stopped. "You serious?"

"Yes."

"When this is all over, I would *love* to have a very long talk with you." He chuckled and motioned behind me. "This is Jimmy. He's going to cut you free with the jaws of life."

"Hi, Jimmy." I gave a little wave without opening my eyes.

"Seriously?"

"Don't worry. She's a tough cookie. Cut her free."

"Yeah, Jimmy. Get me off this bitch."

The compressor off in the distance whined as my skewer rattled as the jaws clamped down on it. Several noises later, there was a snapping sound as the blade bit

270

through, and then the rail fell to the side. My EMT caught it before it fell and tossed it off to the side. "Come on. Let's lift her off."

"What's your name?"

"Cliff."

"Thanks, Cliff."

He got his hands under my shoulder and cradled my head in the crook of his arm as Jimmy grabbed my hip and knee. "Hey, Kara?"

"Yes?"

"This is gonna fucking hurt."

"Yep."

"One, two," and before he could say three, they yanked me off the metal spike. The scream that followed almost made them drop me. As soon as I was free, they set me down gently on the diamond plate floor.

"You weren't fucking kidding."

Cliff pressed several gauze towels over the entrance wound and handed one to Jimmy. "Guys, bring the stretcher over," he hollered behind me.

"Don't bother. Just give me a few minutes."

He gripped my wrist, felt my pulse, and gave up trying to count. My heart was going like a Hitachi on pummel mode, pumping all that wonderful demon blood to all the parts that needed it. I could feel my flesh stitching itself back together under their hands. "Ahhh. That's the good stuff."

"What is?" Cliff looked at me strangely.

"Healing. Nothing feels better. Well, some things do, but we won't get into that here."

He just shook his head. "Grab some water out of the kit behind you, Jim."

A squeeze bottle with an angled nozzle passed over me. Cliff pulled the gauze away, and squirted some on my wound, washing the blood and gore away. "Jesus fucking Christ."

"What?"

"It's almost healed."

"Thank fuck. I'll stick to the holes I have, thank you."

He handed the bottle to Jimmy. Cool wetness splashed my other side, and Jimmy backed up a few feet. "What is she?"

Cliff looked down at me. "What are you?"

"You'll sleep better if you don't know."

He looked back up at Jimmy. "A hero."

Jimmy nodded and moved back to my side. "Thirsty?"

"Is the beer tent still open?"

He looked at the water bottle in his hand, got up, and walked away.

"I'll take that as a no."

"It's four in the morning, Kara. It took us that long to clear the rubble."

"Did somebody take my kids home?"

He laughed and pointed off to the side of the wreckage. There, behind the barrier, was my family. Ryn and Karl were surrounded by Brady, Daniel, and Alana. On this side, sitting on the barrier was Grendel, rubbing the bridge of his nose. It took every ounce of strength I had, but I lifted my arm and waved. I could hear their collective sigh over the sound of the rescue machinery.

"You're all closed up. Come on, let's get you to the hospital."

"Fuck that. I don't want to end up dissected in a lab. It's going to be hard enough to pack my shit and move away before the tabloids show up."

He laughed.

"It's not funny. I like it here."

"Good. Because if you move, the people of this town will find your skinny ass and drag you back."

"Huh?"

"You can thank Lieutenant Grindel and the chief."

"The chief of what?"

"His boss. The Chief of Bickering PD. You were already a hero to the guys in blue. As soon as the dust settled and we began rescue operations when your kids swore up and down that you were still alive, he cordoned

272

off the area, kept everybody here, and gave a speech about how lucky they were to have such a special person living in their city."

"How'd that go?"

"About as well as you would expect. People were still doubtful until all those kids you rescued told their parents about the angel that had pulled them from the ride."

I gulped and then made a face, the taste of blood still prevalent. "Ugh. Can I have some water?" Then a squirt bottle of beer appeared above my head. "Jimmy, you're my fucking hero." I opened my mouth, and he squirted a heavy dose of hop-flavored painkiller into it. "Thanks."

"You're welcome." He grinned and set the bottle next to my head.

"One last thing?"

"What?" Cliff gave me a concerned look.

"Would you help me stand the fuck up? My ass is frozen."

They chuckled and each took an arm, lifting me agonizingly slowly to make sure I was, in fact, well enough to stand up.

Thankfully, I didn't have to support my own weight. Grendel, Brady, and Daniel were there before I even straightened up. Gently, they pushed the EMTs out of the way and held me for a moment before wrapping me in the biggest hug. When they pulled away and started walking me toward the kids, someone in the crowd started clapping. Then another. Before I got to the barricade, the gathered audience was full-out cheering and screaming my name.

"Demon blushes are pretty fucking cute," Grendel whispered in my ear. "Come on. Let's get you home."

I leaned against him as we walked to his police car, the crowd parting around us. I wanted to crawl in a hole and die. I'd managed to live sixty years without anybody *finding out* my secret. Now, the whole town knew. They seemed okay with it, but that was heat of the moment. It was only a matter of time before Uncle Sam or the

Enquirer showed up at my door. It would be a cold day in hell before I let that happen.

There was just one more thing I needed to do before we left.

Find the son of a dickwad that could melt steel and put them in a coroner's cooler.

∞ ∞ ∞

The infamous doorbell scene in Christmas Vacation. Everybody in the house is off preparing for the big holiday, and the doorbell goes off. It echoes loudly through the house, slowing with each reverberation as the impending sense of doom washes over each member of the family. Slowly, the door opens, and the parents are standing there just before rolling into the house like a tidal wave of annoyance. I loved that scene.

Until it happened to me.

I was lying in bed, still encased in my comforter cocoon, when the *ding dong* snapped me out of my slumber. Crawling, literally, out of bed, I headed down the stairs slowly. The bell chimed four more times as I fearfully reached for the door.

Thankfully, it was just Karen, but the tidal wave of annoyance was no joke.

Leaving the door open, she backed me all the way into the kitchen as I crested the wave of her litany of questions, tirades, and speculations.

"Karen!"

"What?"

"Deep breaths. Coffee?"

"Yes, please." She sighed, and sat down at the kitchen counter, resting her head on her hand as she drew little circles over the granite with the tip of her finger. "Why didn't you tell me?"

It was my turn to sigh as I popped a pod into the maker and hit the flashing brew button. "How do you think you would have reacted, Karen?"

She thought about it for a moment. "I would have understood and thought nothing of it."

"Bullshit."

"I'm serious, Kara! I've known you for over a month now. We've shopped at Target together! We're practically *sisters*."

"Karen, you either would have thought I was crazy and tried to have me committed, or you would have believed me and told everybody and their mother I wasn't human."

"Is that what you think?"

I cocked an eyebrow at her over my shoulder.

"Well, maybe. But I wouldn't have tried to have you committed. I would have just *told* everybody you were crazy."

I sat her mug down in front of her. She got up and grabbed the milk and sugar on her own. Which was good, because I wasn't fucking getting it. I needed caffeine. She was lucky I surrendered the first cup to her. "What the fuck time is it anyway?"

"Six."

Sighing once again, I rubbed my forehead and debated between the butcher block of knives or the bamboo skewers in the drawer beside the fridge to kill her with. "Karen. It's fucking Sunday. Why are you in my house before noon?"

"Because I couldn't stand it anymore. I had to have some answers."

Growling, I waited for my coffee to sputter before gutting her. Taking a sip, I counted down backward from twenty before I turned around and swallowed.

She was sitting there with doe-like eyes, and I could see the thirty-seven thousand questions in her eyes. She opened her mouth to speak, but I held up my finger to silence her. Then I guzzled my entire mug of coffee and turned around to make another. When it was brewing, then and only then, did I turn around and motion for her to continue.

"I guess you not being human explains why you can guzzle hot coffee like it's iced tea."

"Yep."

"So?"

"So what?"

"So, what are you?"

"How much did you see last night?"

"The whole thing. My kids were on the Ferris wheel, too."

"Really? I didn't see them."

"They were toward the bottom. The firemen pulled them off with the ladder truck while you held the damn thing up."

I nodded and took my second cup out of the machine, turned around, and let my wings come out. She stared in wide-eyed amazement. "What do you think I am?"

"D-d-d-demon…"

I didn't blame her for the reaction. Not too many mythological beings had wings like a bat, and I sure as shit wasn't no fucking gargoyle. Those guys were boring, but surprisingly good in bed. They just needed to loosen up. "You guessed it. Good. Now I don't have to tell you."

"I don't get it. Kara, you're a *good* person. How can you be a demon?"

"Not everything under heaven and earth is as you believe, Karen. There are decent, law-abiding demons. I wouldn't go so far as to say *good*, but not 'slaughter your whole family and munch on your bones' bad, either."

She gulped. And then gulped her coffee, burned her tongue, sputtered, and made the most Karen face I'd ever seen. "Do some demons actually eat *people?*"

"Some."

"Do you…eat people?"

I shook my head. "I'm a succubus. I just fuck 'em."

A little tiny Christmas light went off in her head. She smiled, her eyes got wide, and she pointed a finger at me. "That explains *everything!*"

"What does?" I narrowed my eyes in confusion.

276

"Why you're so hot, why you have so many boyfriends and a girlfriend. Why all the guys absolutely fucking adore you when they see you. Why everybody drools over you. That explains everything!" She was actually ecstatic she had deduced that all on her own. I thought it was pretty self-explanatory when I said that I was a succubus.

"Yep."

"Oh, thank God." She blushed furiously. "Is it okay if I say that?"

"What? God?"

She nodded reverently. Which was hilarious because she was an official member of the congregation of the First Church of Target. "Yes."

"Yes. I just said it, too. Though I tend to think of him or her more as the Creator instead of God. But what do I know? I'm just a demon."

She visibly relaxed after that. "One last question?"

I nodded.

"Are we still friends?"

I set my coffee down and hugged her. She didn't pull away, either. "Yes, Karen. We're still friends if you wanna be."

"Oh, thank Go-goodness."

Pulling away, I put my fingers under her chin and lifted her head. "But if you ever ring my doorbell on a Sunday before noon again, I'll kill you."

Chapter 25

I set another mug down on the counter in front of Grendel. At least he had the decency to wait until eight to show up at my door. I still wanted to dance in his entrails, but not as much. "So, what brings you to my neighborhood on your day off in uniform?"

"We have a problem."

"No. We have two problems. What's yours?"

"Somebody called the newspaper claiming a demon caused the Ferris wheel to break last night."

"They did."

"Excuse me?"

I grabbed my fifth cup of coffee and stood on the other side of the counter from him. "I noticed just as the whole fucking thing came crashing down on my head last night. Somebody melted the support. There's only one thing on God's green earth that could have done that."

"A demon?"

"Yep."

"So, you're saying there's another one in town?"

I nodded and sipped, while my heart sang that he hadn't jumped to conclusions and assumed that I had done it.

He blew out the breath he'd been holding and stared at the mug in his hand. "Fuck."

"Maybe not. They might not be a succubus. There are hundreds of different kinds of demons."

It took him a moment to understand my joke. He didn't laugh. "Think the demon and the Bickering Bandit are one and the same?"

"I know they are. I was attacked, and I thought it was a vampire at first."

"But now you think it's a demon?"

"I know it is. Consider it a fact."

He sighed and sipped some more coffee, still looking at nothing and thinking. "So, how do we find them?"

"We don't. They find us."

"What do you mean?"

"I mean a trap."

"Will it work?"

"It had better. I'm running out of time."

He frowned. "What do you mean by that?"

No more lies. "Josh, everybody who was at the Fall Festival knows I'm a demon. The newspaper printed an article that said a lot of peoples' kids almost died last night because of a demon. How long do you honestly think it will be before they come knocking on my door with pitchforks and torches?" I blew out at the absurdity of it.

He grinned at me.

"What?"

"One, you called me Josh."

"That's what you're all excited about?"

He shook his head. "Two, I never said they printed the article."

"What?"

His grin turned into shit-eating epic proportions. "I have a friend at the paper. Told them to give me a heads up if anything demon related came across their desk. No worries on that front."

"You sneaky bastard." I grinned back at him.

"I think that deserves a kiss, don't you?"

"Sure. But I get to pick where that kiss goes."

"Deal."

Sunday morning dick kisses and a bellyful of lust were way better than Karens.

∞ ∞ ∞

"Are you sure this is going to work?" I whispered the words, trusting that the ear mic would pick it up. Now if Grendel could hear it over the chattering of my teeth, it would have been a fucking miracle.

"Honestly? No. I'm not sure. But the bandit seems to have a hard-on for you. So, you get to be the bait."

"Lucky fucking me."

"Does he?" Daniel sounded a little unsure.

"Does he what?" Josh's voice crackled in my ear.

"Have a hard-on for Kara. She was only physically attacked once. Might have been random. Her house had attempted burglary. Are we sure it was the bandit? Could have been somebody completely different."

"What about the Ferris wheel with her kids on it?"

"There were a lot of kids on that Ferris wheel. Maybe that was just a coincidence, too?" I saw where Daniel was going with his thread of logic, and I hated to admit it, but it made sense. Maybe I was outside, walking through the frigid Bostonian cold for nothing.

"But why would they call in to the newspaper that a demon attacked the carnival, if they weren't trying to pin it on Kara?" Grendel interjected his own logic. Which was just as sound.

"Well, let's stick to the plan and find out," I answered the both of them.

Daniel and I were using a date as bait. Brady had wanted to come, but he was stuck coaching a night game in Salem. Alana, too. So, the two of us were walking the mile to the closest restaurant with Grendel keeping an eye on us with binoculars.

"You two make good bait. If I were a demon, I'd eat you."

I chuckled. "You already did. This morning." A stifled groan escaped Daniel's lips. Reaching down, I rubbed the front of his trousers and smiled. "You're having happy thoughts now, aren't you," I whispered in his ear.

"Yes," Grendel replied, thinking the question was for him.

I was about to clarify when I felt something slip from the shadows behind us. "Fish on," I called softly into the mic.

"I don't see anything," Grendel replied.

"Switch to thermals."

"What the fuck are you talking about? The department can't afford shit like that."

"My tax dollars, not hard at work." I sighed and let Daniel get a half-step ahead of me.

"Just saw a flash of red. Looks like eyes," Grendel chimed in. "Big sucker. You sure silver will work?"

The department couldn't afford thermal imaging *or* silver bullets. Luckily, Grendel was all into guns n' ammo and had all the shit to make his own. He said it saved money going to the range, I think he just enjoyed it. So, I donated half my jewelry to a worthy cause and a warning that if he accidentally shot me, no more nookie.

Silver wouldn't kill a demon like it would a werewolf, but it fucking hurt, and the wound healed slow. Shoot the demon enough, and they would be in enough pain to give you the chance to cut their head off. Which *did* work on demons. I gave the bullets to Grendel and took my silver dagger out of storage. It was in a sheath on my back. It was either that or my claws, and getting flesh out from under my nails was a bitch.

"How close?"

"Thirty yards or so," he replied.

I relaxed a little. It still wasn't close enough to draw. If I went too early, the bandit would probably just run if it saw the gleam of silver. I would have. Saying it fucking hurt wasn't a joke. "Let me know when it gets less than ten."

"You're assuming I have eyes on it. I just see flashes of red. Fuck! Five!"

I pushed Daniel forward with my left hand, drew the blade with my right, and swung. On the biggest fucking hell hound I'd ever seen in my life. "Run!"

"What?" They both shouted in my ear.

"Run! Hell hound! *Not* the bandit!" Throwing the knife at the thing's head, I scooped Daniel up and ran.

Hearing the clank as it batted the blade with its massive horned head, I yelped when I heard it pound the earth right behind us in pursuit. There was a squeal of tires and a crack of thunder as Grendel shot the thing from the car as he pulled alongside us. "Get in!"

"What part of fucking run didn't you understand?"

"You didn't say which way, and driving is faster."

"Yes, but hell hounds can't *fly*." I jumped into the air and batted my wings. "Now get going!"

I heard the engine roar to life as he gunned it. Giving up some altitude, I shook my ass at the demon doggy about thirty feet in the air. "Who's an evil puppy?" I taunted it, trying to keep its focus on me instead of the lieutenant. Cars were fast. Hellhounds were faster. Maybe not on the highway, but through residential neighborhoods, definitely.

I breathed a sigh of relief when he turned off on one of the side roads and Fido followed me.

"What do we do?" Grendel's voice crackled a bit more with the distance between us.

"Keep running and flying until we figure out what to do."

"What do we do?" He reiterated.

"I don't fucking know. Hell hounds are damn near impossible to kill."

"Fire?"

"That would be like trying to burn a kitty with a sunbeam. He might curl up and take a nap, and *then* eat us when he woke up."

"Freeze it?"

"In October?"

"Ice rink?"

Nodding appreciatively, I answered. "That might work. Won't hurt it, but that might slow him down a bit. How far?"

"Two miles. Know where the mall is?"

"Concord?"

"Yep."

"Yes."

"Okay, I'll meet you there."

"Great, but where's the ice rink?"

"In the mall."

"Fucking yuppies. Wait, the mall is still open!"

"Not on Sunday. They close at six."

The lieutenant skidded to a stop just as we flew over the entrance to the mall parking lot. The hell hound was literally right on my tail. "Grendel, I don't care how you do it, but get on the fucking roof of the mall. Let me know when you're there."

"Okay, but why?"

"We're gonna trade."

"What?"

"I give you Daniel, you give me your gun."

"Do you know how to shoot?"

"I'll figger it out. Do it. Let me know when you're there."

One thing I had noticed about the Concord mall was how beautifully it was illuminated during the day with all of the skylights lining the place. I didn't notice the fucking ice rink, but I knew there were plenty of skylights.

To give the lieutenant time to get on the roof, I started circling the lot, dipping low enough to keep the hell hound interested. Not that he would have lost interest, but I just wanted to make him think he had a chance. They weren't much different from dogs in the intelligence department, but once they had the scent of their intended target, they didn't stop until the remnants of that target were nestled safely in its belly.

If I needed any further proof that the bandit was a demon, the hell hound was it. Like dogs, they bonded with their owners for life and would do anything—and I mean kill anything—they were told to by their masters. The other demon wanted me dead in a bad way and wasn't afraid to bring in a lot of help.

On my third pass around the mall parking lot, I caught sight of Grendel climbing an access ladder on the south wall. "'Bout time."

"What?"

"Nothing. Let me know when you're ready."

"You're sure it's going to follow you and not us?"

"It got my scent somehow. When it followed us instead of you, I was certain. Until I'm dead, you could strap grenades to its ballsack, and it wouldn't give a shit."

"If the ice rink doesn't work, we'll try that next. I'm here."

I landed on the roof as soon as I saw where Grendel was hiding. Unceremoniously, I dumped Daniel next to him, grabbed the gun, and ran to the center of the roof to the closest sky light. The hell hound made it on the roof in one leap, scrabbling its paws over the ledge. Taking one look at me, it growled and stepped forward and stopped, sniffing the air around it.

Its focus turned from me to Grendel, but that didn't make any sense...

"Daniel!" I screamed his name and took after the already bolting hell hound, wings pushing me along the rooftop. Grendel, weaponless, stepped in front of the confused Daniel and held out his arms, bracing for the impact he probably wouldn't even have time to feel.

I aimed the gun, sighted down the barrel, and shot it in the fucking butthole just as it was leaping to attack.

The massive demon dog's hindquarters curled beneath it, the pain of silver ammo splitting its sphincter too much for it to ignore. It yelped and bleated as the wound sizzled. I twitched as my butthole puckered in sympathy. Landing next to it, I unloaded the entire clip in the thing's forehead. It stopped moving for a moment and then started shaking.

"Is it dead?"

"No. And it's going to be really fucking pissed when it wakes up."

"How do we kill it?"

"Cut off its head, or kill its master and send it back to Hell. Come on. We're fresh out of chainsaws, and I want miles between us before this fucker comes to."

"Where do we go?" Daniel didn't sound half as worried as he should have. If he had ever seen a hell hound gnawing on the torso of a Bane demon, he would have. Not a pretty sight.

"We go to an airport. You get on a plane. You go to the fucking Bahamas or some shit until this all goes away one way or another."

"Are you serous right now, Kara? I'm not going *anywhere.*"

"Yes. You are. Come on." I picked him off the ground and threw him over my shoulder. Grendel, I just encircled around the waist. I pushed us up into the air and over the edge of the roof until we landed by the cop car. Pushing Daniel into the back, I shut the door as he pounded helplessly against the prisoner-proof glass.

He was still yelling when I got rid of my wings and slipped into the passenger seat. "I'm not fucking going, Kara."

"Yes. You are. You don't understand, Daniel. That thing is a literal killing, fucking, and eating machine. The other demon gave your scent to it and told it to kill you. It won't stop until you're kibble. You have to go someplace where it can't smell you. Do you have any relatives in California or anything?"

The lieutenant got in the driver's seat and put the still running car into drive, pulling away from the mall with a squeal of tires.

"No."

"Then go to my place in Florida. I'll buy your ticket. Texting you my address, now." I pulled out my phone and did just that. Then I texted him the door code to get in. "Go there and hide. I'll call you when it's safe to come back."

"I don't see why you can't keep me safe."

I turned around and looked at him through the sheet of plexiglass. Putting my hand on it, I met his eyes. "Because

I *can't*. I just got lucky and bought us a little bit of time. Get on the first plane. You need to stay alive."

"Why?"

"Because I'd take a bullet for you." I let my hand slide slowly down the glass. Just before I pulled it away, he reached out and pressed his hand against mine.

"Fine. Because I'd take a bullet for you, too, I'll do it."

"Thank you." A real tear formed in the corner of my eye and he smiled.

"Straight to Logan?" Grendel swerved around a corner.

"And no stopping for donuts."

Chapter 26

One nice thing about travelling by cop car was the good parking. Grendel stopped at the curb right outside the ticket counter and slammed the car into park, leaving the lights flashing.

"Come on," he said impatiently, heading for the automatic glass double doors.

"Are you sure about this?" Daniel looked utterly dejected.

"Positive. If you're not safe, I won't be able to fight, think, or anything."

That made him smile. "Fine." He sighed and headed for the doors, reaching behind him to take my hand. "I'd just love to know how the son of a bitch got my scent to begin with."

"What did you say?"

"The bandit. I'd love to know how he got my scent."

"That's a good fucking question, Daniel." I stopped and stared at him. "Did you see anybody today? I don't mean just see, interact. If it didn't happen today, the scent probably wouldn't be strong enough to track."

"Samantha came by to pick up a check. She might be the devil, but she's no demon." He paused to think while I thought about the possibilities of Samantha actually being a demon. It *was* possible, but highly unlikely. She wasn't aging well, and demons didn't do that. It had to be somebody youthful in appearance and very healthy. Plus, if she were a demon, she wouldn't have run off with her personal trainer. And as far as I knew, succubae were the only demons *remotely* interested in long term relationships, and even then, very seldom. "Oh, and the Donaldsons stopped by to bitch about the grass."

"Definitely not them. *Nobody* else?"

"Oh! And Marissa stopped by this morning to pick up some camping gear I'd been promising to lend her for her trip next weekend."

"Marissa. Stopped by your house?"

He nodded.

"The Bitch of Bickering?"

He nodded again, chuckling.

Everything clicked into place. Unfortunately, it was in the pit of my stomach.

"Daniel?"

"Yes?"

"Where do you keep your camping gear?"

"In the garage."

"Do you keep…say laundry out there?"

"Yes. The utility rooms are kind of small with those massive washer and dryers. I have bins for sorting just inside the door to the garage…" He finally understood where my line of questioning was going. And what it meant. Marissa was the bandit… She had gotten Daniel's scent from his laundry basket.

"What?" Grendel was still a little bit concerned over what we were worrying about.

"She's not sure she can kill me, so she's going after everyone I care about. She already tried to kill my kids. Now Daniel. Oh, shit…"

"What?"

"Brady and Alana… My kids… The soccer game!"

The three of us ran back to the police car, got in, and Josh punched it. "Where are we going?"

"Soccer field in Salem!"

"Can you narrow it down a bit?" He hit the siren and started weaving through the exiting traffic. Luckily it was Sunday, and the airport was *kind* of slow. The highway, too. Otherwise, it would have been bumper to bumper for thirty miles.

"No, but I can find out. Karen is there."

I started frantically texting her on my phone, asking which field they were at, and if everything was okay.

Fine. We're at McGrath Park? Why?

Just wondering. On my way. Stay away from Marissa. Tell the kids and the coaches, too. She's wacko and has a gun. Cops on the way so don't call them, either. Don't want her to get spooked and start shooting.

I probably should have just texted her the truth.

I spoke too soon about the traffic. At the edge of the city proper, there was an accident and it was bumper to bumper. Grendel drove off the shoulder, lights flashing and siren wailing until we were past the overturned semi. The rest of the ride, people actually got out of the way, and he had to have hit the one-thirty mile-an-hour mark.

There was nobody in the parking lot. A shit ton of cars, but no people, which probably was a good thing, or Grendel might have mowed them down with as fast as he was going when he stopped in front of the concession stand. Shutting off the lights and siren, we piled out of the car and headed toward the field.

"You want the gun?"

I blinked in surprise. "Uh, you hang on to it. If moms start shooting people at soccer games, things can only go downhill from there."

"Your call. This is your show."

Again, he surprised me.

"I'll take the gun," Daniel said eagerly.

"You're staying in the car."

"What if she's in the parking lot?"

"Good point. Lock yourself in the men's restroom." I implored him with my eyes.

"Well, I guess it's better than Florida." He chuckled and headed toward the stone restrooms.

"Or a porta potty!"

"That was you?" Grendel just shook his head.

"Heard about that one, huh?"

"She filed a police report."

"Surprised she didn't say my name."

"She did. I just didn't think you'd stoop that low."

"Uh...demon? Hello."

"I didn't know at the time."

"Come on. Let's get this over with."

He put his hand on the weapon in his holster but didn't draw it. Probably a good idea. Panicked parents would be a hassle to deal with at the same time as a demon. Hopefully, she was waiting until after the game to try and eat my boyfriend and girlfriend. Possibly my kids. "I get that she needed the laundry for Daniel's scent, but if she's here, why did she need Brady and Alana's?"

"The truth is she doesn't if *she* attacks outright. But I'm willing to bet Fido was supposed to make quick work of Daniel, put a hurting on me, and then meet her here to eat the coaches. Then she could stand there, enjoy the show, and act all heartbroken after the fact."

"So, we have to watch out for Fido, too?"

"Yep. Hopefully, we can kill her quick enough that Fido goes back to Hell without much fuss. No master, no ties to the human realm."

We emerged between the concession stand and the aluminum bleachers. I was kind of pissed. Their field was *way* nicer than ours, and we had the better neighborhood. "How come we don't get bleachers?"

"You think the people in Bickering want to put their asses on cold metal bleachers when they can use squishy lawn chairs?"

"Good point."

"There's Karen." Grendel pointed to the closest set of bleachers, halfway up. She was glancing around nervously and finally spotted us before whispering something to Rick and pushing her way through the row of spectators and bouncing down the stairs.

"What took you so long?"

"Traffic. Have you seen her?"

"No."

"Is the game almost over?"

"They both are. The girls are playing on the back field."

"Did you see her over there?"

"No."

I narrowed my eyes at Karen. "Did you go over there and look?"

"Yes!"

"Then where the hell is she?"

The ref blew the whistle, and just like that, half the parents stood and started cheering. "That's it. The game's over. We won." Karen started clapping excitedly.

"Good. Get your kids and go home." I leaned in closer to Karen and whispered, "She's not a crazy with a gun, she's a demon. The *bad* kind."

"Oh. Oooh." Her eyes widened, and her already pale flesh whitened even more.

"Keep it together. Go. I'll come see you when it's over."

"Rick! It's time to go. Get the kids." Her shrill voice probably could have been heard over the crowd in the back field.

Shaking my head and rubbing my ears, I smiled and nodded at her.

"Mom?"

Ryn was standing behind me, confused. "Hey, sweetie. Is your game over already?"

"Yeah. We finished first. I was just coming to find Karen, since she's our ride home."

I *wanted* to send her home with Karen. But I also wanted her to be safe. With the bitch on the loose, the safest place was with me. For all I knew, Marissa was waiting back at Daniel's. *None* of them were leaving my sight until she was dead. Or back in Hell. Or both.

"You haven't seen Marissa? Or Jason and Mandy?"

"Jason's right there," she answered, and pointed to the boy standing next to Karl as Brady gave them all a kudos speech. "Mandy never comes to the games, but their mom should be around here somewhere." She glanced around the bleachers. "There she is," she said, and pointed at the very end of the last row.

Marissa was sitting calmly, watching us as she filed her nails nonchalantly. I'd almost have thought we were barking up the wrong tree, until her eyes flashed red and the woods around the field cracked as two more hell hounds stepped out under the lights over the field.

"Fuck me."

"No thanks," Marissa answered from the end of the bleachers, clear enough that I could hear her.

"Change of plans," I whispered. "Gimme the gun, you get the kids, the Drakes, and Daniel out of here."

"Where?"

"Anywhere but here. Drive. Don't stop. Get on the highway."

He turned, drew his weapon, and pressed it against my stomach as he calmly walked away. As soon as my hand was on it, he let go and stopped. Out of his pocket, he pulled two more magazines of silver ammo and slipped them into my hand.

"Coaches? A word, please?"

"What's going on, Mom?"

I knelt down in front of her. "Keep everybody safe, okay?"

"That's not an answer."

"No, but I'll fill you in later, okay? I love you." I kissed her forehead and pushed her toward the exit.

Grendel caressed my arm as he walked past me, two confused looking soccer coaches in his wake. They both shot me questioning looks, but I was watching the hell hounds. With every step Brady and Alana took, they took one to match.

"Mom?" Karl followed my gaze and stopped in front of me. "What the fuck are those?"

"Grab your sister. I told her to go with the lieutenant and the Drakes, but go home with Karen. Go inside and lock the door. Don't answer it for anybody but me or Lieutenant Grindel. Go now before Karen leaves, please."

"No, Mom. I'll help!"

"Go!" My voice echoed off the bleachers. He blinked, nodded, and did as I asked.

He left, and the hell hounds slowly crossed the field while Marissa filed her nails. Her son was nowhere to be found. My phone buzzed in my pocket. Pulling it out, I had two texts.

One from Ryn. *Go with Karen?*

Yes.

And one from Grendel. *On our way.*

I stood there watching Marissa and the hell hounds until the last human left the area. The hounds took off running and leaped over the fence by Marissa, chasing the speeding police car I assumed. I loved everybody in that car, but I didn't trust my chances against Marissa enough to send my children with them. If I didn't kill her, they were all dead.

Sighing, I started walking toward her.

"I'm assuming Daniel is still alive and kicking since my third pet never came back."

"Yep. He's on a plane to Hawaii. Put him on there myself, then I figured out you wanted all my lovers dead."

"Well, I wouldn't have had to kill them if they had chosen me. So, it is *technically* your fault. Not that they stood a chance against a literal fuck demon. Your pussy is all they can probably think of, stupid humans."

"Well, we know I'm a succubus. What flavor are you?"

"Ifrit."

"Well, that explains the fire."

"You saw my handiwork on the Ferris wheel." She laughed and let flames dance over her hand.

"You did it to kill my children?"

"Yes. I can't have that little whore of your loins constantly tempting my son. He is weak. He is only human, after all."

"Cambion?"

She nodded and continued filing her nails, flames dancing over her flesh. "Unfortunately, my son didn't inherit any demonic traits. Just a normal boy. Not even of remarkable intelligence. But I do love him so, and I would do anything to protect him. I was going to live and let live, until your daughter sank her fangs into him. Now he's quite madly enraptured with her below average beauty. So, I figured I would kill everyone around you, and then you."

"Because your son likes my daughter?" I stared at her incredulously.

"Well, when you put it like that, it sounds kind of silly!" She put her nail file back in her purse and set it on the ground before standing as I got closer. "But no. It's because she's a whore, you're a whore, and the sight of the both of you makes me sick." The walkway between us erupted in white hot flame as she used her ifrit magic. They were literal fire demons, basking in the hottest flames of hell.

I screamed as they erupted around me, my flesh charring on my bones. I shed my human flesh and withstood their heat, but my skin still sizzled and crackled, unable to deal with the intensity of the flames. Me, a demon, burning in fire. That was not how I was expecting to end my earthly existence.

Pulling the gun from the waistband of my leggings, I fired rapidly at her until the gun clicked empty, hoping to end my anguish.

She laughed as the silver melted before it got close enough to touch her, let alone pierce her. The aluminum benches around her melted into slag and dripped to the ground below.

"You can't kill me, bitch. I *am* fire."

Launching myself into the air, I finally spread the wings I didn't dare open in the flames. The tender membrane would have crisped immediately and turned to ash. The heat below propelled me even higher as she rose into the air before me. She didn't have wings, but stood atop a billowing square of pure power. It was where the legends of flying carpets were born.

"Don't think you can run. I'm going to burn you to ash right here and now." She pushed her hands together in front of her and pulled them apart. A shimmering ball of fire appeared between them and grew in size the farther she pulled them apart.

I had nothing. Like any demon, I could call fire, but it was no match for hers. It might even feel cool to her touch. The gun was useless, the bullets evaporating before they could pierce her aura of flame. My knife, not that it would have fared any better, was lying on the ground on my street somewhere.

It was official.

I was fucked.

And not in the good way.

It was my own damn fault, too. I'd been so sure of my power and my abilities, I hadn't even assumed I couldn't best her in a fight. That was the biggest problem with being the toughest kid on the block. Every once in a while, you came across somebody bigger and badder than you, and you got your clock cleaned. Except, she had no intention of cleaning my clock. She wanted to recycle that shit. Melt it down. "Fuck me."

"As I said. No thanks." She laughed and launched the fireball at me.

I'd had every intention of dodging it. Unfortunately, when she released it, it doubled and then tripled in size. There was no way in Hell to dodge it. Folding my wings, I crossed my arms in front of my face and chest and took it.

It fucking hurt and blasted me across the park. When I hit the trees, they burst into flames that scorched my back as I slid slowly down and fell to a heap at the base.

She extinguished her flames and dropped to the ground, laughing maniacally as she walked slowly toward me, enjoying my screams of agony. "And now, you die, bitch."

She stood over me and gloated.

And she was as surprised as me when the nine-millimeter silver bullet burst through her chest, the report of the gunshot sounding a moment later. It was her turn to scream as pain laced through her. There would be no second shot though, her body burst into flames as she spun around. Through her legs, I saw Ryn standing where I had dropped the weapon, shaking badly.

"I told you to run," I said disappointedly.

"Oh, good. I get to kill both whores in one night." She clutched her hand over the gaping hole in her chest. Unfortunately, she would heal, it would just take a while. We'd both be dead before it happened, though. Might as well go out fighting.

"What did you call my daughter?" I coughed and gagged at the soot and smoke that filled my lungs. Or maybe they were just charred.

She stopped walking and smirked at me over her shoulder. "A whore. Just like her whoring mother. You think you're so beautiful? Guess what. While you're a charred corpse, I'm going to fuck all your boyfriends before I turn them to ash."

"Then kill me. At least I can get laid. You might want to turn them to ash before you fuck them. You might have a shot that way."

My taunt worked. She was so focused on me, she had completely forgotten Ryn.

"Run," I yelled and stood up, charred flesh making the smallest of movements pure agony.

"No."

Well, if I wanted my daughter to live, I was going to have to take the bitch down with me. I steeled my nerves and charged just as she brought her hands together to make another ball of fire. I got to her just as she pulled them apart. The flame hit my chest and exploded between us just as I got my claws around her neck. That did more damage to her than anything else, and I felt a few of the bones in her neck snap as we were blown apart.

She writhed on the ground as they reknit. Ignoring every charred nerve ending in my body, I rolled over and crawled to her. As soon as my hand grabbed her ankle, I started pulling myself atop of her. When she realized her peril, she turned up the heat, turning her own body into a pillar of flame.

Just as I was about to give up, a column of water cooled the flames. Not enough to douse them, but enough to keep my flesh from igniting. Inch by inch, I dragged myself up her torso until my face was just below her chin. Concentrating on the cool water instead of the scorching flames, I dug my talons into her soft human-like flesh, slowly shredding everything I could reach until there was nothing left but bone. Over the crackling flames and the whooshing water, I couldn't hear her gargled screams as I ripped her flesh and *finally* got my fingers around her spine. With all the strength I had left, I yanked, snapping the bone beneath and collapsing with a smile as her head broke free and rolled away.

My head, pressed against her chest until her body turned to ash, smacked against the water soaked charred field, and I surrendered to the oblivion.

Epilogue

I woke up in my own bed, my children at my feet. Literally. They were curled up in little balls like chihuahuas. It was the middle of the day, but I didn't know which one. Gently, expecting massive amounts of pain, I nudged Karl with my bright pink toe.

He lifted his head and blinked. "Mom?"

I tried to speak, but only a rasping sound came out.

"Don't talk. The demiurge said it would take a while for your insides to heal. Something about temporal magic not being that effective on internal energy lattices or some anime sounding shit like that." He sat up and shrugged.

"What happened?"

"You killed Mrs. Hodgins. But she was a major bitch."

"Demon."

"Whatever. She's gone. We won."

"The water? It was you?" I sounded like a Muppet with asthma. But at least I was getting the words out. For the most part.

Karl nodded, and Ryn lifted her head to see what the commotion was, smiling when she saw me awake. Gently, she crawled up the bed and lay next to me, trying hard not to touch my tender skin, but wanting to be close to me. I ran my fingers gingerly through her hair.

"Yeah. She looked like burning magnesium. I knew I wouldn't be able to put her out, but I might be able to keep you from turning to ash. Kind of like putting a water balloon over a fire."

"You're a pretty smart kid. You both are. But next time I tell you to fucking run, run. Got it?"

"We'll see," they said in unison, and looked away.

"Is everybody else okay?" I braced my heart for the news I was afraid of hearing. I had killed Marissa, but whether or not I got to her before the hell hounds got to them...

Karl's face fell, and he looked down at the bed.

My heart cracked.

"Just kidding!" He lifted his head and smiled.

I refrained from kicking him in the head.

"She's awake!" He yelled through the open bedroom door, laughing as I struggled to call him dirty words. The little fucker. I loved him.

All four of them poured through my door, smiling as they filled in around the bed. Then Karen came in and started clapping. "Told you she was going to be fine!"

"You were crying two seconds ago!" Daniel laughed.

Indeed, she had been. Her eyes were puffed out, and her cheeks were wet. Typical Karen. I wanted to laugh, but it hurt when I tried.

"Hell hounds?"

"I was watching them chasing us in the rearview mirror. I looked back at the road and then back up, and they were gone. Back to hell, I assume?"

I nodded and smiled, a huge burden lifted from my chest. My family was safe. Now, if I could just stay with them, things would be fine. I looked at Grendel. "Any repercussions?"

"From?"

"Dead soccer mom?"

"What dead soccer mom? There was a missing persons report filed by the ex-husband who didn't seem too thrilled at being granted full custody of his two teenage children he hasn't seen in ten years, but there was no body to make the police department think anything was amiss."

"Oh, good." I chuckled through the pain. "Her kids okay?" I blinked in shock at *myself*. Where the hell the thought had come from, or how it worked itself into my brain was a complete mystery. One better left unexplored.

302

"The daughter seemed indifferent. The son...was a mess and will probably need some therapy."

I frowned at that news.

"Their father took them to New York."

"Oh."

I glanced at Ryn, but she just nodded stoically.

"What was the weirdest thing was the arson case at the park right after the game. Salem PD is clueless about what could have caused that much damage. Weird, I tell you." He winked at me.

"Anything else I should know about?"

They all looked at each other and shrugged. "Nope," they answered quickly. Too quickly.

"Wait a minute. Demiurge? How the hell did you pay for that?" I glanced at my children, fearing the worst. They were the only ones with any power that would be accepted by the gangly demon with horrific powers.

They shrugged and pointed at Grendel.

"Yeah. We forgot to mention that part."

"I'm sure. How did you pull that one off?"

He looked at the Drakes and Daniel. "We uh...we didn't."

"Spill it."

"Michel did."

"Michel? The vampire?"

All four of them nodded. Karen just looked confused. More so than usual. "He paid for the magic," Grendel admitted reluctantly.

"Oh, great. I'm going to end up teaching his dancers for the rest of my life for free.

Daniel shook his head. "No."

I narrowed my eyes at him. "So, what's it going to cost me?"

"A date..."

The end.

Author's Note

Reviews are important for new authors, and I greatly appreciate everyone who takes a moment to leave one, even a line or two! Thank you so much for reading my book! I'm writing away, and more books will be out soon!

Follow me on Amazon to be sent updates on my new releases!

Flip the page for my bio and all my other stalking links.

For 18+ readers who like a lot more steam and don't want the girl to need to choose just one guy, check out my reverse harem series, Lovin' the Coven!

About the Author

A late comer to the writing game, Jacquelyn had always been a fan of romance novels and lately become addicted to the reverse harem category. I mean seriously, who wouldn't? Sitting alone one night she flipped open her laptop and said, "I'm going to give this a whirl." And thus, the Lovin' the Coven series was given life. She has designs on other series as well, but only time shall tell.

As for her, she is five-foot-something, with graying hair, wicked eyes, an eager smile, and an annoying laugh. She lives at home with her dog, a cat, and that is about all she is comfortable sharing.

Other Works

Lovin' the Coven Series
(Reverse Harem– 7 book series)

First Moon
Second Blood
Third Charm
Fourth Rite
Fifth Essence
Sixth Sense
Seventh Seal (Coming Soon!)

The Fox and the Hounds
(Reverse Harem– trilogy)

A Tail of Woah
A Tail of Two Kitties
The Tell Tail Heart (Coming Soon!)

Other

Girlfiend (standalone YA Paranormal Romance)
Succubus Soccer Mom (Reverse Harem Standalone)

www.ingramcontent.com/pod-product-compliance
Lightning Source LLC
Chambersburg PA
CBHW060532180626
46817CB00002B/534